The Time Rip Chronicle

The Tarot Legacies
Book 6

Victoria Belue

For everyone who chooses to live in the wow. And who knows this is the moment. The only moment.

Contents

Chapter One

Once again, no choice was offered.

Vesta floated on the edge of existence where reality felt like a rumor. She sensed her body dissolving into microscopic shards, but it didn't matter. Contentment swept through her like a dreamed kiss, so brief, maybe not real. Nothing mattered for that infinite split second. Non-physical, non-local, infinite. The shift back into her body was so complete that she wasn't even sure anything happened.

She opened her eyes but instantly closed them. Swirling dust landed on her lashes in tiny clumps and tasted acrid on her tongue as she struggled to speak.

"Where did all this dust come from?" she asked, wiping her mouth.

Hurricane-force winds directly aimed at the cave opening would have been necessary to stir up the kind of storm surrounding her. The likelihood of that happening was remote. Barely a breeze had blown all day while she and the rabbit sat on the ledge of the butte. There was no way the white rabbit could have created the gritty tempest. A logical explanation had to exist, but Vesta didn't know what it was. Her third eye was buzzing like a bee stuck in her forehead, yet the twinge of pain at the base of her skull distracted her the most from any further critical thinking.

"I need to walk outside to get some fresh air," she said rubbing her head.

"That's going to be difficult," Luna replied in her tinkly voice. "We're fifty feet underground in a sealed tomb."

"What are you talking about?" Vesta's voice was sharp with confusion, her brow furrowing as she swatted at the dust clinging to her lashes.

The maelstrom began to die down allowing the image of Luna to come into view in the dimly lit space. Vesta noticed that instead of standing beside her as she had been a moment earlier, the young woman now sat cross-legged on top of a wide stone box. She stared at Vesta, her round face and large gray-blue eyes resembling the full moon on a clear spring evening. The tight silver curls clustered around her head created a halo effect, striking in stark contrast to the camouflage pants, combat boots, and short-sleeved black T-shirt she wore.

Moving her attention to the wall next to Luna, Vesta realized the images of the trionfi she had seen earlier had vanished. Deeply carved symbols she didn't recognize covered the space in their place.

"What happened to the drawings of me and the others?" She leaned closer in the dim light to inspect the carvings.

"You said you wanted to see the Elders' inscription." Luna stood up tousling the ringlets on her head setting free little puffs of dust. "So here you go," she said sweeping her arm toward the wall.

Vesta studied the young woman's face letting her words echo in her mind as she tried to understand what she meant.

"Wait, are you saying you engaged Point Revision and brought me to Egypt?" She finally asked.

"No. It's not that. I can't alter anything on a set timeline like you can," Luna said. "But I can hop around on it. So, I popped us in here."

"Hop around?" Vesta asked, wiping her jacket sleeve across her gritty face. "Like in time?"

Luna nodded. "Yeah, through the vortexes."

"And so, you just popped us into – where did you say? A sealed tomb fifty feet underground through a vortex?"

"Yeah."

"I guess that explains my headache," Vesta said rubbing her temples. "I would have appreciated you asking me if I wanted to come, if I was ready to come here so I could prepare for it."

"Oh, my bad. But here we are," Luna said pulling out a thin stick from a pocket on her pants leg. She ran her hand across its knotted surface causing the stick to glow with the magnitude of a floor lamp illuminating the room. Luna tossed it into a corner. "Your headache will go away soon. You just aren't used to the vortex friction, that's all. It stirred up some dust too."

Vesta brushed the remaining residue from her face as she looked around. She stood in a room dominated by stone walls and the color beige. A large sarcophagus sat in the center. The air was thick with heat. She pulled off her jacket and wiped her forehead again.

"Okay, let me understand this clearly, you hopped into the cave in Monument Valley to add your little artist's signature to the rock wall in there, then hopped with me to some tomb in the Valley of the Kings in Egypt."

"No, we're not in the newer tomb area of the valley. I brought you to Memphis. Or what used to be called Memphis near the much older Saqqara pyramid. Really different place."

Listening to Luna speak, Vesta had to admit she was envious of her ability to physically move herself—and obviously others—to a different location instantly. Aside from pain in her head, now no more than a mild throb, she had easily traveled an enormous distance and through fifty feet of earth within a single breath. The brash young woman hadn't asked her if she wanted to travel through a vortex, but now that she was here, it was time to get some answers.

"So, who's this?" Vesta asked pointing to the stone coffin.

Luna stepped toward it. "This is Meri," she said brushing sand from its surface exposing a face like others Vesta had seen in museums. Large black pupils resting in their sockets of brilliant white stared at the ceiling. Thick black eyeliner surrounded each eye and stretched out from the corners in a dramatic fashion. Black eyebrows and a placid expression completed the stoic face.

"He was the keeper of secrets for the king."

"What secrets?" Vesta asked.

"Sacred rites and rituals. That sort of thing," Luna said walking across the room to a wall covered in limestone dust. "But it was during his time, during the reign of Unas, whose temple we're in now, that the Elders showed up. They had already been here before of course when they juiced up the First Blood. That little posse of superhumans started trying to kill each other almost right away to gain power. Real badasses," Luna said with a laugh. "The Elders realized they had given them way too much power, so, they came back to try to fix it."

Luna swept her delicate hands over the wall causing a flurry of thick dust to take flight. Images of wavy lines, birds, snakes, arms, feet, and crude human figures in ancient Egyptian hieroglyphics emerged, carved in long neat rows. Vesta had seen the symbolic language before in the tomb of Seti I. Although she didn't understand the message carved into the walls there or where she stood now, she did recognize one symbol, the ankh representing eternal life, but the lower half of the symbol was missing, replaced by what looked like a skirt with legs sticking out at the bottom. How that factored into the message, she had no idea.

"What's going on there?" Vesta asked pointing at several of the same-looking ankh figures in a line whose arms and legs seemed to be reaching for something in front of them.

"That's you and the other trionfi."

Vesta felt her eyebrows raise as a reflex to Luna's answer. Why were images of her and the other trionfi carved in a tomb thousands of years ago? Luna swept more limestone grit from the wall revealing the falcon-headed god Horus next to the ankh figures.

"Do you know who this is?" Luna asked.

"Him, I know. We had an interesting conversation in another pharaoh's tomb once."

"Cool. Well, here's what you wanted to see," Luna said giving the carved images a final swipe with her hand so they could see more detail. "The message from the Elders. Well, it's really a warning."

Vesta felt her heartbeat pick up speed as she scanned the symbols on the wall. There was an arm bent at the elbow next to a vase with a human face on it, and it sat next to a large eye with eyeliner trailing off it which was carved beside a creature that looked like a bull. She shook her head.

"I have no idea what this says. I can't translate hieroglyphs. Can you?"

"Oh, sure. It's really a simple language. Some characters actually represent sounds while others just mean complete thoughts," Luna began.

"Okay," Vesta said flatly. "Just tell me what the message says."

"Yeah, I get it. It's the whole 'this is my destiny being spelled out here' thing making you a little anxious. I understand and would probably be acting the same way. Right?"

Vesta inhaled deeply rather than speak the words of irritation she felt from Luna's exhausting, pointless prattle. She exhaled and measured her response. "Right," she said.

"Yeah," Luna pointed at a symbol on the wall. "So, this arm here that looks like it's waving at us means this message is being recorded by Meri. That guy in there." She pointed at the sarcophagus. "Which means the Elders came to Meri and trusted him to record their message. And next to the arm, you see a guy leaning over holding a big stick that's forked at the end. That means the elder, as in the Elders. I don't know if that means the beings who gave us our gifts were old, or maybe they walked with sticks..."

"It doesn't matter. Just tell me what the message says." The shrillness of Vesta's voice came through despite her best efforts to suppress it.

Luna shrugged. "Sure, so, the bottom line is the Elders bestowed their gifts to you including everlasting life–that's this little group of ankhs wearing skirts with the two legs and two arms sticking out–causing you to reincarnate life after life as the same person with the same gifts, until..."

She paused and tapped her finger on an image of two bent arms joined at the shoulder pointing in opposite directions.

"Until what?"

Luna turned toward Vesta and stared at her for a moment.

"Until you forget," she said.

"Forget what?"

"Who you are."

Vesta's heartbeat sped up. "Does it say what makes us forget?"

Luna nodded. "It sure does." She dragged her finger from the symbol of the joined arms to the image of a seated man with what looked like a vase on top of his head. Next to him carved deeply into the stone was a leg from the knee down. A huge knife was depicted lying across the leg. Beside that was a final image of a long horizontal line with a diagonal line crossing through it.

"It's all right there. You forget when he mutilates the timeline."

"Who mutilates the timeline?"

"Him," Luna said tapping on the little seated man with the vase on his head.

"Do you know who that is?"

"I do." Luna began dusting off her hands. "It's Cornelius Agrippa."

"Who's that and why is he able to mutilate the timeline?"

"Agrippa is an alchemist living at the beginning of the sixteenth century."

Luna sauntered around the tomb as she spoke inspecting various objects left for Meri which, according to their sacred rites, he would need in the afterlife. She inspected a miniature stone statue of a man, a large necklace made of hammered gold, and a piece of ivory fashioned into the shape of a comb lying on a table. She leaned over the table dusted off a flat, round object, and held it up to her face. Luna tousled her curly hair as she gazed into what had to be a mirror.

"He discovers how to travel through a portal and lands during this time. He finds a device here that he takes back to the sixteenth century and uses it to change everything from that point forward which includes you and the others not being members of the trionfi any longer."

"That didn't happen," Vesta said. "I've never heard of this guy."

Luna laid the mirror down. "He hasn't done it yet. And here's the killer part, you're the only one who can stop him. See, it shows it here." She pointed to a crescent moon shape above the man with the vase on his head.

Vesta shook her head. "How do I stop him?"

Luna shrugged. "I have no idea."

"Well, I have no idea either. Maybe it won't happen."

A deep scoffing sound which shouldn't have been possible from a person as tiny as Luna rumbled from her throat. "Oh, it will if you don't stop him."

"What will happen?" Vesta asked walking closer toward her.

Luna's moondust eyes resembled two translucent marbles as they opened wide. "The world is a super different place if it happens. We're all just regular people. The trionfi doesn't exist anymore. We're RanChans. And the Alliance rules everything. And it's really strict about everything. We can't go anywhere or do fun things. It's boring. And hard. We all have to work all the time while the Cousins watch everything we do."

"Who's the Alliance? Who are the Cousins?"

"The Alliance controls everything and everyone. They tell the Cousins what to do," Luna said. "It's really a bad deal. A lot of people die because of them."

Vesta eyed the objects lying on the table picking them up one by one not to inspect them but to hold some piece of reality in her hand as she mulled over what Luna said. Her fingers grazed the smooth teeth of the ivory comb. She felt more grounded.

"You know this for certain because you've actually been in that time?"

"I've seen the projection of how it goes if you don't stop him."

Vesta set down the comb and picked up the mirror. "How do you know I can change this projected future you saw?"

"Because I was there when you did it. The Elders knew you could keep it from happening and wrote it out here. It will go the bad way unless you change it."

"I stopped this Agrippa guy from severing the timeline?"

"Yep."

"How did I do it?

"I don't know. I wasn't there for that part."

"Hold on!" Vesta said gesturing toward Luna. "You said you saw me change the future from the bad one."

"I did, but it can go lots of different ways. I just know that you must stop Agrippa or it's going to be bad, really bad."

"You've said that already. But I need some help here."

Vesta intuitively knew Luna was telling the truth, that she had witnessed an alternate future. Her third eye had begun to throb, a sure warning sign of something negative about to happen.

The only logical thing for her to do was to find Cornelius Agrippa and stop him. An hour earlier she had been sitting with the white rabbit on a butte in Monument Valley with no discernible direction forward in her life, feeling useless and lost. Now she was tasked with saving the world. Such a situation would have been unbelievable to her, and she would have dismissed it as complete nonsense, except that her life as the High Priestess of the tarot for the past few years had proven anything was possible.

What was Agrippa looking for in 1999? How could she stop him? Vesta could feel frustration building inside of her and glanced into the mirror she held in her hand to bring a sense of grounding back.

"Oh my God," she shrieked. "What happened to my face!" The mirror clattered to the floor of the tomb.

Luna leaned toward her. "What's wrong with it?"

Vesta's heart was beating so hard inside her that she felt like it was going to pop out. Sweat beaded up on her forehead.

"My face is covered in wrinkles!" Her hand quivered so badly she could barely pick up the mirror to look into it again.

"And oh my God, look at my neck! Those deep lines and that crepe skin. Look what traveling through the vortex did to me."

Luna frowned and cocked her head. "I don't know what you're talking about. The vortex didn't do anything except give you a little headache for a minute. You look normal. It's what you're supposed to look like in 2024."

"What?" Vesta glared at Luna. "Are you saying we jumped from one place to another, and in time as well? Twenty-five years?"

Luna nodded. "That seems about right."

Vesta placed her hand on the table to steady herself. Her knees felt weak, and her breathing became shallow. "That means I'm sixty-five years old." She let her body slide down to a sitting position on the dusty floor. "I need a minute here."

As she steadied herself, she realized the appearance of her hands was different too. Vesta turned them over, investigating every detail. Thick blue veins bulged under the skin, and its thickness had also changed. It felt like tissue paper, and several tiny dark splotches dotted their surface.

She ran her hands over her face and neck, feeling the loose, pliable skin. She didn't want to look into the mirror again, but she couldn't stop herself. An involuntary grimace moved into place as she inspected the image staring back at her. Furrows ran from the bottom of her nose along each side of her mouth almost to her chin. Her jawline now included fleshy jowls while her eyelids appeared to be made of crepe paper, and there was a distinct wrinkle midway across her forehead.

"I look so old."

"You look beautiful," Luna said softly.

Vesta looked up at her. "Easy for you to say. You haven't aged a minute since we were in the cave in Monument Valley in 1999. Why is that?"

"I don't know why." Luna shrugged. "Maybe it's because..."

But before Luna could finish her sentence the floor and walls of the tomb began to shake. Swirling dust began permeating the thick, hot air again.

"What's happening?" Vesta asked ducking under the table.

"Someone's in the portal. I bet it's Agrippa coming from his time to this one. You must stop him from cutting the line."

The shaking grew more intense causing the comb and little statue to rattle off the table hitting the floor. Other objects in the tomb jostled around causing more dust to stir.

"I don't know how," Vesta said, the pleading tone clear in her voice.

"Well, it'll be the dark times then. Try to remember to get on a ship to the new world so they don't burn you at the stake this time."

"What do you mean, this time?" Vesta shrieked.

Luna walked to the corner of the room where her glowing stick lay. She picked it up and ran her hand across it. The tomb fell into a heavy darkness.

"What are you doing?" Vesta asked feeling a surge of panic.

"Jumping of course."

"You have to take me with you."

"I can't. You must stop him."

"You're leaving me here, in the dark, fifty feet underground in a sealed tomb in the middle of the Egyptian desert?"

"I've never been good about staying in any one place too long. But it was fun hanging out with you." Luna's voice cut through the dense air like champagne glasses tinkling on a server's tray. "Stop Agrippa. Find the way."

A swooshing sound filled the tomb as though the air was being sucked out of the room. The swirls of limestone grit doubled in their intensity coating Vesta from head to toe. Then it was still and silent. So silent, Vesta could hear dust settling onto the floor.

Time had no relevance to her as she sat under the ancient table in the darkness. Was it ever relevant? This is the moment, the only moment, she repeated to herself. What she did now was all that mattered. But what could she do? She was trapped in a tomb with no way to dig herself out. Point Revision wouldn't help either because she would still be in the room. She wondered how long it would take before someone came to look for her. Why would anyone look for her in a tomb sealed five thousand years ago? Thirst was already an issue because of the swirling dust she'd swallowed. How long would it be before it became critical? A dull ache crept into her awareness. Maybe it was a headache; perhaps it was fear.

Turning loose at last of conscious thoughts, Vesta closed her eyes and stretched out her awareness beyond her surroundings. Act like the High Priestess that you're supposed to be, she chided herself, drawing in deep breaths. Focus, Vesta, focus. Even though she couldn't recall all her past lives because of the memory spell she cast, she knew situations as dire must have occurred. InSight and pristine intuition were her gifts from the Elders. Allowing those gifts to come forward instead of terror was key because she had a job to do. And above all else, she took responsibility very seriously.

Vesta relaxed into the moment. No anticipation, no struggle. Just being in the moment. She had no idea how much time had passed, but the shift came, like a cosmic click, sliding her into that delicious place of being part of everything. Her third eye sparked to life, glowing like a lantern on her forehead. Even though she was unaware of it, the room was illuminated once more, this time by the light within her.

She called out for her trionfi brothers and sister with her inner voice. Please come assist me, was her silent plea. Yet no response came from Liam, the Fool, nor from Peter, the Hanged Man, the two most connected to her in that telepathic way.

Neither Amara, the Empress, nor Jared, the Emperor picked up on her psychic wails. Even Sandor, with his Magician's impeccable timing, didn't plow through the yards of sand and rock to the tomb door. But Vesta stayed focused on her request for unmeasurable moments until a shuffling sound finally brought her attention back to the small room.

Her inner light faded out as she held her breath listening intently. A presence had entered the tomb. Could it be a rat searching for food? Maybe Cornelius Agrippa as he traveled through the portal had landed there on a mission to destroy her. Perhaps a vengeful pharaoh had awakened, angered by the disturbance of his tomb. Anything was possible and Vesta knew it.

She opened her eyes to see a faint glow hovering beside the sarcophagus of Meri, the secret keeper. As the light grew stronger, a crack of thunder exploded through the tomb. A gust of wind roared, shaking the walls once again, this time with such a force she was sure they would crumble. Still crouched under the table, she watched the form of a huge man covered in hair take shape, or was it a demon? His eyes locked with hers, and he bellowed out her name.

Chapter Two

Vesta's body trembled uncontrollably as her name ricocheted off the tomb walls. Each echo grew sharper and more deafening, stabbing at her eardrums like shards of glass. She clamped her hands over her ears, but the sound still clawed into her mind. Her connection to the higher plane, steady and luminous a moment earlier, crumpled like brittle parchment.

"You," the monstrous voice continued to boom. "The priestess of the mighty trionfi hiding under a table. Crawl out!"

Vesta knew she had to gain control of her fear. Even if she was facing death, she wouldn't cower like a terrified mouse. That would not be her last act in this life, which could also be her last life as the High Priestess. She took a deep breath, telling herself the beast in front of her was right. She was still the priestess of the tarot, and she wouldn't die hiding under a table. As she exhaled, a calm determination took hold. Logic was no longer in charge of her actions. Instead, intuition took hold as it always did when logic failed. Vesta tuned into her third eye with its soft whirring sensation, its tiny ball of energy warming her forehead.

She removed her hands from her ears and placed them on the gritty floor. As she slid out from under the table, the tomb became lighter, every corner and crevice illuminated. Now, she could clearly see it was a man standing in front of her.

He had to be almost seven feet tall. His bulging eyes stared at her. They were brown, the same color as the bags clinging beneath them. In between was a beak-like nose, too thin for its fleshy face. Yet the feature standing out most on him was the tangled beard. It resembled some sort of matted forest animal hanging from his face more than any human whiskers. Vesta's gaze took in the full view of the snarled thatch of hair as it extended below his neck in front of a tie-dyed Grateful Dead T-shirt slowly dwindling into a thin, messy braid with frayed ends resting against what appeared to be a filthy plaid kilt.

"You're not Cornelius Agrippa," Vesta said feeling fairly confident of her statement.

A laugh loud enough to crack the tomb walls roared from the man. "Only in his most preposterous dreams could he be me," he bellowed in a British accent with theatrical flair.

Vesta sized up the figure in front of her more fully. He stood barefoot with monstrous feet displaying gnarled toes. Layers of what looked like thin cotton robes hung from his broad shoulders. He reminded her of a homeless man she'd once given money to in Battery Park.

"Then who are you?" she asked.

A guttural snort churned inside him before he spoke. "I am your loyal servant here to fulfill your every request," he said.

"Really?"

"No. But I did answer your rather pathetic distress call," he said before hoisting himself up to sit on top of the stone sarcophagus lid. A distinct popping sound followed his landing.

"You cracked it!" Vesta gasped.

"Ol' Meri and I go way back. He wouldn't mind me resting here."

"I think you should have some respect for the dead," Vesta said.

"Dead? He's reincarnated twice as many times as you, scattering his starseeds across the planet."

"Starseeds. What's that?"

"Your friend Lucy Jane is a starseed."

"You mean half human and half extraterrestrial?"

"I prefer to call them starseeds. It's more respectful."

Vesta caught the chiding implicit in his remark. "Okay, sure. I'd just never heard that term before."

It had been a long time since she'd thought of her father's partner, Lucy Jane. The last time she saw her, she handed over Cyrus's ashes to her. There wasn't any reason to keep in touch after that. Lucy Jane was busy helping the U.S. government with matters she couldn't discuss working with NORAD deep inside a mountain range in Colorado.

"So, you're here to stop Agrippa?"

Even at a normal volume, the man's voice had a nerve-rattling quality to it. Vesta brought her thoughts back to the present moment.

"Yeah, how'd you know?"

"Why else would you be here?"

"I'm obviously trapped, and I have no idea how to get out. Let alone how to stop someone I've never met from doing something I have no clue about."

"You are dreadfully unprepared, aren't you?"

"Wait," Vesta gestured toward him. "Who are you? And did you come here to help me?"

"I came here because it's my job. Trust me, I'd much rather be enjoying a good joust somewhere right now."

"A joust?"

"A true gentleman's sport. Like dueling but it's not over and done with as quickly. More time to appreciate the skill."

Vesta shook her head. "Are you serious?"

"Madam," she could hear the exasperation in his voice. "What do you require?"

"Who are you?"

"I'm a chronicle," he replied.

"That's a thing, not a person."

"It's a thing and it's beings. I'm the one compelled to show up when a time rip has the potential to occur."

"You're talking about the inscription here on the wall, right?" Vesta asked pointing across the room.

"Of course."

"So, you know about that, and you can tell me how to stop this Agrippa, right?"

"Wrong. You either stop him or you don't. If he rips the timeline, then everything changes. It's as simple as that —and that dangerous."

Vesta ran her fingers through her hair setting free a shower of dust. "Look, someone named Luna brought me with her through a vortex and left me here. She told me if I don't stop Agrippa the world would turn into some kind of nightmarish place."

"It is the nastier of the two routes. I'll grant you that. But the superior beings who bestowed you your gifts trust that you're up to the task to stop the alchemist."

"I need some help because Luna wasn't any."

"Luna is a twit of the highest order," he said leaning back on the sarcophagus lid causing another pop to echo in the tomb. "She flits from one epoch to another willy-nilly. Her whole purpose in this scheme mystifies me."

"So, there's no help you can offer me either? I just literally fell into this mess with no direction from this point. I don't even know if I will get out of this place."

"Oh, well, I can get out you."

"That's good to know, but then what?"

"Then you thwart Cornelius's plans," he said before he shook a long finger at her. "But be warned, he's a tricky one."

"You know him then?"

"Oh, well," the chronicle huffed and mumbled a few unintelligible words.

"What are you saying? Speak up," she said, a sense of confidence growing inside.

He cleared his throat. "We may have crossed paths once or twice."

Vesta frowned. "What are you not telling me?" Her third eye felt like it was bulging from her forehead.

"Nothing really. He's good at card games. That's the long and short of it."

Vesta eyed him carefully. "He's good at card games because he has beaten you before. Is that right?"

A word appeared to form on his lips, but it froze in place. He returned her gaze for a long moment before nodding.

"You know what Agrippa looks like and probably where to find him. You can take me through a portal to where he is so I can figure out a way to stop him from severing this timeline."

"No, no!" The chronicle shoved his hands toward her. "I want no part of this scenario. It matters not one whit to me how this plays out. And I certainly want no further dalliance with Agrippa."

Vesta continued to study his face, the tense muscles around his mouth, the darting of his eyes, the licking of his lips. "What was the bet in the card game you played with him? What did you lose?"

"I, um. It was minor, a minor thing." He slid off the sarcophagus and turned his back to Vesta. "I don't remember. I also don't have to tell you."

Vesta walked around the coffin to face him, her breathing steady and determined. "If you're a chronicle, someone that records events exactly, then you must tell me exactly what happened because that's what chronicles do."

He turned away from her again, but she jumped in front of him, staring into his eyes. "Tell me. Now!"

The chronicle winced. "You must understand, he plied me with liquor—lots of it. And I'm as sure as the sun rising in the east that he let me win the first few games. Priming me. Making me overconfident of my abilities. Oh, he's evil."

"What did you lose?" Vesta locked her gaze on him.

The chronicle pressed his lips together so hard they turned white before he finally spoke. "It's not so much what I lost as what he gained."

"Tell me," Vesta commanded.

"The portal. All right?" The chronicle let his hands drop to his sides. "I taught him how to travel through it.

Chapter Three

Vesta stared at the chronicle, her brain trying to process his statement logically to piece together a cohesive thought. But her emotions gouged a hole in any attempt, as the reality dawned on her.

"You're the reason I'm here," she said, her words weighed down by a palpable hollowness, "why I've lost twenty-five years of my life." She thrust her arm toward the hieroglyphs on the wall. "It's because of you that the Elders told Meri to inscribe this message."

The chronicle scoffed and mumbled again. "Hardly my fault. It was inevitable. He's a clever man. One way or another he would find a way."

She shook her head. "They knew you were going to do this."

Vesta's line of reasoning had returned. A clear picture glared at her.

"You didn't come here because it was your job. You came here because you need to make sure I stop Agrippa. You're not rescuing me. I'm supposed to rescue you."

The chronicle stroked his mangy beard, his fingers tangling in the long gray hair.

"And the shaking I felt in here the first time was Agrippa traveling through the portal. Right? And you came to find me because Luna probably told you she left me here." Vesta cocked her head. "But why me? Why am I the only one who can stop Agrippa?"

The stroking motion stopped as the chronicle stared back at Vesta. His dull brown eyes vacant doorways. "I honestly don't know," he murmured.

Vesta pursed her lips while nodding her head. She looked around the ancient tomb of the secrets keeper not because she thought she would find any answers there, but to allow her thoughts to align into a plan which had the best chance to succeed. Her focus moved back to the chronicle, her thoughts crystallizing.

"Agrippa is in this time right now, correct?"

"Unfortunately, yes," he said.

"Alright, you're getting me out of here and taking me to where he is."

"I don't want anything further to do with that conniving alchemist."

"Too late," Vesta said, raking more dust from her shoulders and pants. "You created this mess, and you're going to help me stop him."

"I refuse." His haughty tone Vesta had heard before from others like him. People who knew their last defense was to feign superiority and finality. The shadow of a smile grazed her lips.

"Oh, yes you are. Luna told me that I could stop Agrippa. She said she was present when I did it."

"That meddlesome twit."

"You're the only one who can help me." She pointed at the message carved on the wall. "The Elders knew. That's why they had Meri leave this here for me." She leveled her gaze at the hulking man. "You're the chronicle. You must accurately record what happens as this prophecy plays out. You have no choice."

The chronicle scowled; his fleshy cheeks pushed tight toward his nose. "Alright, alright," he said after a long pause. "I'll take you to where he is, but then you're on your own."

* * *

The second voyage felt easier for Vesta. Though her headache had returned, at least there was no dust this time. A swirling wind whipped her short blonde hair in every direction, but only for a moment. The dimly lit tomb disappeared as if she had stepped through a doorway into blinding sunlight. Vesta blinked against the sudden glare of the sun reflecting off water. As she rubbed the back of her head, she realized she and the chronicle were now standing by a body of water—a lake or maybe a river.

"Where are we?"

She turned around to see they were standing in front of a statue of the musician Stevie Ray Vaughn. The chronicle leaned against it, fanning himself.

"We're in Austin, Texas."

They stood in a park setting. On the other side of the river, steel and glass buildings stretched skyward. She had been to Austin once before for a party thrown by a former Sybarite board member. Willie Nelson had performed at the outdoor barbecue. It was one of the best parties she had ever attended. Beads of sweat gathered on her forehead.

"It's really hot here."

"It certainly is. I'm going to walk over to find one of my favorite watering holes nearby to cool off."

Vesta glared at the chronicle. "A bar? No way unless that's where I'll find Agrippa. You're going to take me to him."

He began walking toward a gravel trail a few yards away.

"I have no idea where he is in this city. I knew he came to this place at this time, but that's all I know," he said over his shoulder.

Vesta followed close behind him. "You're not leaving me like Luna did. I don't know what Agrippa looks like. You must find him."

"He's a needle in a haystack here. Use your talking device to enlist the aid of your other trionfi. They will be more help than me."

The other trionfi? Vesta stopped walking.

"Do you know where they are?" She called out to the chronicle who kept walking. "Hey!" she shouted. "Answer me."

The chronicle turned around mopping his forehead with his sleeve. "They're here. They're all here," his voice weary and taxed.

Adrenaline raced through her. Her trionfi family was in Austin? Amara would help her, so would Jared, maybe even Liam.

"Take me to them," the words raced out of her mouth.

"I don't know exactly where they are," he said lumbering down the trail. "I told you, use your talking device."

"I don't have my phone with me. As a matter of fact, I don't have anything with me except what I'm wearing." She stopped. "Oh, no. I left my jacket in the tomb."

The chronicle waved his hand in her direction as he kept walking. "Puzzling artifact if the tomb is ever opened. Do you think you're the first time traveler who's left something behind either accidentally or on purpose? Let's cross the river. I know someone who can help you find your trionfi."

They came to a short flight of stairs that led to a paved pathway at street level above. There they were met by parents walking with strollers, people with dogs on leashes, and runners weaving in between the throng. As they walked across the bridge spanning Lady Bird Lake the chronicle talked. He told Vesta she needed a primer on time travel, its potential ramifications, and consequences. The first thing she needed to know was that the Vesta of 2024 was already living in Austin.

"That's fortunate," he said. "Things can get messy if someone has already died. But you don't have to worry about that because you're alive and well."

"Yeah, that's good to know. Am I working in the fashion industry?" She was hopeful she had regained a place in the world she loved so much.

The chronicle cut a sideways glance at her. She caught the hint of a smirk that grazed his face. "No," he said. "You, um, are involved in a profession more aligned with your historic duties."

Vesta gave him a confused look. "What does that mean? I'm a consultant? Using my InSight to guide a corporation or something."

They reached Cesar Chavez Street and stopped. The chronicle pressed a button on the traffic light pole to summon clear access to the crosswalk.

"Well," he began. "It's essential you understand now that you are here, you are the only one here. You've superseded the you of 2024. There aren't two priestesses of the trionfi. Only one. But you are fully enveloped in the world you've created in this time. You must remember also, there are consequences for changing too much at once if you choose to do so."

They crossed the street. The heat from the asphalt below and the cloudless sky above felt merciless. Cars waiting breathlessly for the light to change to green added to the stifling temperature as they walked in front of them. Once they reached the other side of the street the chronicle raised his arm and began waving. The driver of a pedicab further down the block waved back. He pedaled to a stop at the curb in front of them.

"Your carriage awaits, madam," the chronicle said, sweeping

his arm out with a grand gesture. Vesta gratefully climbed aboard.

The breeze gliding through the maze of downtown streets felt more like a hairdryer being held in front of her than anything else but at least the air was moving. Within minutes, they pulled up to the corner of Sixth and Brazos Streets. The chronicle hopped out of the pedicab.

"Young man," he said. "Wait here. I intend to compensate you most generously."

Vesta realized at that moment neither she nor the chronicle had any money for the driver who was sweating as though a water faucet had been turned on him.

"I'm sure he will be right back," Vesta said as she climbed from the well-worn seat. The truth was she wasn't sure at all.

Dressed in her black T-shirt and khaki pants, which had traveled with her from 1999 but still looked current with the attire she'd seen on their jaunt, Vesta walked into the Driskill Hotel. Built in 1886, the wide lobby boasted enormous paintings from that era in Texas history and its well-heeled, even in cowboy boots, society. Fashionable women of the time in long dresses and conspicuously prominent men with their close-cropped hair and long beards called out from the walls. Her third eye itched as she walked past them. They wanted to tell their tales to her, but she didn't have time to listen.

A grand double staircase sprawled out in front of her as she approached the center of the lobby. There, she saw the chronicle as he came puffing down one side of the staircase.

"I'll find you in the lounge," he panted as he stalked past her toward Sixth Street.

Vesta walked up the stairs, where a cool breeze rushed up to her on the landing. She felt as though someone was anxious to greet her before a blast of immense sadness barreled through her. The emotion was so brief she wasn't sure she felt it at all. Yet the sensation of a presence, however fleeting, wasn't her imagination, she was certain of that. Did the hotel have a ghost? Most definitely, her intuition replied. But again, she didn't have time to dwell.

"I'm sorry," she whispered as she climbed the remainder of the stairs.

At the top, sofas and chairs grouped around coffee tables were scattered around in a huge lounge. At the end of the room, a stately bar constructed of dark wood stood majestically anchored in a corner. Laughter and loud conversation mingled into a lively din as she walked to an empty seat at the bar and sat down.

"What'll you have, Miss?" The bartender with sparkling green eyes smiled at her.

Vesta drew in her breath, not sure what to say at first, and surprised by her hesitation. "I would like some water," she said. "And vodka martini," she added quickly. "Do you have something Russian?"

"I'm sorry, we don't currently offer anything from Russia. How about an Austin vodka? Tito's is made right here and it's one of the best."

Wanting water more than vodka at that moment, she nodded her head. "Sure, that's fine."

The bartender slid a tall glass of iced water toward her and began making her martini. Vesta drank all the water before placing the glass back onto the bar. She could feel the chill of its serpentine path course through her body, the exquisite sensation caused an audible sigh.

The chronicle heaved himself onto the seat beside her with a mighty huff. "Admirable boy out there. Earning an honest living. I tipped him well," he said.

"He must have incredible stamina," Vesta replied.

"Thank you for your help, Isaac. You know I never travel

with money," the chronicle called out to the bartender. "I will refund you shortly."

"I know you're always good for it Gus," the bartender replied as he set Vesta's martini in front of her.

Vesta eyed the chronicle. "Your name is Gus?"

He picked up a paper napkin from a stack on the bar and mopped his forehead and neck. "That's right. Named myself after the greatest of Roman emperors, Augustus Caesar."

Vesta waited until Isaac moved further down the bar to help another patron before she leaned into Gus. "It seems you know this bartender pretty well."

"Well enough," he said.

"Does he know who you really are? Maybe I should say *what* you really are."

"He knows I'm a loyal customer who has helped him out on certain occasions. We'll leave it at that."

Isaac returned with whiskey and placed it in front of Gus.

"Thank you, sir." The chronicle said picking it up.

"What kind of whiskey is that?" Vesta asked.

"Old Crow," he said before throwing back the shot.

Vesta wrinkled her nose.

"Alcohol all tastes the same after a while." He motioned to Isaac for another. "Good memories of drinking this on some raucous nights with Ulysses."

"Ulysses?" Vesta arched her eyebrow. "Like from the Odyssey, Ulysses?"

"Fictional character from that bore Homer? No, I'm referring to the former president of the United States. That man won his war while pickled like a cucumber."

"The Civil War?"

"I believe that's what you called it. But is any war ever civil? None that I've ever witnessed," he said.

"We agree on that point. Now, we need to get a mobile phone for me. We're wasting time."

Vesta paused while Isaac slid another whiskey to Gus. He picked it up and leaned toward her.

"You aren't ready for your assault on this era yet priestess." He threw back his shot and let out a satisfying sigh. "You must get a feel for what is acceptable now, what advances have been made, as well as what you and your fellow trionfi are up to now. Diddling with the current moment too radically will cause some drastic consequences."

Vesta blew out a long exhale. Patience was not one of her strengths. She understood that from countless times of acting before thinking. Some of those times had paid off, others had failed in monumental ways.

"That makes sense, and I believe you. Okay, let's make short work of this. You said earlier I'm now a consultant of some type. Where do I work? If not in the fashion industry, I hope it's at least in something interesting in finance like Sandor, or tech with Jared."

Gus studied her. Once again, she spotted the hint of a smirk play upon his lips.

"You read tarot cards," he said.

She frowned at the prospect of a lengthy and tedious explanation in the works. "Yes, of course I do. But what do I do professionally now?"

"I just told you. You read tarot cards."

Vesta leaned back in her seat and frowned. All his facial signs showed Gus was telling the truth. This was confirmed by the soft whirring of her third eye.

"Professionally?" She asked trying to make sense of what seemed like nonsense.

"Indeed."

Before remembering she was the High Priestess of the tarot,

Vesta had regarded all tarot card readers as fakes. There was no way, she believed, that a person could predict another's future with a deck of cards. The garish shops they worked out of made the entire premise even more implausible. Neon signs or crude hand-painted ones proclaiming tarot, palm reading, or psychic contact with dead loved ones were a sure location to throw away money. Only the weak-minded or desperate would fall for such a ruse. She had been the CEO of Sybarite, an international couture and luxury goods brand based in New York City. How did she end up making a job out of reading tarot cards in Austin, Texas? Even though she did see the future with her cards, it didn't make her newfound career any less repugnant. She rubbed her forehead.

"That's not really what I do," she said.

"It is."

She shook her head. "What happened to me that I would resort to a job like that?"

"Ah," Gus nodded at Isaac further down the bar for another shot. "You've had some interesting moments in this life."

Vesta took the first sip of her martini. "So, what went wrong?"

"Is it necessarily an onerous circumstance that you read your trionfi cards for those seeking their futures and your advice? It's an honorable profession. A querent could only be so lucky as to be read by you."

After taking another deep sip of her drink, Vesta leveled her gaze at Gus. "You've obviously seen everything, everywhere in the history of the world. Tarot card readers have always been portrayed as charlatans."

"Not always, but your assessment is understandable."

"Why did I decide to do that?"

"I may witness many events in the human story but reasons behind that particular choice I do not know," he said.

"I must have lost my damned mind," Vesta took another long sip. "Do I have to keep doing that? Because I really don't want to."

Gus nodded. "You must continue to read cards for clients at least until you can logically segue into something else. But you must be careful. Even the smallest changes too soon can create seismic ramifications. You cannot, under any circumstances, let your trionfi know you've time traveled to fix this little problem."

"But I thought that was the point of me being here now, losing years of my life." She put her hand on her face. "Having wrinkles, to stop Agrippa from changing the timeline."

"Absolutely. That's your mission. But you must be cautious in the changes you make. Telling them about jumping from 1999 will set a chain reaction into motion that could cause much bigger problems than the one you're trying to solve. Cataclysmic problems like vicious time loops."

The combination of vodka and physical exhaustion had worn her down.

"Alright. I get it." Vesta exhaled as she ran her fingers through her hair. "What are the other trionfi doing? And why are we all here in Austin?"

Gus began speaking about Amara first. As the Empress of the tarot, throughout her many lives, Amara sought out endeavors and organizations promoting the welfare of the planet and its inhabitants. She was still deeply involved with Conscious Evolution Partners, the nonprofit she founded in her twenties. However, she had handed over many of her responsibilities to a brilliant young woman who had worked with the organization for the past ten years.

Her passion project now was designing a new way to collect rainwater. The climate in Austin and many other parts of the world was changing, becoming hotter and drier. Droughts lengthened, and the scarcity of water was a critical issue. When it did rain, it was vital to collect as much as possible. Amara's current focus was on manufacturing an effective and affordable way for homeowners to capture precious water drops when they hit their roofs. Creating a system that worked not only in collecting but also in the storage and purification of the water was her goal. At the same time, CEP was negotiating with several local and nationwide homebuilders to incorporate rainwater collection systems into their home designs. She had already achieved several victories in her quest, but there was much more to be done.

Amara and Jared were active in the city's civic and social circles. Accomplishing her visionary projects took major funding, and the deep pockets of wealthy Austinites were a lucrative resource. A large portion of the technology sector had relocated from Silicon Valley to the more tax-friendly city. Houses cost less in Austin and usually came with more land attached. Jared was one of the first disruptors in the tech industry to move to Austin. Others soon followed. Industry giants Apple, Oracle, and Facebook, who had recently changed their corporate name to Meta, all occupied dozens of floors of downtown office space. Jared's Odin Labs, simply called Odin in 2024, had shifted its focus from software and hardware products aimed at augmented reality and virtual reality to the development of artificial intelligence.

Vesta bristled. The Terminator had been a terrifying film to watch. Its sequel was even worse, in her opinion.

"Why is he messing around with that?" she asked. "No good can come from creating robots smarter than us."

The chronicle's eyes widened. "Oh, you have no idea." He wiped his mouth with another cocktail napkin. "Yes, well, we should be getting on our way."

He motioned to Isaac who nodded in return.

"My good man. I'll return with money for the tab and more," Gus said.

The bartender nodded again. "Always good to see you."

Vesta left the remainder of her martini and followed the chronicle out of the hotel. The pedicab driver still sat at the curb. They climbed into the backseat again and took off toward Congress Avenue. After navigating the one-way streets downtown for a few blocks, the pedicab pulled up to the W Hotel. Gus patted the driver on the shoulder and thanked him. Vesta stepped from the backseat and felt sweat roll down her back.

"I can buy a phone here?"

"Oh, no, no. This is a hotel," Gus said over his shoulder as a doorman swung open the door.

She caught up with him. "I know it's a hotel. Why are we here then?"

"Instead of buying a talking device, why don't you just use the one you already have?"

"Because it's in Monument Valley, Utah," Vesta leaned in closer to Gus. "Twenty-five years ago."

"You also have one upstairs in your condominium," Gus murmured to her as he walked through the bustling lobby to a bank of elevators and followed a man onto one. Vesta stayed close behind him, brimming with questions she couldn't ask at that moment.

The man got off on the nineteenth floor, but Vesta noticed Gus had pressed the button for the penthouse level on the thirty-seventh floor. The moment the man made his exit, her questions began.

"Why didn't you bring me here to begin with? What am I supposed to know about this place that you haven't told me? How do I afford this place if I read tarot cards for a living?"

Gus gave no reply but raised his hands in a gesture for her to be patient. The door opened to a long hallway with a door on either side. The chronicle walked up to one, fumbling in the layers of his clothing.

"What are you doing?"

"I'm trying to locate your key," he said pulling it from a pocket of what looked like a lightweight cardigan hiding beneath his larger outer robe.

"How did you get a key to my home?"

"I stopped by when your maid was here. Told her I was your weird uncle."

"I obviously need to have a talk with her."

"Don't be too harsh with her. I can be very persuasive," Gus said as he turned the key and pushed open the door. "Welcome home priestess."

A vast space sprawled in front of Vesta with the ceiling of the living room soaring twenty feet high. A modular sofa bathed in the finest camel-colored mohair anchored the room as a gargantuan white chandelier, no doubt from Murano, Italy, hovered above it. Artwork from Sandor's Manhattan apartment hung on several walls. Her favorite Lichtenstein, Mondrian, and Pollack from his collection were present, along with other paintings she had never seen before. Sandor lived there, too, that was obvious. She had never taken the time to collect or curate anything for her apartment beyond her clothes, shoes, and handbags. Nothing else mattered to her. Her clothes and accessories reflected her important job as CEO and chairman of the board at Sybarite. She loved her career, and she loved her clothes.

Floor-to-ceiling windows revealed an expansive view of Austin beyond the room. Vesta smiled to herself. Her Manhattan apartment was on the eighteenth floor, boasting a view of downtown. The assortment of shorter and taller buildings close by created a jagged, cramped landscape. Here, the vista from her Austin penthouse extended ten or fifteen miles across a prostrate plain of one- or two-story buildings. Lady Bird Lake wound like a lazy serpent at the bottom of her view. Technically, it was the Colorado River, but within the confines of the city, it had been renamed after the former First Lady who had worked tirelessly to preserve and nurture the natural environment of Austin.

The living room connected to the kitchen through a twelve-foot-wide opening. Vesta walked in. It looked rarely used but held her favorite De'Longhi espresso machine on a spotless white marble counter. Familiar and unfamiliar objects eased into her line of sight. In the sink sat a water bottle covered in tiny silver crystals she didn't recognize. But next to it was one of the espresso cups she'd purchased at Café Florian in Venice in the early nineties.

Turning around, she saw a row of drawers under another marble counter. She felt her heart skip a beat when she noticed two drawer pulls were the amber pieces from Enid's herb cabinet. They were the only things she'd kept from their Crested Butte home after her mother died. Vesta let her hand rest on one. A vivid memory popped into her mind's eye of pulling on that piece of amber to open the rickety old cabinet door as a child. Mysterious odors wafted toward her, warm and comforting but also acrid and pungent. She recalled reaching her hand inside to touch a jar containing a golden liquid.

"That will ease the pain of a sore throat," she heard Enid say. "It has goldenseal and honey, plus a pinch of orange rind."

Vesta's memory deepened as she watched her mother gather an herb from another shelf before crushing it with her mortar and pestle and sprinkling it into a small white cotton pouch. She told Vesta it was a special kind of oregano she could only find in the fall on the southern side of their mountain. The herb was excellent for clearing up respiratory infections, she said, especially when combined with the other herbs and oils in the pouch. As she spoke in the memory, Vesta studied her face. It had been a long time since she'd recalled her mother's unusual beauty.

Enid's eyes were pale turquoise and captivated anyone who looked at her. Her skin was the color of alabaster, like one of Michelangelo's divine statues. Her hair was also white and formed a halo of soft curls around her head. Enid only wore white clothing which added to the overall effect of otherworldliness. The children who came to see her with their mothers and fathers who sought Enid's remedies called her The Ghost. They weren't afraid of her though. She would give them lollipops she made from berries she collected in the woods. A wistful smile grazed Vesta's face.

"I think you have a modern and posh abode. Don't you agree?" Gus asked.

His clipped British accent jolted Vesta back to the foreign yet familiar residence. She nodded as she looked around. "Yeah, I like it so far. Where's my phone?"

"How would I know? It's not like I went through your closet and your privies when I was here before."

"Are you sure?" Vesta gave him a sideways glance as she headed across the living room to the other side of the condo where she assumed the bedrooms were located. "Why did we go to the Driskill Hotel then if my phone was here? What purpose did that serve in helping me find Agrippa?"

The chronicle plodded over to a section of the pristine sofa and plopped down. "None. I required a little libation."

"Don't waste my time any further Gus. You need me to fix this situation as much as I do."

Vesta walked down a short hallway confidently passing two

doors to arrive at a door at the end knowing that had to be her bedroom. She would never buy a home where people passed the primary bedroom to get to the guest rooms. "But I would never read tarot cards for a living either," she mumbled to herself wondering just how different her older self was. But stepping into the room, she knew she was indeed in a home of her own.

The black and cream harlequin patterned wallpaper commanding one wall had long been a favorite. Why that specific geometric design resonated with her on an almost emotional level, she didn't understand. It didn't matter; she loved it, and she had found a place for it in her home. Other familiar and treasured objects grabbed her attention as she looked around the room. The 18th-century Japanese cabinet she purchased when she was promoted to head of marketing at Sybarite stood against one wall. The Art Deco club chairs covered in midnight blue leather she splurged on with the announcement of her position as CEO at Sybarite sat beside a massive window overlooking the city. Last, but far from least, the mirror rescued from the Versailles boudoir of Marie Antoinette she acquired after she became chairman of the Sybarite board reigned above a black lacquer table loaded with books.

Vesta basked in the memories for a long moment. Reminders of her former life. The life she loved more than anything or anyone. Dead to her now. Tarot card reader. Gus's words echoed in her mind. How could she have possibly embraced that professionally? It was clear her life over the past twenty-five years had spiraled into a dank abyss where she had given up trying to accomplish anything formidable. She shook her head. No time to go down that road of questions now. There was work to be done. Focus. Where's the phone?

She turned toward the bed. A simple black brushed metal headboard stood next to her harlequin wall. Below, a cream-colored damask bedspread lay on top of the queen-sized bed. Large antique Chinese pots covered with clear glass tops stood on both sides. Matching Art Deco-looking lamps sat on top of the glass. Each had a pile of books sprouting from them. One held art books from the Renaissance, while books about movies from the 1940s and a biography about someone named Elon Musk lay haphazardly stacked on the other.

Vesta nodded. The idea of using large fish pots from the Qing dynasty as nightstands had occurred to her in the 1990s. She smiled at the fact she finally found a pair and put them to good use. Their shades of blue complimented the blue of her chairs exquisitely, a nod to her intuitive, excellent taste, but no phone lay on either table.

Outside, beyond the expanse of the floor-to-ceiling window, the late afternoon had settled in. Awakened from a heated-exhausted blue, the sky had roused itself into shades of orange and purple. Adrenaline spiked through Vesta. It was getting late. Where was the phone? Next to the bed stood the entrance to a bathroom. She hurried inside to find all she would expect in a luxury penthouse: Italian marble countertops, high-end faucets and fixtures, another spectacular view of the sprawling Texas landscape, and a door leading into the closet. She hurried inside. It was twice the size of hers in Manhattan. Racks of clothes lined three walls, and the fourth held shelves filled with shoes and handbags. At least she hadn't lost her love of fashion.

Vesta picked up the Louis Vuitton Neverfull tote sitting on top of the ottoman in the center of the space. She thrust her hand inside it and let out a relieved sigh. A familiar shape cradled in her hand. Being a creature of habit had its rewards. The handbag currently in use always sat on the ottoman in the closet, and the phone was always in the interior pocket. She pulled it from the bag but froze as she stared at it. The device she held–was it actually a phone–was unlike anything she had seen before. No buttons existed on its surface for dialing a number. It was all screen, like a tiny television screen.

A deep frown crept into place. "What the hell?" she mumbled to herself.

When she put her thumb on the screen, it lit up, startling her for a second. An image of the Chartres labyrinth came into view with a date at the top, Sunday, September 17, along with the time beneath it, 7:08. At the bottom, the instruction read, "Swipe up to open." Vesta swept her finger upward over the screen. The image shifted again. Numbers 1 through 0 were lined up in rows on a black background. What was her password in 2024? Maybe it was the same as in 1999. She typed in Liam's numeric birthday and watched the numbers skyrocket upward, revealing a screen filled with rows of tiny squares of different colors. Again, she congratulated herself for being a creature of habit. A green square at the bottom displayed the image of a telephone receiver. Vesta touched it, and a list of her trionfi family's names appeared on the screen. She let out a satisfied sigh.

Who should she call first? The stern admonishment by Gus returned to her thoughts to not let anyone know about her time traveling. Yet a plan was necessary to gain the trionfi's help in finding and stopping Agrippa. That was certain. What was the most logical way to accomplish that without divulging her secret? Mentally stepping back to view the big picture, she realized the first step was to understand fully who she was now so she wouldn't behave bizarrely around them.

Vesta scanned her closet, grateful to see no bohemian clothing hanging from the racks. "Thank God," she whispered. Every tarot reader she'd ever seen had been adorned in either rough cotton, lace, or God forbid, crochet with tassels and bangles in bright colors hanging off them. Vesta shuddered. That really would be too much to handle and clear evidence of her having lost her mind. A true sense of giddiness bloomed within her as she viewed the handbags lining the top shelves. Heartwarming labels of Louboutin, Dolce and Gabbana, and a black leather tote proclaiming the name Fendace in bold gold letters above a Medusa head. She nodded with approval at the obvious and stunning collaboration of Fendi and Versace. Nothing seemed foreign or heinous here. The iron grip on her shoulders loosened a bit.

Walking out of the closet, she noticed another smaller closet on the other side of the shower stall. Inside, two racks of men's suits, jackets, and crisp button-down shirts hung in tidy order. Vesta grabbed a suit jacket to inspect the label. Ralph Lauren. A sure sign of Sandor. The books about movies from the 1940s on the bedside table were his, too, no doubt. He was still enamored by that era of their previous lives when they lived in the tony new neighborhood of Beverly Hills and produced films with the top actors of the time.

Since Sandor lived there, he could walk in at any moment. What else did she need to know about herself in 2024 to be acting normal when he arrived? She read tarot for a living, and what else?

Vesta hurried out of the bathroom, back into the bedroom. It was a beautiful space; nothing screamed that she was now someone peddling fortunes. The tarot cards. Where were they? If she read them professionally, they must be lying around somewhere. Vesta scanned the bedside tables again. No cards in sight. None on the low, round table between her Art Deco chairs. Wouldn't she keep them close at hand? She needed to look more carefully. Where would she put them? Her eyes landed on the hand-painted Japanese cabinet from the 1800s. She walked over to it and removed the lacquered chopstick holding the doors closed. A palpable breeze carrying an exotic aroma of frankincense and myrrh danced around her as she pulled the doors open. There, sitting inside one of the black cubby holes was a velvet pouch, a reproduction of the High Priestess card from the Rider Waite Smith deck printed on top of it.

Despite her best efforts to be matter-of-fact about seeing the pouch, an effervescence coursed through her like a champagne cork had popped open. What was this feeling? Vesta felt almost embarrassed about it. As she reached for the pouch, her fingers began to tingle even before she touched it. Her third eye whirred gently as she picked it up. From a logical standpoint, this sentimentality irked her. However, it was undeniably there.

"Well, I am the High Priestess," she said out loud before catching herself. "But that doesn't mean I have to be ridiculous about it."

It had to mean, she thought ruefully, that she'd lost her edge in her old age and embraced this seriously. She shook her head but wasn't exactly sure what to do beyond that point. Outside, she could see the Austin sky had admitted the brightest stars of the constellation Cassiopeia onto its nighttime stage. Panic rushed into her. She needed to move faster to implement a plan. Vesta dashed toward the living room.

"What else do I need to know about myself in 2024?" She held up the pouch of tarot cards to Gus, who sat on her sofa, sipping what looked like red wine from a glass tumbler.

"How would I know such a thing?" he replied, wiping his mouth on the sleeve of his robe.

"You knew where I lived. You've been here before, obviously seen me during this time. Why didn't you tell me Sandor lived here too?"

"Minor detail," Gus swept his hand dismissively, almost spilling wine. "I had no doubt you would figure it out."

"What else do I need to know before Sandor walks in?"

But it was too late. Vesta heard the front door open and

spun around to see Sandor MacFarland, the Magician of the tarot, walk in. She shot a glance toward Gus, hoping he would impart some helpful information to her in the last remaining seconds before she was Vesta 2024, but Gus, the chronicle who ripped time, had vanished.

Chapter Four

"**H**ey, doll," Sandor said, walking toward a bar tucked into the corner of the living room. Vesta tried not to stare, but she couldn't help it. His hair, neatly swept back as usual, was no longer just the color of espresso. Now, it was finely woven with silver threads. He still retained those Ken doll-like good looks, though, the regal jawline and the patrician nose with mesmerizing amber eyes. His lightweight lapis jacket and open-collared white shirt revealed a healthy tan, further accentuating the sparkle in his eyes.

"Hey," Vesta responded, not knowing what to say and realizing even that one word she uttered sounded out of place, uncharacteristic. Where was Gus? Damn him; he knew she needed his help.

Sandor dropped a squatty ice cube into a highball glass before a two-finger pour of scotch from a bottle of twenty-five-year-old Macallan. He sipped it as he looked at her.

"Why aren't you dressed?"

Vesta froze at the question. Sandor walked over to wrap his arm around her waist but paused.

"Have you been digging ditches?" His nose wrinkled. "You smell like you've been outside all day." He ran his fingers through her hair. "And you're covered in dust. What have you been up to?"

She wanted to say, 'Yes, I've been outside—buried in an ancient Egyptian tomb fifty feet underground before being whisked thousands of miles and twenty-five years into the future. How was your day?' Instead, she stammered, trying to pull her wits together. "I, um... I volunteered at the park to help build a children's playground."

"Really. At Zilker?"

Vesta paused, she knew she had heard the name before, somewhere a long time ago when she visited Austin. "Yeah," she said, hoping that would cover her lie without the need for further explanation.

Sandor looked down at the glass coffee table beside them. "It must have been incredibly stressful."

Vesta followed Sandor's gaze to see the large tumbler filled with wine. Damn it, Gus. "Right. It was. I mean, we got a lot of work done."

"Well, you need to hurry because we have to be at Jared and Amara's in forty-five minutes and you know traffic is going to suck."

Vesta swallowed hard. The unsteady sense of being on a conveyor belt that was speeding toward an unknown destination blasted through her thoughts. She must stay calm.

"Okay. I'll be ready in thirty minutes." She paused. "Will that work?" she asked, having no idea how long it would take to get there.

"It'll be cutting it close."

"Right, I'll hurry."

Vesta turned toward the bedroom, but Sandor gently took her arm, pulled her close, and kissed her. "Even though you smell and look like you've been playing in a sandbox all day, you're still gorgeous."

If Sandor only knew how close he was to the truth.

As she walked across the living room, she realized she didn't know what to wear. Was it a leisurely gathering or something requiring her to dress up? How could she ask Sandor without being obviously ignorant about it?

"Is that what you're wearing?" she asked casually over her shoulder.

"Since it's an investor meet and greet for Odin, I'm going to put on a clean shirt and jacket. Probably a tie too."

Excellent. Her stealthy approach worked. "Sounds good," she called out walking into the bathroom.

The warmth of the shower water splashing on her skin had never felt more incredible. The long day, years, and eons washed down the drain. Working quickly, she scrubbed her body and shampooed her hair. She grabbed one of the towels hanging on a rack and began drying off. Only then did she catch sight of her image in the expansive mirror above the dual sinks. Shock ripped through her. The woman staring back looked like a stranger. The sagging skin around her neck, her breasts drooping like balloons losing air, and her belly and hips distinctly shifted from what was familiar. It was an apparition standing before her. That couldn't be her now. That couldn't happen to her.

Vesta cautiously ran her hand over the rivulets carved in the skin of her chest. She fingered the flaccid nature of her neck skin and followed the course of the thin aqueducts running from the sides of her nose plunging to her jaw. Her breathing became shallow and rapid. This wasn't her. It couldn't be. Chest skin that felt more like an orange peel than anything else, the loose folds of her neck—these changes were too sudden, too cruel. She was in her early forties just hours ago.

Sandor strolled into the bathroom, unbuttoning his shirt as he headed toward his closet. Vesta snatched her towel with both hands, wrapping her body in it. She wanted to run into her closet but forced herself to slow her steps into a quick walk.

"What's the matter?" Sandor called out.

"Noth... nothing," she said. "I'm just trying to hurry."

Her hands trembled as she pushed dresses and skirts along a rack. Everything felt too abrupt. Too much change, too fast. Focus, Vesta, focus. Do the job, then go home. She would make Gus take her back to 1999 through the portal. If she was able to travel here, then she could travel back. Everything would be okay. Focus on her mission. Agrippa was going to destroy the world. She was the only one who could stop him. The Elders knew she could do it. They made Meri, the keeper of secrets, carve it onto the wall of his tomb. That was all she needed to think about now.

A tentative calmness spread through her. Of course, her body would look twenty-five years older. It was the natural aging process. She should have expected it. Do the job and go home. That was the goal. Her fingers paused, eyes resting on a long dress whose colors echoed the glorious reds and blues of her beloved Chartres stained glass. Its long sleeves and cinched waist harnessed bold patterns, gold scrollwork, and long arched panels reverberating her windows with a dazzling collage. She pulled the dress from the rack. A long slit up the front panel to highlight some leg came into view. Even better. She checked the label. Alice and Olivia. Not a line that was familiar, one that had come into existence during the twenty-five-year gap in her life. Vesta let out a long exhale. At least she still had great taste in clothing.

Twenty minutes later, she walked into the living room, loving the new-to-her dress and strappy gold Gucci platform sandals she found. The shock of applying makeup minutes earlier was fresh on her mind, the loose texture of her eyelid skin unnerving. It was almost impossible to draw a flawless swath of eyeliner. But she fit perfectly into her dress, and at least, that was a small victory.

"You really are spectacular," Sandor said looking up from his cell phone.

Vesta felt a blush rise in her cheeks. Something that rarely happened. She smiled at Sandor, grateful for the compliment. He slid the phone into the pocket of his navy Ralph Lauren jacket.

"I called for the car," he said.

"Okay." Again, the one word sounded awkward coming from her. But she wasn't sure what else to say.

They took the elevator down to the first floor. The hotel lobby was throbbing with people. Some wearing shorts and flip-flops, others ready for a night out. Vesta followed Sandor through the hotel doors onto the sidewalk. A young man ran up to him and handed him something. He patted the young man on the shoulder, sliding a twenty-dollar bill into his hand. Vesta followed Sandor as he walked to a black car parked a few feet away. It looked unlike any car she had ever seen before, sleek, with a silver T embedded at the front of the hood as its only ornamentation. The letter resembled a sword pointing down rather than the actual letter. Her third eye began to whirr, a subtle buzz of awareness sparking within her.

Vesta walked around to the passenger door where Sandor opened it. A slight gasp escaped her lips as she settled into the seat. A large screen sat in the center of the dashboard. It had to be sixteen inches wide, a foot tall, and less than an inch deep. Sandor opened the driver's door and slid into the seat. He touched the screen causing a map to pop into view.

"Traffic doesn't look bad once we get out of downtown," he said pushing a button with the letter D on it below the screen.

He pulled out onto the street, merging with the flow of the other cars. Vesta stared at the parade of unfamiliar vehicles. Her attention soon shifted to the hairstyles of women sitting in cars at nearby stoplights. She slipped on a pair of gorgeous Chanel sunglasses she discovered in her handbag so she wouldn't be too obvious with her gawking. She peered out the window toward young women with a multitude of hair colors. Hair dyed in cartoon shades—vivid pinks, blues, and greens— was styled into high pigtails or cropped short. Some wore it well receiving silent approval from her while others were way off on the color they had chosen for their skin tones. How had this become a style? Was it a new fad, or had it been around for a while?

Vesta brought her attention back into the car as they entered the highway. She almost screamed as she noticed Sandor didn't have his hands on the steering wheel. Not only that, but he was also looking at his mobile phone.

"Oh my God, what are you doing?" Vesta came close to shouting.

Sandor's black eyebrows gathered like a bird in flight. "What? I'm just answering a couple of emails."

She glanced at the steering wheel. It was moving without his hands on it. They were traveling between the white dashes of a lane in a perfectly normal way. The stunning reality hit: they were in a self-driving car. Relief gushed through her like an open fire hydrant. The only problem was she needed to cover for acting so hysterical over something no doubt commonplace now.

"I um... You know you shouldn't be working twenty-four hours a day. Those emails can wait," she said. "Plus, you know I'm old-fashioned about you actually driving rather than letting a computer do it."

"Well," Sandor said laying the phone on a charger under the

screen. "That's one of the best inventions our clever Death came up with in this car."

Vesta gave a slight nod but nothing more. Was the trionfi member Death part of their lives now? She recalled Peter telling her that Death had cast a memory spell even stronger than hers to forget who he truly was many lifetimes ago. He felt the substantial contributions he had made over countless lifetimes were outweighed by the destruction they could cause. Even though his gift dealt with the necessary ending of things so new could be born, he didn't want to be consciously aware of his part in the grand scheme. He wanted to be free to create without obligation to the Elders. Clearly, the estranged family member had been busy in this lifetime.

The landscape outside the car windows had shifted from lanky buildings to the wide expanse of a green rolling hill dotted with scrubby juniper bushes. She let her gaze rest on the scenery until Sandor pushed a button on the screen and put his hands on the wheel. The car turned right, pausing in front of an iron gate. He pushed another button, making sections of the gate slowly pull apart. They drove onto a street dotted with large homes nestled behind elegant driveways and manicured lawns.

At a corner, they turned right, allowing the Austin skyline to reveal itself spectacularly from their perch atop a hill. It no longer looked like the modest little city residents were trying to keep weird. A half-dozen cranes were silhouetted amongst the lineup of skyscrapers. Growth on a major scale had taken place, showing no signs of slowing. Down the hill on the street, three young men sporting ill-fitting black jackets with white shirts mingled in the distance. Sandor pulled up to them. The tallest penguin among them opened her door.

Beyond them lay a sprawling house, its white stucco exterior gleaming in the early evening moonlight. Vesta approached, pulling open one of the massive glass double doors. A young woman stood next to it holding a silver tray filled with glasses. Her long hair the color of polished ebony.

"Good evening and welcome," she said. "I'm Serena. May I offer you a glass of champagne or sparkling water?"

"Champagne, please," Vesta said.

"Make that two," Sandor said sliding up behind her.

Vesta accepted the glass as she surveyed her surroundings. Walls she would later call the shade of AI alabaster sheltered a cavernous room filled with smoky gray sofas, club chairs, and elephantine ottomans. Across half of one wall, a white limestone fireplace stretched languidly. All the interior space seemed geared toward the main spectacle, an enormous expanse of windows on the eastern wall framing the skyline view sparkling in the twilight like a nearby galaxy.

Bringing her attention in closer, she scanned the room. Clusters of people mingled. Their faces were unknown, but their jewelry was another matter. Cartier and Bulgari jewelry hung from ears, necks, wrists, and fingers. Their clothing echoed the same high-quality status with careful attention to tailored stitching. Two men standing near the fireplace wore cowboy hats. Living in New York and traveling mainly to Europe, Vesta rarely saw that style of hat except when someone was wearing a costume. These weren't costumes. They were well-made and expensive. Probably Stetson. Their suits were also expensive. It was clear, Texas oil money had ventured into tech.

"You look radiant tonight."

Vesta swung her gaze toward the familiar voice. Amara approached from a long hallway on her left. Her sister still rocked her slender body, but everything on her looked–how could she describe it without being too judgmental? Relaxed. The sleeveless slip dress she wore revealed arms lacking the tone that had always been a hallmark. Amara's chest bore the same orange peel-like rivulets she now displayed, including some distinct sunspots. Her former Barbie doll mane of blonde hair now glistened with thick streaks of tinsel gray hanging in a long braid over one shoulder. Her easy smile was the same but now encased with age gullies on both sides of her mouth.

"Thank you," Vesta said trying not to stare. "So do you," she added striving for the most casual tone she could muster.

Sandor, who stood beside her, leaned in to kiss Amara on the cheek. "Where are my boys?"

Vesta shot a confused look his way. Boys? Did Sandor have children? Mentally she checked her expression ordering the crease between her eyebrows to ease up.

"Jared had to dry them off. They've been in the pool."

A glaze of sweat rose on Vesta's neck. Children made her nervous. They were unpredictable, requiring much attention. She never knew what to say to them. If Sandor had children, it meant she must know them, too. How could she improvise her way through this? The idea of declaring a sudden migraine occurred to her, which would allow an immediate exit from the party. Other options darted through her mind when, from the corner of her eye, she saw Jared step into the long hallway to her left. Behind him bounded three giant standard poodles in march-step pursuit. The dogs raced past him, the beige one letting loose an excited whine as it rushed to Sandor.

"There they are!" The Magician swooped down to scratch the dogs behind their ears while accepting many licks on his face. Relief burst like a dam through Vesta. She reached down and patted each one.

"They may live with us," Jared said arriving at the group. "But they will always love you the most."

The idea of Sandor being a dog lover was novel. Vesta couldn't recall him ever interacting with pets of any kind. She might have pondered this a bit longer if it hadn't been for the sight of Jared. Even well into his sixties, he was still a handsome man. His blonde hair, now completely gray, had maintained the spiky, carefully messed up look he had mastered decades earlier. The clear blue eyes were as piercing as ever despite the waves of wrinkles around them. He stood tall without a trace of stooping in the shoulders. If anyone deserved to be the Emperor of the tarot, it was Jared.

Sandor stood up. "Have my clients arrived yet?"

"They have," Amara said. "They came directly from the airport here. I invited them out on the terrace to enjoy a drink and the view."

"Excellent. I'll go say hello." Sandor gave the beige poodle a final loving scratch before walking toward the terrace.

Vesta's glance darted toward Sandor, thinking she should follow him so she didn't have to engage in risky conversation.

"Hey Vesta, how are you?" Jared asked.

She slid her attention back to him and Amara realizing her escape window had closed.

"I'm really good," she replied gritting her teeth at uttering another phrase she never would have before. "How are you?"

"Very excited to have all these guests here tonight to try out Gateway. You're still up for it, right?"

Vesta paused. She had no idea what he was referring to but rather than say no and maybe need to explain, Vesta nodded her head. "Sure."

"Great. I'll come get you soon. Now, excuse me while I talk some of these Texans out of a little bit of their money for Odin research."

Vesta watched Jared step into the living room to join a group. He shook everyone's hand wearing that irresistible smile of his. Each returned the gesture, and a lively conversation was immediately underway.

"He'll get what he wants," Vesta said out loud, more to herself than anyone else.

"He always does," Amara replied. She turned to Vesta. "Everything okay?"

The question was unexpected. Vesta drew in her breath. "Yeah, yeah, just maybe tired. And the heat. Yeah, it's so hot here."

"You do look stunning in that dress. You must really like it to wear it two nights in a row. I don't think I've ever seen that happen before."

All the air in the room felt sucked out. Vesta silently cursed herself. Why did she think she could pull off fooling the people she knew best, and who knew her best? She would never wear the same dress two nights in a row even if she loved it. Even if it was the only dress she owned. Had she been around all these same people the night before? The moment felt like the last straw. The last not-so-tiny mistake she had made in less than three hours of living in the future. She had taken only a sip of her champagne but now put the glass to her lips draining the glass to the bottom. Embarrassment and a sense of hopelessness crept close, crouching in the corner waiting for a final gaff.

"I do love it," she murmured, not knowing what else to say. "It reminds me of Chartres."

"You were saying that last night."

Vesta let out a long exhale. "I need another drink."

"Oh, here," Amara said reaching for another glass of champagne from Serena's tray.

"No, I need a real drink," Vesta said walking away from her sister. A small, satisfied smile forced itself into place. At least she said and did something authentic to her true self.

The immense living room held a bar in the far-right corner. She noticed Jared still entrancing the group with his looks and words as she passed by. Outside, Sandor stood on the terrace talking to a young woman dressed in a skintight silver jumpsuit. The soft evening light made them look like they were in an old photograph of Paris. No other faces were familiar around her and for that she was grateful. Behind the bar stood a barrel-chested man with a bushy mustache and long sideburns.

"Madame, what can I get for you tonight?" he asked, laying a cocktail napkin in front of her.

"A vodka martini, please, very dry with a twist."

The bartender picked up the local brand Tito's and began pouring it into a shaker. From her peripheral vision, she saw a slim man about her height slide up next to her. He nodded at the bartender.

"Just a whiskey when you have time." He turned his attention to Vesta. "You are here for the show too?"

She returned the gaze, nodding. By his comment, she found a clue about Gateway. Maybe she could find out more information. "And you?" she asked.

He nodded. "I am here to see it all."

The man's accent was German, and behind his heavy lids were the dark eyes of a hawk catching every movement not only from her but the entire room. His high forehead held back a mane of brown wavy hair that fell below the collar of his shirt.

"Do you live in Austin, or did you come in especially for the evening?" Vesta asked.

"I arrived a few days ago."

The bartender slid a martini to Vesta and a whiskey neat to the man. He picked up his glass.

"To good fortune," he said. Vesta caught her breath, not sure what to say. "You're the card reader, yes?" he asked.

There was no use denying it. They had either met before, or he knew about her current profession. Embarrassment stepped closer from its corner.

"That's right," she said.

"Well, here's to good fortune, for both of us."

With zero enthusiasm Vesta touched her cocktail glass to his.

"So, I have reserved time for a reading with you tomorrow. You may have noticed." He took a sip of his drink, his eyes never leaving hers.

Not only had Vesta not noticed, but she had no idea a schedule of readings even existed.

"No sorry."

"My apologies. We haven't formally met. I'm Henry Page."

"Vesta Beauvais. But you know that already."

"Yes, your gift is legendary. I'm looking forward to what you see in my future."

Vesta pressed her lips together. How could she possibly be doing this as a job? Wasn't she exposing herself and the trionfi? The Vesta of 1999 would never do something so blatant. Now that *she* was here in 2024, she wondered if she should cancel the reading.

Jared approached them with his beguiling smile before she could decide.

"Mr. Page, are you ready to try Gateway?"

Henry Page threw back the remainder of his whiskey, then smiled with an openness that caught her off guard.

"I am quite ready," he said before looking at her. "And I will see you tomorrow in San Antonio."

Vesta stared at the two of them as they walked away. San Antonio? Why would she go there? Then there was Jared's statement about trying Gateway. Wasn't it a show? The muscles in her back began their angry march. Spasms on the right side then the left. Knives piercing deep within. Vesta winced, grabbed her martini, and slammed its contents. She had taught herself not to rely on excessive alcohol for relief anymore, but here she was lapsing back into old habits. More self-criticism. More stress.

"Relax and focus," she whispered.

"Madame?" The bartender took a step toward her. "Did you say something?"

"Um, yes, could you pour some water for me into this glass?" She handed her martini glass to him.

"Yes, ma'am."

Vesta turned around to face the room of people who murmured and mingled. Hoodies chatted with Stetsons. Poodles received appreciated attention. A hulking man with a long beard stared at her. Gus! He winked from his position across the room next to the fireplace. She grabbed her martini glass and strode toward him.

"A wise choice drinking some of that after knocking back your hefty libation."

"Where have you been? And how did you get in here? You look like a bum."

"I put on shoes." He nodded toward his feet, couched in a pair of flip-flops. "One thing I admire about this city is the lack of judgment about one's clothing choices. Keeping it weird, as the locals say. Humans worth their weight in gold are dressed in a multitude of ways here tonight. Haven't you noticed?"

"Why did you disappear when Sandor arrived?"

"My presence would have been difficult to explain."

"Has he met you before?"

"No, none of your trionfi have except you, Luna, and Death. Interesting that despite his willful ignorance he has chosen to live here too part of the time. A nexus, no doubt."

"Why are you here now?"

"To illuminate you, dear priestess."

"Good. What's the deal with San Antonio? Why am I going there tomorrow?"

"Trivial matter. That's where you set up shop. The greater significance is who you're reading for."

"You mean that guy, Henry? What's his story?"

A smile edged its way across the chronicle's face. "His story is your story."

Vesta fixed her gaze on him as she spoke slowly. "Are you saying that was Agrippa?"

"One and the same."

Vesta set her martini glass on the mantle and took a step away from Gus.

"I wouldn't go after him just now."

"Why not?"

"What are you going to do? Have him arrested? Punch him in the nose?"

"I'm... I'm going to tell him I know who he is. Who he really is. That I'm going to stop him from doing whatever he's planning to do to change the future."

"And that will send him scurrying back to the sixteenth century?"

Pain surged in Vesta's back pushing the knife deeper. "You have a better idea?"

Gus lifted a highball glass that had been obscured within the folds of his robes. He threw back its contents of whiskey. "I do. Meet with your fellow traveler and read his cards. Find the way to thwart his plans."

"There's no guarantee I can see his plans through the tarot."

"Well, do your best."

Amara moved through the crowd toward them, the black poodle at her side.

"Vesta, it's your turn with Gateway. I'll show you to the lounge."

"Enjoy your odyssey." Gus nodded toward the bar. "I believe I'll head for another wee tipple."

Vesta leaned into Amara as she walked with her. "Do you know who that guy is I was talking to?"

Her sister replied without hesitation. "He's not completely human, I can tell that, but he's harmless. I can also sense that."

Vesta touched Amara's arm pulling her to a stop. "What do you mean he's not completely human? You don't know who he is?"

"No, Liam probably invited him. I'll say a proper hello to him after I drop you off."

"And the not completely human part?"

"He's probably one of the hybrids I haven't met yet. Jared has been working with several on the fluctuating timeline tablet Horizon."

She gripped her sister's arm tighter. "The what?"

Vesta saw the confusion registering in Amara's bright blue eyes.

"The tablet whose history of the past and future world updates instantly according to even minor shifts of the timeline."

Vesta shook her head even though she knew she was risking exposure. "A forward-looking time machine?"

"Of course." Amara paused, the confusion still present. "It's the one you suggested to the board."

Chapter Five

V esta followed her sister through a long hallway off the living room, down a short flight of stairs at the end, and into a windowless room. She paid little attention to any detail in the space other than the basics: sky-blue walls, a small desk, and a big comfortable chair. She paid even less attention to what Amara was saying. Something about Gateway being a prototype. The battery will never die, and it was called Lithium Energy Synthesis Tangible Activity Technology. LESTAT, for short. The battery was in all their new products. Her words were babble and background noise to her earlier words, *"It's the one you suggested."*

How did Vesta come up with the idea of a tablet that could look into the future? As she thought about the concept, as Amara prattled on, she only had a vague idea of what that could possibly mean. It sounded like something to do with the plot of the movie *Back to the Future* where Marty McFly's mother falls in love with him instead of his father, therefore wiping out his existence. Beyond that, she had no clue. Did it involve the prophecy in the tomb and Henry Page, who was, in reality, Cornelius Agrippa traveling to the twenty-first century?

Vesta snapped back into the present moment when a young man in a blue hoodie walked up to her and handed her a clipboard with a piece of paper on it.

"This grants us permission to record your session both internally and externally," he said. She took the pen from him and signed the printed form.

What did he mean by internally, she wondered. Would it be recording her brainwaves? What was she being exposed to, something that could affect her memory or cognitive skills? It was a prototype, after all. Before she could ask any questions, another millennial man in a faded red hoodie guided her to sit down in the large, comfortable chair and dimmed the lights in the room. He placed a helmet with a large pair of high-tech-looking goggles attached to it onto her head and slid the goggles over her eyes. Complete blackness filled her view. The blackest of black. He slid a pair of headphones under her chin rather than over her head. Just before he put them over her ears, he said, "Now, sit back, Think of someone–anyone–living or dead you would like to have a conversation with."

"Someone I know?"

"It doesn't matter," he said. "I'm going to turn on some chill music for a minute or two to help you relax to get the process started."

Soft ethereal sounds began floating around her. A slight scent of amber mixed with maybe myrrh danced at the tip of her nostrils. The nubbiness of the leather on the chair arms beneath her hands felt grounding. She felt safe. She knew she was safe. As far as any adverse reaction to her brain, she trusted that Jared and his team of engineers weren't going to put her in danger. Plus, she was too curious about what the device could do to refuse it.

Who did she want to talk to? Living or dead. Her thoughts immediately pointed in the direction of Enid or Cyrus. Talking to her parents would be a gift, but also painful. Vesta bit her lip. Visiting with them wouldn't accomplish her mission either. Nor would it answer her question about time travel. Who did she know who would be an authority, someone she could trust?

As the music tiptoed into a hypnotic rhythm, she noticed her thoughts unmooring from their rigid place of logical thinking. The sounds were sending her on a journey. But to where? Did it matter? Relax, Vesta thought to herself. For once in your life, relax.

She exhaled. Blackness surrounded her in a velvet void, her senses retreating inward. A mental release began that seemed to last for eons. Across solar systems, galaxies even. Slowly, effortlessly, out of the blackness, an image began to take shape. Vesta watched it passively as a casual observer in no hurry. The face of a man whose large dark eyes protected by thick brows came into view. A mustache thick, thicker than his eyebrows. A thoughtful face, wearing a touch of sadness perhaps. Then came the tumbleweed of white hair surrounding his head.

"You're Albert Einstein," Vesta whispered as if she'd made a great discovery.

The image blinked as if no verbal response was necessary to such an obvious statement.

"I guess I conjured you because of my questions about time travel."

"What is it you seek to know?" he asked.

"So many things. I've traveled physically through time. I've gone backward and made it stand still to repair damage done to an ancient tomb. It's called Point Revision; maybe you know what that is. And today, I traveled forward in time twenty-five years. It wasn't my choice. I didn't even know what was happening. I do know huge consequences can happen—terrible paradoxes—from it. My main question is, is it possible to create a device that constantly updates what's going to happen in the future due to events in the past constantly changing, and can it be free of paradoxes?"

"Everything is energy. That's all there is to it. Match the frequency of the reality you want, and you cannot help but get that reality. There is no other way. This is not philosophy. This is physics."

Einstein spoke in such a matter-of-fact way that he seemed bored. His words sounded true to Vesta. She could feel herself nodding in agreement.

"But what does that have to do with time travel?"

"Energy equals mass times the speed of light squared," he replied.

Another thought she could understand and agree with. "So that seems to explain how theoretically time travel exists going forward–into the future. But what about going backward?"

Einstein looked even more bored when he responded. "It's the same."

Vesta realized he must feel as though he was talking to a child, and he had little patience with children, she could tell. But she wasn't going to give up so easily despite his attitude.

"So, you're saying if you've linked to the frequency of the reality–the time and place–I want, I will be there? And paradox-free?"

"It can be no other way." His droopy eyelids and push-broom mustache barely moved as he spoke.

"How do I link to the frequency?"

"Priestess," his heavy brows lifted. "You know how, but you made yourself forget. I understand. The gift from the Elders is a great burden."

Vesta sucked in her breath. She had forgotten that Albert Einstein had been a trionfi member. He was Death during his life, but centuries earlier, before that life, he had cast a powerful memory spell on himself in another life to forget how he was related to the trionfi. His gift from the Elders was still present in all his incarnations since bringing ground-breaking theories and inventions into the world. He was still the Death card as represented in the old Visconti-Sforza deck created by their patrons centuries ago. It was clear he remembered their relationship and his position within the trionfi now. She thought of his current incarnation, who was busy reinventing the electric automobile and who knows what else while oblivious to his gift. Or was he? She could ponder that more later, but at that moment, she wanted the answer to her question.

"So, all I need to do is remember how to link to the frequency I want, and I can avoid any paradoxes? And that's what Jared has done in his invention of this Horizon tablet, right?"

Einstein gave the slightest nod and seemed to look relieved that the conversation was at an end.

"Just one more question." Vesta felt herself wince knowing she was pushing his patience. "Did you feel like you made the best decision in casting that spell on yourself?"

"It eased some of the pain."

Vesta nodded. "Thank you."

Einstein vanished, released from her imposing questions. The black blackness engulfed her again, and she became aware of her surroundings.

"Hey," she said lifting her arm. "I'm finished with this."

Blue hoodie removed the headgear and headphones bringing the windowless room back into view. "How was it?" he asked.

"Interesting," Vesta said sliding out of the chair.

"Did you talk to somebody famous?"

Vesta thought about whether she wanted to share anything. "Yeah. Einstein."

"He seems to be popular with your generation."

She wrinkled her nose at his statement and wanted to say, "Well, maybe so, but I bet the others of *my generation* didn't have the discussion I had with him." Instead, she caught her recoil, so there was only the slightest tension of her neck, and volleyed the question back to him. "Who's a famous person you've spoken to with that?" She pointed at the headgear.

"Jobs is one of my favorites. Man, he had some ideas about the metaverse that really slap. Even better than Zuck's."

"Slap?"

"Yeah."

Vesta set a courtesy smile into place as she walked out of the room and back upstairs. There she found Sandor guiding the woman in the silver jumpsuit and a man dressed in Armani down to the room.

"They're having a go with Gateway," he said as they passed each other. "It really slaps, doesn't it?"

Vesta shook her head as she walked back into the living room. Maybe using the word *slap* to denote that something was wonderful was no more obscure than when an older generation began using the word *groovy*.

Neither Henry nor Gus was anywhere to be found in the living room, terrace, or other open rooms of the house. Exhaustion hit Vesta with a full body slam as she considered what to do next. No more alcohol. All she wanted was a bed. Out on the terrace, the heat was still pressing down with its unrelenting grip but at least it was tolerable without the sun. A lounge chair with plump cushions lay next to the infinity pool. Vesta eased herself onto it. The skyline glittered in the distance. She raised her gaze to the deep blue sky above. Only the brightest stars were visible, the others obscured by city lights and hazy air. It was then she realized that the last time she had slept was on a hotel bed in Monument Valley. Twenty-five years ago. All she wanted to do was close her eyes. They were refusing to stay open.

At some point, Sandor fetched her from the terrace, and they drove home. Vesta recalled very little after that, but she awoke feeling refreshed. Grabbing her mobile phone, she found the little square on the screen denoting a calendar. Touching it revealed that she had a tarot reading scheduled with Henry at eleven o'clock that morning. The place was called Hotel Emma located in a renovated Pearl Beer brewery in San Antonio. The questions about why she would choose such a venue would have to wait. She had to get game-ready for Henry.

After a shower, Vesta chose a pair of gray Akris pants with a lighter gray long-sleeve top from L'Agence from her closet. She aimed to dress as unbohemian as possible and was satisfied she achieved her goal.

The next challenge was to drive a car. Sandor had departed an hour earlier. He didn't mention driving so maybe he didn't, but the prospect of driving the computer car was scary. She couldn't take a train, or fly. Out of choices, she picked up her phone. Resourcefulness has always been one of her strengths. If she had to, she would pay someone to drive the car. She tapped on the square with the image of the phone on it. A screen titled Favorites popped up with Concierge listed. She pressed on it and requested her car when a woman answered.

"Do you prefer the Tesla or BMW today Ms. Beauvais?" she asked.

Relief swept through her. "BMW please," Vesta quickly replied. Even if it was a computer car too, she had owned several BMWs and had a feel for them.

After typing in the address of the Hotel Emma she checked

the map on her phone. She had to admit this was a handy tool. The drive would take a little over an hour meaning she needed to leave immediately. Vesta picked up her handbag and walked toward the door before drawing to rigid stop. The tarot cards. She couldn't forget those. Opening the door to the Japanese cabinet in her bedroom, she found many decks of tarot inside. The Rider Waite Smith deck she knew and grabbed them. She would inspect the others later.

When the valet pulled up in front of her in a white convertible BMW she almost shouted for joy. It looked somewhat like the one sitting in her Manhattan garage in 1999. The interior echoed the display screen of the Tesla but still had a gear shifter in the middle so she could put it into Drive without asking for help. The journey south to San Antonio was easy. So was finding the hotel, pulling into the parking lot at ten-thirty.

Any question she may have had about where to sit was answered the moment she walked into the cavernous hotel lounge.

"Hi, Ms. Beauvais!" A petite redhead with shining blue eyes said. "I saw you were scheduled for a reading today. I put the reserved sign up early, just in case. Would you like your usual cappuccino?"

"Um, sure. Thank you."

"I'll bring it over."

"Great," Vesta said.

When the young woman headed out of the lounge, Vesta began hunting for the reserved sign. None of the tables in the center of the room had one. Several people were already sitting around the coffee tables scattered along the perimeter, but no sign was in sight. Vesta walked further into the space. The wood and brick walls soared twenty-five feet high. The antique wood floor creaked as she stepped on it. Odd and end remnants of the old brewery were displayed—a rusty cart, beer barrels, and the like–throughout the place. A double row of windows had been cut into a brick wall to let in the outdoor light. The space felt inviting despite the tinge of melancholy she sensed reaching out to her.

Why had the Vesta of 2024 chosen this place to do tarot readings? The formidable bar to her right wouldn't be the reason. She doubted she had altered her rule of not drinking alcohol while conducting a reading. Pivoting her attention to the left, she noticed three huge vertical tanks that must have held beer during the brewery's working days. Half of the metal tank on the left had been sliced open on the side to allow entrance. A semi-circular banquette filled with cushions now rimmed the interior with a small round table in the middle. Clever idea. The tank in the middle still looked original, with no alterations made. She glanced to the right of it, and noticed the third tank had also been cut open to hold a banquette and table. Her gaze slid above the entry. There on the yellowing white paint, written many decades earlier in crude print, was the word Spirits. Vesta smiled. Peering inside, she knew she would see the sign sitting on the little circular table informing everyone that the space was reserved. Spirits, indeed, were held in the tank in liquid form at one time. Now, she could feel the spirits of another sort.

Vesta climbed three steps into the semi-circular space. Dark gold quilted fabric covered the wall to reduce noise and obscure rusting metal. Another thoughtful touch. She sat down just as the red-haired woman appeared with her cappuccino.

"Thank you so much," Vesta said pulling out her wallet to pay.

"Oh, no Ms. Beauvais," the woman said. "This is on the house. You were exactly right. Or maybe I should say the cards were exactly right about me ditching Brian and going back to college. I've enrolled for the fall semester and even received that grant you told me to go after."

A mixture of surprise and happiness bloomed on Vesta's face. Maybe she was doing good by reading the cards for others.

"I'm delighted to hear this. Thank you for telling me."

"You're welcome. Also," she leaned in closer. "That was my aunt trying to contact me. You were right about that too. You're amazing."

"So glad I could help," Vesta replied cheerfully trying to hide the fact she had no idea what transpired during the reading.

"Yeah, I told my mom what you said, and it really helped her too. She's been missing her sister a lot."

"*What?*" Vesta wanted to say but stopped. Had she begun communicating with the dead? This sounded like a bad turn of events. The former CEO and board chairperson of Sybarite now a card-throwing psychic medium? What a source of pulpy gossip she must be back in New York. Maybe that's why she moved halfway across the country.

"That's great," Vesta murmured half to herself.

"Look at me yammering away. You need to get ready for your reading. Thanks again!"

Vesta nodded. "You're welcome."

She turned away from the sprawling room to stare at the quilted fabric on the wall. Her mind needed some place to rest for a minute to regroup. She was obviously in this fortune-telling business deep. Why? Why would she do this? Maybe this was the only job she could find after resigning from Sybarite. The fact remained; she was here now. And an alchemist from the sixteenth century would arrive any minute for a tarot reading. She had to stay on track with her goal; to send him back to his time without him—or her—causing any time travel paradoxes.

Vesta pulled the tarot cards from her handbag. It was the same deck Amara gave her right after the memory spell had been broken. She'd used the cards several times for her own purposes of enlightenment but only on special occasions for anyone else. They felt like her own personal resource, sacred almost. The tool of the High Priestess to be called into service sparingly. It was clear she had changed her mind over the past twenty years. She began side-shuffling the cards, sensing the tingling warmth of them when she heard his voice.

"Ah, the High Priestess in the tank of Spirits, fitting," Henry cooed as he climbed the steps. "Shall I sit across from you?"

"Should I dispense with calling you Henry then since we both know each other's true identities, Mr. Agrippa?"

Surprise flickered across the alchemist's face so briefly that most wouldn't have caught it, but Vesta did.

"No, I rather like Henry," he said touching the collar of his expensive polo shirt to make sure it lay in place. "I certainly cut a finer-looking figure than that toady king in England with the name."

Henry knew he was handsome, no matter the era he found himself in. His high forehead, Patrician nose, and well-mani-cured mustache composed a face pleasing to all who looked upon him. Once satisfied the collar met his approval, he placed his hands in his lap. "So, that drunken old wizard spilled about our little game, did he?"

"He's a chronicle, not a wizard. Why did you book a reading with me? You know I'm going to stop you from doing whatever you're planning."

"Actually, I have nothing planned. That braggadocio—what did you call him? Chronicle painted this epoch so lively and intellectually stimulating that I chose a little visit here as payment for beating him at cards."

"We both know that's not the truth," Vesta said, her stare frozen on him.

"It is true. The wonders I've seen are beyond anything I

could have dreamed. I only want to live peacefully in this time. To absorb all it offers. That's all."

As he spoke, Vesta activated her InSight to determine if he knew about the prophecy on the wall of Meri's tomb. It confirmed what she already suspected; he did not. Neither did he know she had traveled twenty-five years forward in the future. When she probed about his plans, what he might do to cause chaos, the disaster the prophecy foretold, nothing came forward.

"How did you know I was the High Priestess?" She pressed further releasing the scan of his thoughts.

"Why?" Henry spread his arms wide. "Look at where you're sitting, looking to all the world like the High Priestess of the tarot." He studied her stone gaze for a few seconds. "Okay, that's not the truth. The wiz... Chronicle..."

"Call him Gus. What did he tell you about me?"

"Well," he shrugged as he spoke. "During the course of a long evening's play, he mentioned odd bits here and there of things."

"Odd bits?"

"Yes. You and the other... what are you called? Trionfi? That you lived in this place called Austin. And that there were many wonders here. I was intrigued."

"Uh-huh." Vesta realized she wouldn't get any substance or truth out of Henry. It would be only generalities layered with platitudes aimed at assuaging any fears she had. "Okay. Let's do this reading."

"Wonderful. I want to know what fate has waiting for me."

After shuffling the cards several times, she felt the *shift*. That subtle movement of energy from the tingling to the whole stillness of the deck telling her it was time to look at the top card.

"I will pull three cards," Vesta began. "The first is the overview. This is your energy from a broad standpoint right now." She turned over the first card. The Magician. His arm raised holding a sword pointed to the Heavens while his other tools–wand, cup, and pentacle–lay ready on the table in front of him. Dressed in the colors of the alchemist white and red trimmed in black he stood confident of his abilities.

Vesta and Henry's eyes lifted at the same moment from the card to lock gazes with the other. No words needed to be spoken. Henry had been an alchemist since he was a teenager. Magic, in its most ritualistic sense, he had performed countless times with a confident hand. His tools included not only his understanding of science during his natural time but also the street smarts of a card cheat and master manipulator. The total package was rounded out by his good looks and impeccable manners. Qualities any magician would envy.

Sandor exhibited similar characteristics being the Magician of the tarot. Vesta was well acquainted with his tricks, talents, and pitfalls. But Sandor bore no malicious intent with his actions. Vesta knew she was dealing with basement qualities of the Magician in this alchemist.

"The next card represents your challenge," she continued. Vesta slid the second card from the deck, The High Priestess. Hairs on the back of her neck rose. Again, she felt Henry look from the card to her. She did not meet his fixed stare. The gauntlet had been thrown. They both knew it.

"And finally, this is your course of action called for," she said keeping her voice as impassive as possible. From the deck, she pulled the Moon card. Her gaze slid up slowly to meet Henry's hawk eyes. "Deception. Confusion. Illusion."

"Well," he said leaning back against the quilted wall. "That is enlightening."

Vesta replied with a slight nod.

"I'm not your enemy. Despite what these cards say. I want

to live in peace here in this marvelous age. Don't the cards show that as well?" Henry pointed at the tarot spread.

Before Vesta could answer she caught a flurry of movement to her left outside of the tank. A gaunt figure wearing black jeans, a black shirt unbuttoned halfway down his chest, and jet-black hair pranced to the bottom of the steps.

"I know I'm way beyond my fifteen minutes of allowed tardiness but I..." Liam froze, his mouth open, his eyes glued on Henry.

Vesta almost gasped but stifled her reaction. While the other trionfi members looked older after her twenty-plus-year jump, Liam looked younger. But younger in an unnatural way. What was it that was so off about him? It wasn't just the dyed hair, even though his normal chestnut locks were drenched in sledge-hammer black. No, it was something else. The reality dawned on her as she scanned his face. Not only were no wrinkles visible after sixty-plus years but his skin was pulled as tight as a drum from ear to ear. The shape of his mouth reminded her of the Joker's smile from the old Batman television series; its corners stretched out to a point and turned slightly up. Then there was the matter of the texture of his skin. It possessed such a smooth glossiness. Vesta stared at him while he stared at Henry.

"Um..." Liam stammered. "Could I talk to you for a minute?" He repeatedly curled his index finger with a beck-oning motion toward Vesta.

"I'm fairly certain William wants to tell you he and I have met before. A very long time ago," Henry said, leaning forward.

"It's Liam now. What are you doing here?" The Fool said sweeping a hunk of black hair away from his forehead before it defiantly fell again obscuring one eye.

"I'm having a reading with Vesta here in the Spirits tank of course."

"No. What are you really doing here you nasty alchemist? I could tell the second you laid eyes on me that you remembered me. You're not a RanChan. How did you get here?" Liam's crisp British accent punctuating the last words.

"Are you keeping secrets from your secret society brother Priestess?"

"What? No." Vesta frowned wanting to be careful how she answered any questions. "I haven't talked to Liam since Gus told me about you."

"Who's Gus?" Liam said.

"I'll explain later. In private," she said. Vesta moved her attention to Henry. "We've concluded your reading."

"That was it?" Henry gestured toward the cards lying on the table. "Isn't there more you should tell me? Who I'm going to fall in love with? How many children I will have?"

Vesta's eyes narrowed as she drew a tight smile across her face. The alchemist was trying to belittle her. Did he know it would be easy to strike a nerve this way? Never would she give him such satisfaction.

"That's all." Vesta placed her cards back in the deck, the deck into her handbag, and stood up. She paused. "I will find out and stop you from doing whatever you have planned."

Henry shrugged. "I don't have anything planned. What are you going to do? Follow me everywhere?"

"I have other ways."

"Oh, that's right. You have the sight." Henry pointed toward his head. "You foresee what I'm going to do. I must always be on alert then knowing you are on watch when I relieve myself or take a trollop to my bed."

"You're disgusting!" Liam hissed.

Vesta walked down the stairs. Hooking her arm around Liam's she guided him away from the Spirits tank.

"How did he get here?" Liam loudly whispered to her.

They walked to the bar on the opposite side of the lounge. Vesta eased into one of the high stools at the end. Liam plunked down next to her.

"Now, tell me what's going on," Liam said pulling a small blue tube from the pocket of his shirt. A wrinkle wiggled across Vesta's forehead while she scrutinized the curious device. Liam pulled the black cap off an end before taking a deep drag from it. A small cloud of smoke billowed from his mouth when he exhaled like a genie emerging from a bottle.

"Don't give me that wicked look," he said. "It's better than a cigarette."

"Is it?"

"Who is this Gus person? And why were you reading for that reprobate Cornelius?"

Vesta surveyed the length of the bar searching for the bartender. She spotted him crouched down at the other end, loading bottles of liquor into a cabinet. He looked up and headed toward them. She knew she shouldn't have a cocktail. She didn't need a cocktail. That having a cocktail was not a good way to handle stress. Especially when on a mission to save the world. But it was a chance to relax for a few minutes with her beloved Fool.

"Hey there," The bartender greeted them with sparkling amber eyes and a smile to match. "What can I get for you?"

"A glass of champagne please." She would temper her lack of discipline with wine instead of hard liquor. She felt better already.

"Gilpin's on the rocks for me. And I didn't catch your name," Liam cooed.

"It's Juan," he said flashing another killer smile. "I'll get those to you right away."

"Thank you, Juan." The cooing tone increased.

Vesta turned toward Liam. "That's some heavy flirting there," she said in a low voice.

"He's gorgeous. It's obvious he works out a lot."

From what she could tell, Liam had no problem moving on after Gui's death. Even though it was more than twenty years ago for him, it was only a few months in her awareness. A shudder ran up her back remembering the awful moment she watched him shoot Chloe Deveraux from a point-blank range then profess his undying love to Liam before blowing out his own brains. Vesta didn't think Liam would ever recover from that. He had been deeply in love with Gui. Yet here he was shamelessly making a play for the bartender.

"You were asking about Cornelius Agrippa, who by the way calls himself Henry Page now."

"Hm. Not very clever," Liam said taking another puff from his vape pen. "His first name is Heinrich."

"What do you know about him? How did you two meet during his time?"

Liam waved his hand dismissively. "He was trying to suck up to Francis I in France and Henry VIII in England. Purporting himself as able to create gold in his laboratory. I met him at one of his lectures. He had scribbled several books on the occult and fancied himself a magician, a sorcerer, a seer, all that blather. He liquored me up real good one day. Got me talking more than I should. I may have shared a little too much about who I was and my abilities."

Each of Liam's words steered Vesta closer to the realization Liam might be connected to Gus meeting Henry. She wasn't sure how but the spot between her eyebrows was spinning. The glow a confirmation.

Juan brought their drinks. Liam pulled a fifty-dollar bill out of his jeans pocket and slid it across the bar. "Keep the change," he purred. Juan responded with a demure grin. Liam was about to engage Juan in further conversation, but Vesta reached under the bar to pinch Liam's thigh. He shot a startled look at her.

"What did you tell Henry?"

Juan got the message and retreated to the opposite end of the bar.

"I don't recall exactly," rubbing the pinch point. "He was bragging about how powerful he was. I knew he was just full of flatulence."

"Liam, tell me." She pressed.

The Fool leaned forward on the bar. He took a sip of his cocktail. "I may have told him that I was a real alchemist. Not a pretender like all the rest." He took another sip. "I also may have mentioned how to conjure. Nothing big though."

Vesta exhaled. "Conjure what?"

"You know, simple things."

"No, I don't know. Like what?"

Liam picked up his drink, staring at Juan but not seeing the handsome young man. His thoughts instead traveled across centuries to a specific day he met with Cornelius Agrippa, the newly minted Henry.

It was all about coalescing energy. It has always been that way. Liam realized that early on after the Elders bestowed their gifts on him. Those arrogant alchemists were directing all their attention toward something that would never pay off–trying to convert base metals into gold. Liam laughed at Henry when he boasted about being so close to mastering the process.

"You will never succeed!" he said.

"Why are you so certain?" Henry demanded.

"Because I am a bonafide alchemist. I can manipulate the greatest power in the universe."

The pupils of Henry's eyes dilated, begging for more information. "Tell me," He spoke breathlessly. "I will give you anything."

"You don't have anything I want or need."

"Tell me and I will be your steadfast servant for the remainder of your life."

Liam threw his head back laughing so hard he thought he would faint. "I don't want a servant."

"Then you jest with me. You boast. Every man needs something. If you say you do not, then I think you lie about this magical ability."

Henry pushed the button igniting Liam's ego. He would show him. That evening the Fool took Henry to the ruin of an old Medieval castle at the edge of the newer Renaud family castle where they were currently guests. The quaint village of Alleins lay below wrapped in docile dreams. With tremendous showmanship drama, Liam leaped upon the remains of a low crumbled wall. He cast his arms into the air fingers splayed before they started moving in a rhythmic, calculated way.

"I call upon the elementals, the fairies, and elves who spirit away gold. Bestow upon me a coin or two. To prove how real alchemy is manifest from the masters. In return I will create a fairy ring here at this very place in your honor which all will treat with the deepest respect," he intoned.

Liam swept his hands together then flung them wide again, repeating the pattern many times. The frenzy of motion created an audible tone so low the human ear could barely pick it up. Accompanying this sound was the faintest visual distortion of Liam as he swooped his arms back and forth. His image seemed to waver with a slow velocity. At last, with seemingly great effort, he pulled his hands close together yet not touching. After drawing in a great breath which he held for several moments he released it with a howl. The sharp sound startled Henry who had been standing transfixed watching the spectacle. Liam looked down at the fellow alchemist letting himself drop from the wall to the ground. He walked over to Henry with hands held out. They sprung open revealing a shiny gold coin in each hand.

A smirk coiled on Henry's face. "Fancy illusion, that's all," he puffed. "You possessed the coins in your pockets before you began."

"I did not! It's real," Liam's voice high with indignation.

"The waving around of the arms, nothing but theatrics. And what were you doing with your fingers? Silly child games."

Liam thrust his head toward Henry. "I was conjuring. That's how you do it." He replicated the finger movements. "These movements condense the energy into your very hands. You can summon anything with these."

Henry's focus was glued to the Fool's gestures. A maniacal smile slipped into place. "I just needed to see the sequence once more." He tapped his finger against his head. "Now, I've got it."

Horror replaced indignation on Liam's face. "You tricked me!"

"Easy enough to do." Henry grabbed the coins from Liam's hands. "Thank you for this. And thank the fairies."

"You can't use my conjuring."

"Of course, I can. And will." Henry said walking away.

"Wait. We must create the fairy ring. Gather stones. Clear the ground. Set them in a sacred circle."

"It wasn't my promise," Henry replied without looking back.

"And so," Liam said looking at Vesta with a dreary expression. "I behaved like the Fool once again. Duped by an inferior."

"What did he do after that?"

"I don't know. I left for Paris the next morning. I wanted nothing to do with him. My guess is he began coaxing gold coins from the elves."

Or Vesta thought, he brought Gus into his time to cheat him at cards, travel to this time turning the world into a hellish place.

"But how did Cornelius–er–Henry end up here?"

"What year did that happen between you and Henry?"

Liam tried to furrow his brow as he thought about the question, but his forehead muscles refused to move. "Well, I would be lying if I said I could remember the year, but I do recall you were in London around then visiting poor Thomas More while he was locked up."

Vesta wished she could recall more details about her past lives, but the memory spell she cast on herself obliterated most of them. Maybe forever.

"Look it up on your phone," Liam said as he waved to Juan for another cocktail.

"On my phone?" Vesta gave him a quizzical look. What was he talking about? She pulled her phone out of her handbag, typed her code in then stared at a dozen little squares looking for what? Names underneath them gave her clues as to what they were, Settings, Mail, Calendar, and Camera. Vesta smiled. She recalled thinking during her time how useful it would be to have a camera attached to her mobile phone. And here it was. But there was no clue about Cornelius Agrippa, Thomas More, or anything related to the 1500s in Europe.

She frowned. How could she find out what Liam meant without giving away the secret about her time travel? The last thing she wanted to do was cause one of those paradoxes erasing her or Liam from history.

"So, what did it say?" Liam asked.

"Ah..." Vesta stammered. "I'll find it later."

"What's the matter with you? You're usually Miss Know-It-All whipping out that phone of yours."

Liam took his mobile phone from his back pocket. Vesta watched him hold it up to his face then press a button and begin typing. "There," he said. "1534. That was when you left Chartres for London. It was early spring. That part I do remember."

Vesta grabbed Liam's phone from his hand. There on the screen was a biography of Sir Thomas More. A vague recollection slid into her awareness of the kind and gentle man who held steadfast to his beliefs. Who would not accept Henry VIII as the head of the Church of England. Who lost his life because of it. The wisp of a chill swept through her recalling the drafty cold of the horrible Tower of London. A fleeting image of her gathering up long heavy white cotton in her hands to climb dark stairs. Black scuffed shoes peaked from behind the folds as she took each step. Vesta blinked. She looked down at the shiny patent leather bootlets from Chanel covering her feet now. Had she really been so different from who she was in this life? The premise seemed wholly impossible. Thoughts for another day.

Juan handed a fresh Gilpin's to Liam. "Would you like another glass of champagne?" He asked her.

"No. I'm fine for right now." Vesta looked back at Liam's phone trying to figure out which square he pressed for the information. Feeling frustrated she began pressing one square after another. One titled Facebook brought up an endless stream of photos of random people doing random things. Comments unfurled beneath each photo along with a stream of ads. Another square titled Instagram was basically the same thing. Did Liam know all these people? There seemed to be hundreds as she scrolled through the apps. Vesta kept looking filtering through weather, banking, and airline apps. Finally, she pressed a square looking like a compass on the bottom row next to the phone icon. Two rows of rectangles displayed a variety of topics in each rectangle. The majority were articles about cosmetic surgery, and something called Botox which looked ghastly. In the bottom rectangle, she found the article about Thomas More. This was the internet on a mobile phone! It was genius.

Liam was purring to Juan about an upcoming performance at Austin City Limits. He was saying he was personal friends of the Black Angels and might even get on stage during the show. Would Juan be interested in joining him backstage?

Vesta knew she was about to lose him for the remainder of the day if she didn't rein him in. She laid her hand on top of Liam's squeezing it just enough. "Remember, we need to finish discussing that little matter?"

Liam tried to frown at her, but his forehead muscles refused to budge. "Oh, alright," he said. He motioned to Juan with his hand to call him. The bartender smiled before moving back to the other end of the bar.

"He's adorable, isn't he?"

"Sure," she said dismissing the thought. She had to get as much information as possible from Liam about their current lives. Henry was determined to do something, acquire something, alter something that would change the course of history. She had to stop him. Magician. High Priestess. Moon. The tarot cards laid out the story. Stopping him wasn't going to be easy.

"You didn't answer me," Liam said. "Who the bloody hell is this Gus person?"

Vesta pressed her lips together. If she revealed who Gus was Liam might figure out the truth. That could bring disaster. But she needed his help. As an alchemist, he could know things she didn't. Plus, he was her best friend. Her only friend. She didn't want to lie to him. A partial truth was better than a lie, she decided.

"He's someone I met recently. Henry knows him too obviously. What could Henry want in this era? Why do you think he came here?"

Liam sipped his cocktail. "The question is how did he come here? How did he hook up with you?"

"I don't know. He booked a reading with me."

"But he knows you're the High Priestess. That's clear as the nose on my perfect face."

Vesta shrugged. Their conversation was going nowhere. Amara and Jared would have more answers. That's where she needed to start.

"Okay. It was good to see you." She stood up.

"Where the hell do you think you're going?"

"Back to Austin."

"Oh, no. You're going with me to that thing."

Vesta held her breath trying to decide how to answer. Should she ask what thing? Should she just agree to go? Or maybe she could come up with an excuse not to go.

"Let's go," she said.

Liam laid another fifty-dollar bill on the bar and made the call-me hand gesture once again toward Juan who was busy serving other customers. He may have been smiling at Juan, but it was hard to tell because Liam's revamped face looked like it was kind of smiling all the time now.

They headed out of the lounge area into the entry lobby. Vesta continued walking out of the hotel when Liam called out to her. She looked back to see he wasn't behind her.

"Hey! It's this way." Vesta spun on her heel catching up with him. "What's the matter with you today?" He asked.

"Nothing. I just couldn't remember where you said it was."

Liam shook his head. "What are you talking about? You wrangled me into this."

"Right. Just feeling a little off balance since that reading."

"Bloody maggot. He's up to no good that's for certain. Now, where's the girl and her parents?"

Liam stared at Vesta's pursed lips. He knew she had no clue what he was asking. "What is going on? Did you majorly tie one on at the Odin party last night?"

"I was exhausted." Vesta fumbled for words. "I..."

"Mr. Spencer! We're so honored to have you," a voice called from behind them.

Liam and Vesta looked to their left to see a middle-aged couple dressed in formal attire approaching from a ballroom. The man reached out, shaking hands with them.

"I'm Fernando Gonzales, and this is my wife, Gloria. I can't tell you how excited we are that you are the entertainment for our Bianca's quinceanera!"

Vesta's eyes grew wide. She had heard about this ancient custom, a coming-of-age ritual for girls when they turn fifteen, dating back to the Aztec culture. Spanish and Latin families still celebrated in modern times. Some of the parties were astoundingly grand with custom gowns for the young woman and her mother, rental of expensive hotel ballrooms, and hiring of world-class musicians. Vesta let her gaze slide over to Liam who was being barraged by a wave of compliments and instructions on what to do next. He stood with that polite but glazed look of his which meant no more information was getting through to his Fool brain. He would ask her to pare it down in bite-sized morsels after they left. It was obvious she set it up. But why would Liam agree to it? He was a legendary rock star who would have never played a child's party in 1999. What happened?

Following another solid two minutes of telling Liam when to play following the father's speech, their daughter's favorite songs, and calling her out by name for the first dance, the couple shook hands with Liam and Vesta again before heading back into the ballroom to speak to the catering crew.

Liam glared at Vesta as he pulled the vape pen from his pocket. "Don't ever do this to me again! I know I need money, but this is too much." He drew a long drag from the pen. "You did get a tidy sum for me though. But that doesn't mean you can leave me here alone. You're staying for the whole damn thing."

"I'm not dressed for this formal event." Vesta looked down at her slacks and sweater.

Liam stomped his foot on the floor. "Stop it! All you've been talking about is that dress your friend Christian what's his name made for you so you could wear it to this. You took it up to the room they rented for me here yesterday morning." He blew out a trail of smoke, leaned closer to her, and whispered. "I want to know what's going on right now or I won't get on that stage."

Chapter Six

Gus sat on a wide rocky outcrop gnawing on a tasty roasted chicken thigh as the sacking of Rome played out below him. He had witnessed this event many times but as far as sackings went throughout human history, this was his favorite. There were several reasons for his preference. First, and most important, it lasted only three days. He didn't have to invest a lot of time in it. Some sieges took weeks or months. By August 27, 410 AD, the Visigoths picked up all the spoils from their plundering and their newly wrangled slaves to head south.

From his vantage point at the top of Monte Mario, he could observe the entire city. The Roman Forum lay five kilometers in the distance where he could see smoke rising from the basilicas of Julia and Aemilia in its heart. The Gardens of Sallust to the northeast were also ablaze. The carefully landscaped pleasure garden which had enticed guests for more than three hundred years would never be seen again. He watched hordes of the barbarian tribe move as dark shape-shifting masses through the narrow streets of the poor and the wide paved roads of the wealthy. He could hear the cries of the Christians as well as those of the pagans who still worshipped the old gods. All Romans were treated in the same manner regardless of status.

It wasn't that he really enjoyed such blood sport. He was bored. The tedious job of a chronicle was never-ending. A literal fact. His job never ended nor took a pause. Gus had no recollection of coming into being. He didn't have a mother. He wasn't born. He simply burst into consciousness well before the bi-peds ever took their first steps. Talk about boring times. It wasn't until he observed the early form of cave-dwelling homo sapiens in what would become France and Spain that things began to look up for him. The humans would blow ochre pigment through a hollow animal bone onto their hands placed against a cave wall. When they moved their hand, the outline of it would be perfectly visible. He remembered a curious vibration—what he later identified as excitement—coursing through him. As he focused on the humans he observed, the sensation intensified, and his formless state began to shift. Slowly, his essence molded into the shape of the humans, their features imprinting on him as if he were mirroring them. Though the manifestation vanished as soon as the excitement faded, it lasted long enough for him to realize one thing: he could summon it again.

He began following them everywhere to capture the sensation again. When he did, he would focus all his energy to hold onto it. Staring at the humans seemed to help. One particularly large male with a long, scraggly beard drew his attention. The large eyes and slim nose became ingrained in his awareness. Slowly, he took on the form of this man, holding onto the vibration until he became substance. The skin wasn't flesh and blood skin. It was some expression of consciousness in physical form, but it would do.

From that day forward, Gus moved among the humans. He got to know hundreds in dozens of eras, developing the ability to interact, eat, and drink with them. Liquor was undoubtedly his favorite of all the things they consumed. It gave him a peculiar feeling, a blend of contentment and recklessness. The potent combination of these human emotions had gotten him into trouble before, but never as much as this time. He took another bite of the chicken followed by a gulp of red wine from a cask sitting next to him. There was no other choice but to trust the High Priestess of the trionfi, he told himself. He didn't realize that the ones she called the Elders had foreseen his blunder. Going so far as to carve it on the walls of a tomb, they knew the terrible consequences for this species if Agrippa succeeded. If the Elders knew, that meant the chronicle for their planet knew. Not that he cared all that much, but he didn't want to be replaced.

He liked Earth. Other worlds he had heard of weren't nearly so accommodating. The dominant species of countless planets were either so simple-minded and boring or so advanced they lacked anything close to a sense of fun. These humans had found a sweet spot with their lively amusements, tasty food, and drink. Worry was sitting with him there on the sunny rock overlooking Rome though. He knew that planets had dealt with fractures in their timelines, spills from careless time travel that resulted in devastation for the inhabitants, and removal of the chronicle. Where did these chronicles go? He never knew. They just vanished. Gus shifted uncomfortably, reaching for the wine again. Don't worry, he told himself. Vesta Beauvais would stop Agrippa. If that was the fact though why did the carvings on the tomb leave it as a question to answer? And why had he witnessed catastrophic scenes of what this planet would be like if Agrippa accomplished his goal?

* * *

Henry watched Vesta and Liam walk across the wide expanse of the hotel lounge to the bar. He leaned against the padded wall in the Spirits tank, pondering how Vesta knew his true identity. The alchemist Liam remembered him from the little magic show with the fairy coins back in his time. But he had never met Vesta, the high and mighty Priestess of tarot. He hadn't heard about any of the other trionfi until he got Gus liquored up one night. Gus. He told her. That had to be it. Were all the trionfi searching for him now?

Jumping to his feet, Henry left the Spirits tank. As he exited the hotel, he called under his breath for Gus. "I know you can hear me, Wizard. We need to talk. Right now, or there will be formidable consequences to pay."

He strolled next door to the Brasserie Mon Chou Chou, its elegant façade dappled with midday sunlight. The hostess guided him to an outdoor seat shaded by a wide umbrella, the terrace bustling with the quiet hum of conversation. Settling into his chair, Henry muttered his threats under his breath, his sharp eyes scanning the street. Finally, from around the corner, Gus appeared, shuffling into view. The chronicle's layered silk robes faded and frayed with age swayed rhythmically as he moved, catching the bright light with the air of a spectral wanderer.

"I was watching a perfectly good sacking of Rome. Why did you disturb me?"

"Sit, Wizard."

"I'm not a wizard."

"I know. I know. The priestess of the trionfi educated me on that fact recently." He waved his hand for Gus to sit. "How did she know who I was?"

Gus heaved himself into the chair across from Henry. He cocked his head to one side mumbling, avoiding eye contact.

"Spare me any half-truths or outright lies," Henry interrupted. "You told her. That is obvious."

"I had no choice. I was summoned, just as you called me here now."

Henry leaned across the table staring at Gus. His narrowed hawk eyes unblinking. "What does she know that I don't about me being in this epoch?"

The server approached their table. "Can I get you gentlemen started with a drink and appetizers?"

"Bring us your finest whiskey, straight up," Henry said, his gaze never leaving Gus. "We'll begin there."

"Yes, sir," she said.

"You're intending to loosen my lips again." Gus leaned back in his chair. "I have nothing to hide."

"Then speak," Henry replied. "And only the truth or I will make your life hell on Earth."

Guttural laughter welled up from the chronicle's belly, emerging like a deep Santa Claus ho-ho-ho laugh from his mouth. "I do not have a life. I witness life." He poked his large hand with his finger. "This is not human flesh like yours." He grunted with a smirk. "I mimicked this image. Created it from a frequency I caught and held onto. It's merely my amusement. You cannot harm me."

Their server reappeared with their drinks. "Garrison Brothers small batch bourbon, sir," she said setting the glasses on the table.

"Thank you. That's all for now," Henry said nodding at her. He picked up his glass, returning his focus to Gus. "Well, then, let's drink to amusement."

Gus eyed Henry for a moment before picking up the glass. He brought it close to his nose inhaling deeply. The contour of his mouth relaxed. The shape of pleasure, soft and yielding moved into place. He tilted the glass letting the caramel-colored liquid spill onto his tongue. Henry could hear the sigh that followed.

"Is it better than what you drank with your General Grant?"

Gus smiled. "This is the nectar the old gods of Greece would be jealous of."

Henry took a sip. "I must say, those arrogant Bourbon royals would be proud of this."

Gus threw the remainder of the drink down his throat. He set the glass on the table and smiled. Henry signaled for another round from the server.

"Are you hungry?" Henry picked up the menu the server had laid in front of him. He caught the twinkle in Gus's eyes. "The beef and chicken dishes look superb. Let's order both. And the escargot, of course."

When the second round arrived, Henry placed their order. He made a toast to the Bourbon dynasty, and they drained their glasses. Henry ordered another round. Following the next toast, this time to the impressive craftsmanship of spirits-making in this epoch, Henry leaned forward, elbows on the table. Gus's glassy eyes looked like open portals into another dimension.

"How does Vesta Beauvais know I time-traveled here?" Henry's stare pierced the portals.

"It was that meddling sprite, Luna. She took her to the tomb where the prophecy is carved in the stone."

Henry lifted his chin almost imperceptibly. "What prophecy?"

"The one saying you would horrifically mar human history by your actions here if she didn't stop you."

Their food arrived. Gus eagerly dove in with both hands.

"What do I do here that changes history?" Henry's focus was so intense he wasn't even taking a breath.

"You take something back to your time," Gus said wiping his greasy fingers from the chicken on his Grateful Dead T-shirt.

"Something that makes me more powerful and rich than anyone else?"

Gus nodded.

Henry watched the slovenly chronicle eat the chicken and steak then swallow more liquor. His appetite was bottomless. So was his own, but not for food or drink. The Gateway device would be his Sorcerer's Stone. He would rule over the grotesque Henry VIII of England and the silly Francis I of France. No one could stop him. Ultimate power would be his unless the trionfi interfered. He squinted at Gus who was licking his fingers with glee.

"Why haven't the trionfi unified to stop me? I was at the home of the Emperor and Empress of the tarot last night. The Magician was there too. None of them said an unkind or threatening word to me."

Gus looked up from his plate, his sated gaze blurry. "The Priestess traveled here like you. From twenty-five Earth years earlier. I told her she could create a possible paradox if she told anyone of her time voyage. No one else knows what the prophecy says but her."

Henry sat back in his chair carefully smoothing his mustache. He had to act quickly. This window of opportunity would surely close soon.

* * *

Vesta convinced Liam to perform for the quinceanera by telling him nothing was wrong with her except exhaustion and promising him dinner that night wherever he wanted to go. He chose Justine's on the far east side of Austin. Amara and Jared decided to join them. Vesta was glad they did because she needed to understand how they knew Henry Page. Her confidence in maneuvering through her new, unfamiliar life had increased. All she had to do was figure out how to send Henry back to his time, and she could return to her own.

Sandor and Vesta agreed to pick up Liam on the way to the restaurant. Heading into an older neighborhood in the central part of the city, she was surprised to discover he was staying in the guest house of a famous filmmaker. Robert Rodriguez made the brilliant El Mariachi in the early 1990s and then followed it up with several hit films in the same decade. It was obvious he was still making movies and doing well with them by the looks of the whimsical, sprawling castle-like house he lived in. Was Liam acting in movies now, Vesta wondered. It didn't take long to find out. The moment Liam slid into the backseat of the Tesla, he began to whine.

"I'm perfect for a supporting role in the film Robert's working on but he's not going to give it to me."

"Buddy, you've never acted before," Sandor said typing the restaurant's address into the car's navigation system. "Why do you think you deserve a role in a major motion picture?"

"Stop being so cruel, Sandor! I've performed on stage for decades during my concerts. What do you think that entails?" He pulled his vape pen out.

"You can't smoke in my car."

"Ugh!" Liam tried to wince but the overly stretched and Botoxed muscles on his face only allowed him to bare his teeth unnaturally.

"That's the other reason," Sandor continued, eyeing him in the rearview mirror. "You've had too much surgery on your face to play anything other than a drag queen."

"Sandor!" Vesta barked.

"Somebody needed to say it."

"You're jealous," Liam sneered. "I look young and beautiful just like I did when I used to play CBGB. Remember Vesta?"

She pressed her lips together for a moment wondering if she dared be honest with the Fool. His cosmetic enhancements were pushed to the limit, but if he felt as though he had regained his youth, who was she to suggest otherwise? He counted on her for support, and she wouldn't take that away from him.

A soft smile bloomed on her face. "I do remember. Such fun times," she murmured.

The rest of the way Liam rode in sullen silence while Vesta listened patiently to Sandor talking about his belief the U.S. economy had made a soft landing after the COVID-19 pandemic. What was Covid-19? What pandemic, she wondered? It sounded horrendous and like it had made a world-wide impact. Halfway there, Sandor programmed the car to drive itself so he could pick up his mobile phone to type out a text. Vesta used the opportunity to grab her phone and press the little compass icon. She typed COVID-19 into the search bar. Thousands of results began to populate. As she quickly scrolled through the headlines, she became more alarmed by what she read. Could this be what the Elders foresaw in the future? Did Agrippa create it? It couldn't be she decided because both Gus and Luna said it happened beyond the year 2024. If what he would bring to the world was worse than this, then she shuddered at the thought of what it could be. He must be stopped. But from doing what?

Sandor turned onto a dark abandoned-looking street. In the distance hung a modest sign proclaiming Justine's in dazzling white neon with the word Brasserie above it in hot red. The car pulled up to the curb beside the sign. Liam hopped out in a flash slamming the door. Vesta got out and followed him. They walked beneath an enormous white tent packed with diners to an ornate wooden podium where the host stood. She ushered them to a table where Amara and Jared were already seated. Sandor joined them a minute later after parking the car.

There they all sat–the High Priestess, the Magician, the Empress, the Emperor, and the Fool of the ancient tarot–in a splendid space. Giant majesty palms in huge pots sat in front of gauzy white curtains pulled back into sweeping curves. Glittering chandeliers hung in a grand row along the high peaked spine of the tent. Conversations all around them sparkled as fine as the stemware on the table. The servers without exception exuded sensational style with their eclectic clothing choices and fascinating tattoos which almost seemed a prerequisite for the job.

Liam grabbed his vape pen from the front pocket of his half-unbuttoned black shirt.

"You…" Amara began. Vesta sitting across from her sister gave her a nudge with her foot. Amara glanced at her. Vesta gave her head a quick shake. Amara didn't finish her sentence pivoting to a new subject.

"Um, did everyone have a spectacular day?" Amara asked.

"I performed at a children's party," Liam said blowing a steady stream of smoke from his mouth. "Career highlight." He took another long drag.

Sandor leaned back in his chair. "I went for a swim on the rooftop and had a massage."

Liam shot him a peevish look before taking another drag.

"Well, I worked on the underground water storage project Conscious Evolution Partners is involved with. It's coming along quite nicely. Jared, tell them about your amazing day."

Jared aimed his gentle smile at her. "I went to the lab today. Our biomedical engineers wanted to show me the latest stage in the chip we're developing to help people dealing with dementia."

"It has the potential to drastically reduce the effects of that terrible disease," Amara added.

"We're cautiously hopeful," Jared said.

"So," Vesta began. "Who is this Henry Page guy who was at your party last night?" She was afraid Liam would jump in with his recounting of his encounter with him five hundred years earlier, but he was preoccupied with puffing on his vape pen while staring at his phone.

"He's a new investor," Jared said. "I don't know much about him. Why?"

"I pulled tarot cards for him today."

"How did it go?" Amara asked. "You said you were looking forward to it."

"Yeah, fine," Vesta said dismissively. "Is he interested in any particular area of Odin products or research?"

A thoughtful expression faded onto Jared's face. "Not that I'm aware of. But I haven't spoken to him much. He contacted our main office, saying he was a broker for a consortium of wealthy European clients who wanted to invest in our company. He transferred several million dollars to Odin that day."

The server arrived at their table with a bottle of Veuve Clicquot. When Vesta glanced toward her, she realized it was Serena, the woman who handed her a glass of champagne at Amara and Jared's party. Her long hair shone like highly polished ebony. She wore it parted simply down the middle allowing her flawless ivory skin brushed with the reddest of lips to command center stage. With careful yet swift movements she filled each glass, her wide dark eyes scrutinizing each pour to make them exact.

"Is everyone ready to order?" She asked in a polite voice directed at Jared.

"No, I think we'll enjoy our champagne first. Thank you, Serena."

"She's the same person from your house last night. Does she usually work here?" Vesta asked.

Jared squinted slightly at her question. Sandor looked up from the wine list in his hand to study her face for a moment before returning his gaze to the list.

"She does," Jared replied slowly. Her third eye began to spin. What was she missing?

"For crying out loud, what is wrong with you?" Liam blurted. "You've been acting positively crazy all day. How could you forget that you teach Serena a new phrase in French every time we come here, which is all the time?"

Vesta's mouth dropped open as though she was about to say something, but no words were spoken. Instead, her gaze floated around the table to each face of her trionfi family who stared at her. Heat raced to her face. She knew her cheeks had to be aflame. A fine sweat beaded on the back of her neck and a shiver raced through her.

"Excuse me." She bounded for the host's podium, asking for directions to the restroom. She was aware the trionfi was watching her. Moving just shy of a run, she exited the tent to enter the little house, the original part of Justine's. She walked swiftly past the bar, past the kitchen, to the women's restroom. It was thankfully empty. She stepped into one of the two stalls and closed the door before folding against the wall with a sob.

She had screwed up in front of all of them. The entire mission to stop Agrippa seemed doomed to failure. On top of that, she was risking a time travel catastrophe caused by her stupidity. An involuntary shaking began in her legs, spread to her arms, then her fingers. *Get control of yourself*, she demanded. Maybe Agrippa was telling the truth. Maybe he decided to live in this time peacefully. Maybe just being in this time with him, maybe her threat had changed his mind. If so, she could call out to Gus to get him to send her back to 1999.

The Vesta of this time would pop back into their body, sending everything back to normal.

A soft knocking on the door of the bathroom stall caused her to jump. "Vesta, it's me. Open the door please," Amara's calming voice called out.

"No, I'm okay."

"I can help you," she said.

"Amara, I'm fine. I'll rejoin everyone in a minute."

"Sister, let me in. I'm not leaving."

Vesta let out a long exhale. She knew when Amara made up her mind there was no changing it. She would stand outside of the stall until she opened the door even if it meant standing there all night. Vesta slid the little bolt to the side. The Empress of the tarot gently pushed the door open with the toe of her shoe. She stepped in. Vesta could feel the bright blue eyes of her sister soften as she apprised her condition.

Amara reached her hand out to Vesta who recoiled at first but relented to her approach. From her sister's fingertips, a pale shade of rose emerged touching Vesta's hand before the flesh of her fingers arrived. Gentleness, warmth, and what Vesta could only describe as love flowed from Amara into her body.

"You push yourself so hard," the Empress murmured. "I feel stress tied up in every cell of your body. Turn it loose now. Breathe it out." She brought her other hand up to Vesta's chest.

Deep within her, a tight grip loosened. Originating in her belly, expanding through her diaphragm, her heart, shoulders, and neck the energetic vice released. Vesta's third eye exploded with a stream of black smoke billowing out blocking her vision. Fractals of color, shards of jeweled glass, followed dissolving the smoke while creating a matrix around her. A sigh poured out of her as her jaw relaxed.

The matrix slowly faded. In its place, a vision formed. She stood in the same spot, but her surroundings looked vastly different. No women's restroom, no Justine's restaurant with the elegant, tented dining room. In its place, a sooty sky hovered above a desolate space dotted with chunks of broken cement with weeds growing in sparse patches around them. In the distance, a lanky dog ran down the rutted road, a man chasing after it with a stick. A deep rumbling sound she sensed first under her feet rose in volume to a deafening reverberation. Vesta put her hands over her ears, but the roar was in her head.

Screams rose behind her. She turned around to see two young girls dressed in dull gray shift dresses being dragged from a lean-to of corrugated metal. Three men wearing solid black with combat helmets on their heads were striking them with batons. Vesta tried to run to them but couldn't move from the spot. Their wails grew louder with each blow, more excruciating. Anger pocked with hatred boiled inside her. Is this InSight of what Agrippa will cause if he succeeds according to the prophecy? Vesta repeated the question over and over in her mind until the answer came. Yes, this was what the actions of Cornelius Agrippa in the twenty-first century would create.

Chapter Seven

Vesta slept late into the next morning. Sunshine beamed like a laser from a point high in the sky when she at last climbed out of bed. Sandor was thankfully nowhere in sight. After making a double espresso, she sat down on the sofa staring out the wall of windows watching squashed marshmallow clouds march across a swimming pool sky. All the trionfi, even Liam, acted as if nothing strange had happened after Amara and she returned from Justine's women's restroom. They finished the bottle of champagne, ordered more wine, cocktails, and food. Their conversation instead centered on a business venture Sandor was developing in a town called Fredericksburg, west of Austin.

It had been a welcome distraction giving Vesta time to process her terrifying InSight. Luna's warning about what the world would look like after Agrippa's meddling she had finally seen for herself. It still felt as though a rock sat wedged in the bottom of her stomach as she parsed through what she had witnessed. What would he change to cause such a brutal situation? Whatever it was she had to stop him. According to the prophecy on Meri's tomb wall, she was the only one who could.

The gnawing question was how? She couldn't follow him around constantly to find out.

The now familiar click announcing the release of the front door deadbolt brought her attention back into the room. Sandor strode in wearing a Stetson cowboy hat and an expensive-looking pair of cowboy boots. At first, she thought it was a costume because he looked so out of character without his usual Ralph Lauren apparel. But she immediately understood he was presenting a serious side of himself she hadn't met yet.

"Is that what you're wearing to Fred?"

Vesta pursed her lips for only a second before relaxing her mouth. Who was Fred? She refused to make another mistake like she had the night before by asking a question. She glanced down at her silk robe.

"Obviously not," she replied with a note of sarcasm.

"I took my bag down to the car. It's waiting at the valet stand. Did you forget we were going today?"

Vesta swallowed the remainder of her espresso. "Of course not. Give me ten minutes. I was exhausted last night and needed to sleep in this morning."

Her mastery of logic could sort the situation out. Something this simple wouldn't trip her up. Assimilating the facts as she walked to her closet, she knew they were heading to see someone named Fred. It was an overnight trip by car, two nights at the most otherwise he would have called a taxi to take them to the airport. Accessing another trionfi's thoughts through her InSight was impossible. Each maintained impenetrable blocks to prevent that from ever happening. So, she relied on her logic, but she was excellent at reading people without the aid of her InSight. A dress code of cowboy attire seemed mandatory to see this Fred person. Perhaps he was a client of Sandor's who liked to dress in such attire. Whatever the reason, she focused on the task.

Inside her closet, no trace of a cowboy hat or boots could be found. Thinking she might have stored such rarely used items in another closet she checked the two guest rooms. No sign of anything related to the Old West except for her worn-out boots she arrived with from 1999. Sandor was far too well dressed in his Stetson and custom-made snake-skin boots for her to wear those. She raced back to her main closet. A small piece of Louis Vuitton luggage sat in a corner. She began stuffing it with everything that could be suitable with Sandor's outfit. A pale blue shirt with pearl-snap buttons she found hanging from a rack. On a shelf sat a pair of neatly folded black jeans. They looked great together. All she needed was to add the pair of black and white Jimmy Choo platform sneakers waiting patiently on a shoe stand and she was ready.

Fifteen minutes later, they turned west on Highway 290 with the Tesla autopilot switched on. Trusting a computer to safely transport them at seventy miles per hour wasn't easy. Vesta scrutinized every turn and lane change it made until well beyond the town of Johnson City an hour later. Finally, bored with her obsession and cautiously confident the autopilot wouldn't send them careening off the road, she leaned back in the passenger seat to gaze at the changing landscape. They passed one winery estate after another. Some boasted huge garish signs propped in front of dusty caliche rock parking lots filled with cars. Others announced their name on more discreet signage with well-designed logos. Tasting rooms bathed in modern architectural styles neighbored estates exuding old-world European flavor. In between, vineyards with tidy rows of grape plantings sprawled to the horizon.

Vesta recalled reading an article on an airplane flight about Texas wine. Even in 1999, it had begun to flourish as a worthy enterprise. Now, two decades later, it had clearly grown to impressive proportions.

Posted by a column of manicured grapevines, she noticed a road sign proclaiming Fredericksburg lay ten miles ahead. Vesta smiled to herself. They weren't going to see someone named Fred. They were going to a town they had obviously been to more than once. Often enough that it had earned a nickname between them.

Vesta eyed Sandor who sat in the driver's seat focused on his mobile phone reading emails. Only bits and pieces of their past lives together lingered in her awareness. The spell she cast on herself in her previous life wiped multitudes of past life memories away. The only solid recollections remaining about their time together came from this life. In this one, Sandor was a New Yorker born and bred. Seeing him sitting in the driver's seat of a car in his crisp white shirt with pearl-snap buttons and blue jeans seemed so out of character for him. Maybe it wasn't according to his dozens of lives before. But for her at that moment, it was unusual. Attractive, actually.

For a good chunk of this life, she had treated him with disdain and disregard. They had met soon after she graduated from college. She was on the hunt for a job within a company where she knew she could move up. Fortune opened the door for her one night while tending bar. As far as dive bars go Dreamland was one of the nicer ones she'd worked at. Plus, it was across the street from the main branch of the New York Public Library. When she wasn't working or filling out job applications with her newly minted bachelor's degree in marketing with a minor in fashion design in her hand, she could be found at the historic library. Situated at a corner table in the main reading room, a stack of books on various topics were her constant companions for hours.

Dreamland, on the other hand, was as different from the library as Sid Vicious was from Luciano Pavarotti. Squeezed into a narrow space on 40th Street near 5th Avenue, a dark blue wall stretched the length of the bar. Scattered across it lay crudely painted silver stars and an enormous ugly yellow moon with a face, eyes closed as if asleep. But the air conditioning was always cold on sweltering summer days and the clientele seemed to want privacy more than a party.

The evening began as many had before. A couple of the regulars were sitting at the bar. One reading a borrowed library copy of The Stranger by Albert Camus, the other picking through a dog-eared copy of an old Vanity Fair magazine someone had left at a table weeks earlier. Both were nursing stiff bourbon cocktails and in no hurry to be anywhere. She was washing glasses in the sink built under the bar when an elderly-looking man walked in. His tailored suit caught her eye. The tan and navy plaid on both the jacket and the trousers could have gone very wrong, but it didn't. Instead, the tight pattern reminded her of Burberry, but it wasn't. His closely cropped gray hair and wide-set brown eyes peering from behind round wire-framed glasses paired well with his suit.

He stood at the bar carefully avoiding contact with the surface. Taking note of this, Vesta wiped off the bar in front of him with a clean towel sitting next to the glasses. It was a spotless surface already. Neither sticky nor dirty surfaces would ever be allowed to dwell on her bar, but he didn't know that.

"What'll you have?"

"Dry gin martini, no garnish."

"Bombay, okay?"

He nodded.

As she slid the icy-cold cocktail toward him, she noticed the deep lines framing his mouth, dominating his forehead. The man looked exhausted.

"Want to start a tab?"

"Sure," he said picking up his drink. He walked to the two-top in the far corner and took a sizable sip before he sat down aiming his back to the bar.

Vesta fished her notebook out of her handbag. Grabbing her pen, she began scribbling a description of the man's suit onto a blank page. From her periphery, she noticed another man enter the bar. This one her age broadcasting GQ magazine model vibes with every step. Polished amber eyes – the color the ugly moon should have been – an aquiline nose with a chiseled jawline that would put even Brad Pitt to shame. The slicked-back black hair barely touching the collar of his white shirt in a deliberate fashion completed the look. She rubbed a spot on her forehead between her eyes that suddenly itched like a mosquito bite. When she did the pen in her hand scrawled a squiggly little line on her skin.

He walked up to the bar leaning casually on it.

"What's your best scotch?

"Johnnie Walker Black," she said trying to wipe the ink stain away but succeeding only in smudging the line into a splotch on her forehead. "We have Chivas Regal 12-year too but it's expensive."

A smile moved into place highlighting his perfect row of teeth.

"No problem. Neat."

Vesta turned her back to him. With one hand she grabbed the liquor bottle with the other she picked up the bar towel scraping it across her forehead vigorously. She turned toward him pouring the shot.

"So," he said picking up the glass. "You a professional?"

A frosty expression settled on her face.

"Bartender, I mean."

Men flirting with her happened often in other bars she'd worked in but not too often at Dreamland. Old men, punk guys, artsy types, she'd dealt with them all. This one was handsome, but it didn't matter. She had neither the desire nor the time to waste. One night, maybe, but that was it.

"Nope," she replied as she looked toward the opposite end of the bar.

"Hey doll, I'm not coming on to you. I just thought you might want to know about the dude in the corner over there. He's well-dressed for a reason. He owns Sybarite. Ever heard of that?"

Vesta's gaze glided over to the man.

"Yeah," he cocked his head. "He's fed up with his secretaries all being cokeheads. You know, model types who see the job as an inroad to Vogue or the Paris runways. No communication skills with clients, can't type worth a damn, and always late because they've been partying their asses off all night."

"How do you know this?" She brought her full attention to him.

"I just know." His eyes dazzled even in the dull bar light. Two sparkling drops of honey stared at her.

"Why are you telling me this?"

"Because." He tossed the contents of the glass down his throat. "I thought you might want to know." From the pocket of his black Jordache jeans, he pulled a fifty-dollar bill and laid it on the bar. "Keep the change."

Little did she know on that day, she watched Sandor, the Magician of the tarot, walk out the door.

She guided her eyes back to the man in the corner. People came to this bar to be alone. She couldn't intrude on his privacy. What reason would she give for walking over or speaking to him? In front of her lay a Coors Light drink coaster. She picked it up along with the bar towel. The other two patrons remained absorbed by their reading material of choice. Stepping from behind the bar, she approached the man in the plaid suit.

"Um, excuse me, sir," she said just above a whisper.

The man looked over his shoulder. A small pile of fabric swatches lay on the table before him. "Yes?"

"I apologize for disturbing you, but I wanted to make sure the surface of this table is clean. You have all those nice swatches laid out." She held up the bar towel. "There were some college kids here drinking beer here earlier. And I don't want your beautiful suit to get sticky."

He looked down at the table. "Oh, I didn't notice anything of the sort on my own, so thank you." He picked up the swatches.

Vesta wiped the tabletop quickly. "It's also a little off balance. Do you mind if I slip this coaster under it to make it stable?"

"Sure, okay." His tone sounded even, no hint of annoyance.

Vesta knelt on the battered wood floor, slipping the coaster under the shortest table leg. "There," she said standing up. With one hand she pressed on the tabletop to see if it wobbled. It seemed steady. "I think it's all good now." Then came the moment, the only moment. "Your swatches are gorgeous, by the way." She nodded toward them. "I especially like the paisley print in that tangerine tone. Superb cotton quality too, I see."

The man turned his full attention toward her pushing his glasses up on his nose. "You didn't call it orange. Why?"

"Because orange has more red in it than this shade. This feels light, summery," she said. Then prompted by the little voice in her head, she added, "Like a Dreamcicle from my childhood."

The man twitched ever so slightly as his eyes sparkled. "That's the name I gave this color.

Vesta smiled at the memory. Harry O'Connell hired her two weeks later at Sybarite to be his secretary. And he was sad to see her leave the little desk in front of his office two years later, but happy to offer her the job of Junior Designer on the women's clothing team. Sandor's tip had paid off well for her. At that point, she didn't know he had placed the subliminal suggestion to Harry to go to Dreamland. It's a quiet bar with good cocktails close to your office, he'd told him through ironically a dream. The Magician at work on her behalf.

Sandor returned to the bar several times after that evening, convincing her finally to go out to dinner with him. The sex was great, but Vesta recalled how his ego was too big to handle. He was a freshly ordained stockbroker with money and women to spare. Monogamy was never part of her plan anyway. Yet Sandor remained in her life. Now she understood why.

The Tesla turned right on a country road about five miles before they reached Fred. Frequent cattle guards embedded in the road kept the pace slow on the weathered blacktop. Long-horn cattle, their horns stretching several feet in length, grazed in pastures dotted with oak groves on both sides of the road. Vesta stared at their massive heads and muscular necks as they passed. The vestiges of the city felt far away. Maybe she should have worn her old boots.

Ahead of them, a hill drew closer into view. An expansive, beige-colored concrete wall loomed at its top. Seeing something so formidable this far out in the country seemed unusual. Vesta dared not ask where they were going. Both logic and intuition told her she had been there before. But she wondered, why the high walls? To keep something out, or in? And what lay on the other side of the wall? They threaded their way past more cattle guards along a winding road as the slope gradually increased. At last, the car reached the top of the hill, pulling up to a kiosk painted the same color as the wall. Just beyond it, a massive metal gate with an enormous peace sign set in its center banned further entry.

Sandor got out of the car. He looked back at her.

"Well, are you going to wait out here or go inside?"

Vesta wrinkled her forehead for a split second before getting out of the car, staring at the kiosk ahead, a utilitarian structure blending into the tan expanse of the wall. A body scanner stood ominously at its center, a sleek black monolith of technology. As she approached, the faint hum of its power thrummed in her ears, low and unsettling, like the murmur of an unseen storm gathering on the horizon.

Sandor stepped confidently onto the outlined footprints marked on the floor, his boots clicking softly against the smooth surface. He raised his arms above his head, and the panels of the scanner snapped into motion, whirring as they encased him in a cocoon of light. Thin beams, bright as surgical instruments, swept over his body with clinical precision. A green checkmark illuminated on the wall. Next came the second wave of security —iris, fingerprint, and facial recognition scanners mounted on the opposite wall. Sandor moved through them with mechanical ease, like a dancer completing a well-rehearsed routine. Each scan produced soft beeps, indicating he was cleared to enter. But to Vesta, each sound made her shoulders tighten, a physical reminder of how alien this entire process felt.

Sandor gave her a glance over his shoulder as if to say, *Your turn*.

She stepped forward, her sneakers barely making a sound. Her palms splayed as she placed her feet on the outlined shapes. The scanner came alive, its panels gliding around her in a precise, almost predatory motion. Her heartbeat thudded louder in her ears as the beams of light swept over her body, tingling faintly against her skin, like static electricity prickling her nerves. When the green checkmark finally flashed, the breath she didn't realize she was holding escaped in a slow exhale.

The next series of scans was even more invasive. The finger-print scanner felt cold beneath her fingertips, leaving a faint pressure behind as if it had taken something from her. The iris scan was worse—a quick flash of blue light that burned like staring into the heart of a flame. As her facial scan completed, the final green checkmark lit up, and a low click announced her success.

Sandor was already halfway to the car by the time she stepped outside again. The wall ahead groaned, metal grinding against metal, as the massive gate began to slide open. Vesta braced herself, but nothing could prepare her for what lay beyond.

The first thing she noticed were the dogs—or what she thought were dogs. Two silver machines, their gleaming metallic forms crouched low, stood at the entry gate. Their heads swiveled in perfect synchronization, laser-red eyes locking onto her with unnerving precision. They began to move, their steps mechanical but eerily smooth, like predators stalking prey. The faint whirring of servos and clicking of joints filled the air, a metallic symphony that made the hairs on her arms rise.

The robots with their Rottweiler-like heads flanked the Tesla as it rolled forward, their heads tilted slightly as if studying her through the tinted windows. She could almost feel their gaze slicing through the glass, probing her, dissecting her. Beside them, rows of rosemary hedges lined the road, their soft green leaves a jarring contrast to the cold, unfeeling presence of the machines. Every fifty yards, mechanical blue eyes perched on white posts swiveled to follow their progress, their unblinking gazes scanning the car and its passengers.

Sandor seemed unfazed by it all. A small amount of comfort eased through her, but she had no idea what was next.

In the distance, on a slight rise, lay a modern-looking house covered in two stories of gleaming white stucco and topped with solar panels. Two enormous windows on the second level stared at her with their unblinking gaze. Even from this distance, the structure felt alive, as if it were watching her just as closely as the robotic dogs had. A circular driveway lay to their right as they arrived, but she noted that the road continued further beyond the house where another building sat tucked away. Sandor drove halfway around the circle before stopping at the bottom of a wide expanse of steps descending from the front door. Vesta stared at it, wondering what lay beyond. More robotic dogs or mechanical eyeballs staring at her? Or something even more bizarre? The double doors swung open like a yawning mouth. She caught her breath at a full stop, bracing for a dystopian nightmare. But Jared and Amara's three exuberant, flesh-and-blood poodles bounded toward the car. Vesta exhaled as she realized she had been clenching the door handle. Sandor leaped out of the car.

"How's that for a welcome!" The Emperor of the tarot shouted as he followed the dogs out the front door.

"It's the best. These are my boys!" Sandor gushed as he embraced each with hearty love.

Vesta pushed wisps of her short blonde hair behind her ears to solidify her regained composure. She wanted to ask Jared if all twenty-first-century houses in the country had such intense, modern security but she knew that would give away her time-travel secret. She must have been here before. Certainly, Sandor had. It was essential to act as though all of this was normal. She climbed out of the Tesla.

When the poodles approached her, she gave each a friendly pat. She liked dogs but had never owned one–at least in this life. They required too much attention. Her job at Sybarite dominated her spouse, children, and pet space. There wasn't any emotional room for anything else. She never regretted it. But now, twenty-five years after resigning from the luxury brand, she wondered how she filled her time. Surely it wasn't reading tarot cards for lovelorn customers. She frowned at the thought then quickly relaxed her eyebrow muscle. There were enough wrinkles and sags on her face already without creating more.

Find out what Agrippa has planned and stop him so I can return to 1999 when these bizarre robots don't exist, and I don't have wrinkles. The thought reignited her resolve. She must create a plan immediately.

Jared wrapped his arm around her when she reached the bottom of the stairs. Confidence flowed from his hug. Anyone would feel safe with him. She also noted how his blue work shirt and jeans paired stunningly well with his spiky gray hair. The midday sunlight revealed strands of iridescent silver making him even more attractive. His crystal blue eyes smiled at her as she took in the full package. A thought popped into her awareness; had she and Jared had sex within the past twenty-three years? She had lost interest in that aspect of him once she learned about the trionfi and her place as the High Priestess. The fact Amara was her sister no doubt played a subconscious role in that shift. Another memory gap. Huge portions of past lives forgotten because of her memory spell, and now a quarter of a century of this life because of her time jump.

Make a plan. Stop Agrippa. Go back to 1999.

A rumbling whooping vibration interrupted her thoughts. Only a helicopter coming in for a landing could cause such a stir. Vesta looked up. Above the house, a midnight blue unmarked chopper slowly descended. Jared glanced at his watch. A tiny computer screen lit up on its face. He clicked on it.

"Liam hitched a ride with the drop-off," he said. "I'd better make sure he didn't rattle the pilot in one way or another."

He took off on the blacktop road that continued past the house.

"I'm coming with you," Vesta said. What was the drop-off? It wouldn't be drugs. None of their group had touched them since their college days. And then, Jared and Amara smoked weed only occasionally. It was she and Liam who continued post-college at CBGB with smatterings of pot and coke. The punk rock club in the 1970s birthed not only legendary talent like Talking Heads and The Ramones, and of course, Liam Spencer, but it incubated a hardy drug culture. They both stopped cold turkey after Liam's overdose on stage from LSD.

Vesta caught up with Jared who walked at a brisk pace. He always had. It was the commanding air of Emperor energy she recognized. Confident, focused. Behind the sprawling house sat another structure. White stucco also, but this featured only a single-story without windows. A security kiosk identical to the one at the front gate stood by the solid metal door. Eyeballs on posts dotted the pathway leading to its entrance. What did Jared have going on way out in the west Texas countryside?

The helicopter touched down as they rounded the corner of the building. Four robot dogs ran to surround it, their laser eyes scanning its surface. A wiry young male with a slight hunch in his shoulders pushed open a rear door and hopped out. Vesta recognized him and his red hoodie from her Gateway lounge experience. He waved at Jared as he hoisted a bulky backpack over his shoulder. He ran toward them, handing the bag to Jared when he was an arm's length away. He saluted with the Vulcan live-long-and-prosper hand gesture before returning to the helicopter.

The rear door on the opposite side of the helicopter opened. Liam slid out in a Slinky-like motion. Legs first, followed by hips swaying into alignment, then the rest of his body. When fully upright, he paused to grab his vape pen from the front pocket of his half-unbuttoned black shirt. His mop of ebony hair resembled a mini tornado as the wind tossed it in every direction on his head. After taking a long drag, he strolled toward them.

Jared looked down at his watch. The screen illuminated

again. He pressed a button on it and gave a thumbs-up to the pilot. The blades on the helicopter increased in speed. As soon as Liam was far enough away, it lifted into the air.

"I'll never get used to the bloody heat here," the Fool said as he joined them.

"Don't wear black all the time," Jared replied giving him a pat on the shoulder. "Come on. Amara's made some of her special herbal tea to fix you up."

"He even sounds like a cowboy out here," Liam said wiping sweat from his forehead.

Vesta eyed the black backpack Jared carried as the trio walked to the house. Nothing unusual about it but she longed to see what was inside. As they passed the ominous one-door, no-windows building, she noticed no landscaping existed around it. It looked too stark. In contrast, the house's friendly white exterior balanced well with low rosemary hedges interspersed with healthy lantana clusters. Even the glassy blue eyes staring at them from little white posts didn't bother her as they approached. A wide covered porch marked the back entry to the house. Stepping into the shade Vesta could see Amara beyond the double French doors. Dressed in faded jeans and a plaid shirt rolled up at the sleeves, her long blonde hair plaited into a long braid hanging down her back, she fit the textbook definition of a ranch woman. The Empress of the modern Wild West.

"You both look like you could use something cool to drink," she said reaching out to hug Liam once they stepped inside.

"I'm melting," he whined. "Withered like a precious orchid."

"Do orchids wither?" Vesta asked.

"Whatever," he barked. "It's beastly hot."

"Don't wear black head to toe maybe?" Amara ventured.

"It's my brand." Liam grabbed a dish towel from the counter to mop his forehead.

"Well, this will help." Amara picked up two tumblers filled with mint-colored liquid on ice from the countertop, handing one to Liam, the other to Vesta. Liam rushed it to his lips. He gulped half the contents before examining the glass.

"What is this?" A twinge sparkled in her third eye as she turned the glass in her hand.

"My newest herbal recipe. Vesta, take a sip. Tell me what you think."

The High Priestess of the tarot pressed her lips together, trying to get her InSight to tell her about the tea, but to no avail. Nothing specific registered on her psychic radar. It wasn't her habit to blindly trust someone when they told her to do something. Not even her sister. But Amara stood rooted to her reclaimed white pine floors, waiting for her to comply. Vesta gave her a subtle eye roll, then took a sip. The slight bitterness was pleasing. Sweet tea always affronted her palate, masking the true nature of the tiny leaves.

"It's good."

Ready to take another sip, Vesta began to raise the glass but froze. She could hear Sandor talking as if he were standing beside her, but he wasn't. He wasn't even in the room. She scanned the kitchen wondering why he was talking about a merger, business talk, where others, not associated with his business, could hear. A wrinkle rippled across her forehead. Impatiently she rubbed it walking from the kitchen further into the house. The open floor plan took her into a great room filled with sofas, plush chairs, and an enormous fireplace, but no Sandor.

"Where's Sandor?" she asked, walking back into the kitchen.

"Yeah, can't he go upstairs to yammer on about stock prices?" Liam asked.

Amara smiled. "He *is* upstairs."

"You're spying on him with a hidden listening device?"

Liam tried to raise his eyebrows but only succeeded in opening his eyes a bit wider. "Real MI5 intrigue in the trionfi?"

"No." Amara shook her head. "It's the tea." She pointed to a pitcher filled with the pale green liquid. "I've been experimenting with hybridization, working with tea leaves I've cultivated for centuries. Not only does this recipe enhance our hearing abilities a thousandfold but it's loaded with vitamins C and B."

Liam put his hands up to his ears. "So, I'm your guinea pig? How long do we have to listen to Sandor drone on? Plus, now I think I'm hearing one of your dogs lick their bits somewhere. Truly disgusting."

"How would you know what that sounds like?" Vesta cocked her head toward him.

"Oh, do be quiet." He waved his hands. "I wish all of this extraneous noise would stop."

"Calm down. It'll wear off soon," Amara said. "So far, I've estimated about five minutes of enhanced hearing per ounce."

Vesta placed the tumbler back on the counter. "I had only a sip. It's wearing off already. Do you have some non-hybrid water I could drink?"

"That's just great. I drank almost the full glass," Liam blew out a loud exhale. "I'm going to the greenhouse where I won't hear any more chatter about IPOs, C3POs, or UFOs." He walked to the door. "And I'm taking this cowboy hat." He grabbed a black gambler style with a beaded turquoise band from a rack by the door.

"Aren't greenhouses hot?" Vesta asked.

"This one is attached to the old farmhouse which is air-conditioned," Amara said.

Vesta threw her gaze down at the floor. Should she have known if the greenhouse was hot or not? No one called her on it, so she was safe. She wanted to ask Amara how long they had owned the property. She had never heard of the place before. There was the house in San Francisco, the one in Tofino, British Columbia, and the penthouse in New York. They must have purchased this sometime after. She couldn't ask because that would certainly jeopardize her mission and secret.

She sensed Amara staring at her.

"Hey, let's go to the greenhouse too. I want to show you what's new in my garden. We'll have to be quiet though or Liam will run us off."

Amara chose a rounded crown straw cowboy hat from the rack, its black band plumed with a black and white banded feather. Vesta checked the remaining hats. Only one appealed to her: a white wide-brimmed fedora made of lightweight cotton. She picked it up. Stitched inside the headband, she noticed the initials VB. A quick smile grazed her lips. She slid it on her head and followed Amara out of the house.

Heat radiated in tsunami waves as they walked several hundred yards toward a wire fence standing eight feet high. It loomed in front of a sprawling garden. Rows of green plants, some sheltered by fine mesh coverings on poles, others exposed to the full force of the sun's rays, spread out over half an acre. Corn ready for harvest dominated the rear of the plot. Watermelons lounged underneath their leafy canopies to the right, along with other kinds of melons. Spinach, kale, and collard greens dominated one entire long row. Squash, green beans, and tomatoes lined up to her left.

Vesta hadn't seen such an impressive garden since Enid's outside of her childhood home in Crested Butte. Amara clearly inherited the green thumb from their mother.

Next to the outdoor garden stood a restored Victorian-era house. Constructed entirely of wood, its asymmetrical features boasted an elaborate turret on the far end. Dormer windows gazed stoically out from the second floor with gables trimmed in forest green and amethyst. The sandy beige house color echoed the tone of the swirling dirt devils outside of the garden. The only clue they hadn't stepped through another time portal was the ever-present blue eyeballs staring at them as they approached.

Amara stomped up the steps to the front door, releasing tiny dust clouds from her boots with each footfall. Vesta followed her example, amazed at how much amassed on her sneakers and wishing she had worn her old boots. The door was ajar. Amara closed it after Vesta followed her in. While restored on the exterior, the interior was completely renovated. No sign of cramped, formal Victorian rooms remained. The entire house now boasted one large, airy space with dazzling white walls. Sunlight poured in from every window, drowning the room in soft light. Another moment of unexpected total transformation spilled over Vesta. She caught her breath.

Three long tables crafted of the same reclaimed white pine spanned the room from front to back. On top of each sat dozens of rectangular potted tea plants. Their emerald lance leaves bursting on stems pruned in meticulous detail. The Empress greeted each plant as though it was a cherished child. A loving touch accompanied each nurturing murmur as she moved along the rows.

"I think you are ready. Ah, and look at you taking on such a fine gloss." The Empress purred and cooed down each row until reaching a room at the back of the house. Inside Liam sat on one of several tall stools picking through a large wooden box.

"Careful," Amara said taking the box away from the Fool. "Or you will be spilling secrets you may not want us to hear. Or," she said selecting a small teabag from the assortment. "You can temporarily paralyze yourself for a good hour or so."

Liam recoiled. "I was just looking for something to quell the beastly heat."

"Hm," Amara inspected the cubby holes inside the box. "Try this and tell me what you think." She pulled out a little bag tied with a thin white satin ribbon, turned on the Corvo EKG kettle sitting on the counter, and pulled a bone China teacup and saucer festooned with English ivy from a shelf below. When the water boiled Amara set the bag in the cup adding the water slowly. "Would you like some honey? It tends to be a trifle bitter."

"The sweeter, the better."

"This is from our hives near the river," Amara said lifting a jar from the shelf. From it, she pulled out a honey wand carefully drizzling a golden stream into Liam's cup. "May you enjoy beating the heat."

Liam picked it up. "I'm still hearing all sorts of bloody random things. A zipper opening something, annoying crinkling sounds, water running. Will this kill that?"

Amara nodded. "Take a sip. Those will all go away."

Liam took a sip, wrinkling his nose. "It tastes like chocolate without the..."

Vesta gasped. She blinked her eyes hard, staring harder at Liam.

"What's happening? Why are you looking at me like that? I feel... I feel a little dizzy."

"That passes quickly," Amara said putting her hand around Liam's wrist. "Breathe normally."

"What the hell?" he mumbled.

"Oh my God, Liam! You're disappearing!"

Chapter Eight

"**W**here did my arms go? My legs vanished, too!" Liam's squeals of panic soon evolved into trills of glee. "This is actually kind of cool. Ouch! Amara, what did you do?"

Amara held up something resembling a silver thumb tack she had in her hand when she took Liam's wrist. "So I can keep up with you. A little blue dye. Harmless."

Vesta watched as a thin blue outline of Liam's body took shape.

"I'm the invisible man," he said dancing around the greenhouse.

"Almost invisible," Amara replied.

Vesta turned to her sister. "Amara, you surprise me. I would have never expected you to do something like that."

"What?" Her tone wasn't completely innocent.

"You are using him as a guinea pig. Me too, for that matter."

"Not you sister. I knew you wouldn't take more than a sip of my tea. And I would never offer anyone anything I haven't tried myself."

"Still," Vesta felt her eyebrows scrunch together searching her sister's face. "I'm surprised."

An unreadable expression settled onto Amara's face; one Vesta didn't recognize. Confusion? Amusement? She didn't like not knowing.

"This was a mild dose. It won't last longer than ten minutes. Let me show you the rest of my garden then we'll return to the house. No more surprises today. I promise."

Vesta could see the blue outline of Liam pirouetting around the greenhouse while Amara finished the guided tour. She led them through the nightshade section, the biblical herbs and spices, all repurposed and recombined for research, and a curious collection of "forgotten folklore plants," rumored to cure ailments, break curses, or whisper secrets to those who listen. Finally, they came to the plants aimed at combating what Amara called the climate crisis. Were they having a problem with the weather in 2024? Another topic to research when they returned to the house.

"This was even better than the time you gave me Jared's face," Liam called out from across the room.

"Let's see if my concoction has worn off yet," Amara said, turning toward Liam's voice.

By the time they rounded the last table in the last row of plants, Liam's full body had faded back into view.

"I need that tea for my next big performance!" he said. "The crowd will love it!"

Amara laughed. "Always my willing test subject."

The tour concluded; they walked back to the house. Inside, Sandor and Jared sat in leather club chairs in the great room. The three poodles lay stretched out nearby. A tranquil afternoon in full bloom.

"Shall we go to the speakeasy for a drink before dinner?" Jared asked.

"Sounds great. I'll change clothes," Amara said.

Liam drifted upstairs, where more mischief on his part would undoubtedly unfold. Vesta eased onto a distressed leather sofa across from the men. The cool quiet of the thick cream stucco walls momentarily put the heat far away. The Magician and Emperor, handsome in their blue jeans and crisp shirts, chatted with ease about banal subjects. Distilling cucumber-flavored vodka, expanding an orchard of pear trees. Auras of pink and gold emanated from them and the sleeping dogs. Vesta soaked in the tranquility surrounding her. She could only allow the reverie for a moment, though. Agrippa had to be stopped, sent back to his own time before he destroyed theirs. But for the moment, she exhaled long and slow.

Soft thuds on the stairs announced Amara's return. Dressed in a simple prairie-style white skirt accented with bright embroidered flowers and a pale pink T-shirt on top, she looked casual and beautiful. How easily she seemed to accept the wrinkles and orange-peel skin on her body as if they didn't exist at all. Liam followed a minute later, taking the stairs two at a time, vape pen in hand.

"Don't vape in the house," Amara said.

"I bloody well know the rules," he said, heading for the front door. Vesta noticed he had traded his black button-down shirt for an old New York Dolls T-shirt, which must have somehow miraculously survived their CBGB days.

"We can all fit in the Range," Jared said standing up.

The drive along the narrow winding road to the highway seemed shorter this time. Jared drove fast, Tom Ford aviator sunglasses perched on his nose, one hand on the steering wheel. Vesta tried not to stare from her vantage point in the back seat, but he was a glorious sight to behold in the golden afternoon light.

The speakeasy turned out to be another late nineteenth-century house situated two hundred yards off the highway. Its wooden exterior, bathed in a tepid tan, lacked the attention to the architectural detail of Amara's house, but its live oaks, as old as the house itself, welcomed patrons with wide-spreading arms out. Shade blanketed the front lawn like an overturned inkwell, bleeding darkness into the grass.

The trionfi piled out of the Range Rover after Jared pulled into a place in the dusty caliche parking lot. They began the short hike to the entry gate when Vesta stopped.

"I left my phone in the car," she said turning back. "Can you unlock it for me?"

Jared froze mid-stride for a moment staring at her before answering. "It's unlocked," he replied.

Vesta opened the back door and searched for her phone. It lay on the floor, half obscured under the seat. She grabbed it and headed back across the parking lot. From the far-right side of her peripheral view, a red pickup truck kicked up dust as it peeled out from its spot on the outlying edge of the caliche lot. As she walked, she glanced down at her phone, marveling at how quickly she'd become hooked on checking everything from New York's weather forecast to Saks Fifth Avenue sales she could effortlessly order with a single click. Her scrolling, however, came to an abrupt halt when her third eye flared to life like a blowtorch. The searing pain forced her to look up from the screen. The red pickup gained speed, hurtling directly toward her. A young man in a cowboy hat with a long, scraggly red beard hit the gas pedal harder as a wide grin slid across his face. The split second before the truck reached her, Vesta jumped backward, slamming herself on top of the trunk of a car parked next to Jared's. The pickup swerved, missing the car by less than an inch, a spray of chalky dust flying in her face.

"What the hell?" she sputtered from her coiled position.

The pickup fishtailed out of the parking lot and onto the

highway, vanishing from view. Vesta let out a sharp, exasperated breath as she unraveled her tightly clenched legs. Dust clung to her clothes—again—the second time this week. Fury simmered as she leaped off the car trunk, her phone gripped tightly in one hand. Spotting her Louis Vuitton bag on the ground, she swooped down and snatched it up with a sharp, angry motion, then straightened, her glare slicing through the empty parking lot. No moving vehicles or witnesses were visible as she scanned it end to end. Her hands trembled, more out of anger than fear. After trying to brush some of the dust off her pants and shirt but succeeding only in smearing it, she walked through the entry gate across the shady yard to the door of the speakeasy. It opened abruptly, revealing Amara who was headed outside.

"It's too crowded in there," Amara said, pointing behind her. "We'll be able to talk out here though." Her last word trailed off as she looked at her sister. Vesta ignored the inevitable question she knew was coming next, stepping over the threshold and pushing past Jared and Sandor as they followed Amara. She could hear Sandor's voice behind her.

"Hey, what happened?"

She kept walking until she found the restroom, passing Liam standing at the bar, flirting with a handsome, long-haired bartender. He cocked his head as he eyed her appearance but otherwise ignored her.

Once inside the privacy of the restroom, she examined her full image in the mirror. Chalk white dust covered her face, shirt, and pants. While it matched the color of her hair, the fine powder created a halo around her head when she ran her hands through it. Leaning over the sink, she tousled her short locks until no more dust fell. She scraped more caliche from her shirt and pants before saving the best for the last. The fine lines in her face were rivulets of white. Crow's feet stretched from the corners of her eyes, smile lines beside her mouth, and the trio of spidery lines on her forehead were all layered with the chalk.

A tear threatened her left eye, but she ordered back into hiding. For a moment, it felt like it was all too much. The responsibility of nothing less than saving the world with absolutely no plan in place, not being able to get help from the other trionfi for fear of creating a catastrophe, aging twenty-five years in the literal blink of an eye, and now being the target of Agrippa who tried to kill her. She shook her head.

"Focus, Vesta, focus," she said out loud. "Remember who you are."

She cleared her throat, dampened paper towels with water, and began cleaning her face. But that wasn't Agrippa driving the truck. He had hired someone, maybe more than one person. She had to decide on a plan to get him back to his own time before it was too late. Or was it too late already? Maybe he had already done what would alter the course of world history. Maybe it was too late to keep the trionfi together in the next life.

Vesta stopped wiping off the dust. She stared at the face looking back at her. It was tired. And she had to admit it, it looked frightened.

"You've been in tougher spots than this before," she said to herself. "Although I can't think of one right now." She wet more paper towels, cleaning off the remainder of the dust. Following a final inspection, she leaned in closer to the mirror, making unblinking eye contact. "You came this far, now, get to work."

She strode out of the speakeasy, joining the other trionfi on the lawn. They sat in forest-green Adirondack chairs grouped in a circle under the shade of a giant oak. A young man with a forearm tattoo of Willie Nelson's head stood beside them. Vesta heard Amara order something called a Peach Sparkler with gin. Jared, Sandor, and Liam all ordered Manhattans. A hot breeze blew through the circle from the west, waking the leaves above from their doldrums. Liam leaned back in his chair, pulling long drags from his vape pen. Life seemed normal again for the moment.

Vesta debated whether she would order a cocktail or not. In 1999, she decided to cut back on her alcohol consumption. The thought had occurred that her InSight abilities might be hindered by drinking on a regular basis. Whether she was still operating under those restrictive guidelines in 2024 was unclear. It was also unclear whether drinking affected her abilities at all. All she knew for sure was she needed a plan desperately. And the most logical way to begin formulating one was to find out why Agrippa was at Jared and Amara's party. To do that, she would ease into the conversation with a cocktail to not arouse suspicion with her questions. She bit her lip over such a convoluted excuse to have a drink, but when Willie's friendly face moved in her direction, she ordered a vodka martini. Once the server went inside, she turned her attention to the group only to realize they were all staring at her, concerned expressions plastered on their faces.

"What? Why are you looking at me like that?"

"You went into the speakeasy looking like you'd been rolling around in the parking lot," Sandor said. "What happened?"

"I was almost hit by a truck not paying attention to where he was going."

"Oh, that was it, huh?" Vesta noted the sarcastic tone of his voice.

"Yeah, it was."

Jared sat bolt upright in the chair, sitting precisely in the posture of the Emperor as depicted on the Waite-Smith tarot deck. He latched onto Vesta's gaze without any intention of turning it loose, his voice calm and clear.

"So, Vesta, when did you time jump?"

Chapter Nine

Vesta's mouth opened, but no words emerged. She stared at Jared but didn't see him. In his place, a black billowing cloud rapidly formed in her mind, blowing seething hot air over her. She slid down into an empty chair because her legs felt incapable of supporting her. What she would say next could end the world as they knew it, turn everything upside down, inside out. Her breathing turned into shallow puffs, her mind whirling on its side.

"I...," she stammered at last, looking for the right words to sound convincing. "I have no idea what you mean."

"Of course you do," Liam said, releasing a plume of smoke as he spoke. "You've been loonier than me on one of my worst days lately."

Amara leaned toward her, a sympathetic smile smudging her lips. "You're showing all the signs. We aren't sure why you're hiding it though."

If they knew anything about time jumping, they would know why she was hiding it. Vesta wanted to scream this fact to them. Gus told her speaking of it could distort the present into a hideous mess. Her wide-eyed stare moved to Amara as she chose her next words with precision.

"People who time jump can't speak of it because that can cause a cataclysm in the present."

Sandor frowned. "What?"

She locked eyes with the Magician. "If you knew about time jumping, you would know that's what will happen."

Sandor shook his head while rolling his eyes. "Who told you that? I do know about it. We all do. Except you, obviously. And no such thing happens."

Again, Vesta tried to form coherent words, but too many facts were colliding in her mind, not making sense. She squinted her eyes hard, forcing the words out. "But Gus told me..."

"Who's Gus?" Jared asked in his calm voice.

Vesta shifted her glance to the Emperor. "He's the chronicle."

"You spoke to a Time Chronicle?" Sandor's raised eyebrows signaled the gravity of her statement.

She nodded, not knowing what else to do.

The trionfi exchanged cautious glances with each other. Is this when the cataclysm begins? Where the present irrevocably changes into something horrible? Vesta held her breath.

The silence was broken as the server walked toward them with a tray of drinks. Willie's smiling face and long braids handed her a most welcomed martini. When each had their own, Jared stood up. They were alone on the lawn except for the oak trees and the feverish wind.

"Welcome to 2024, Vesta." He raised his glass, and the others followed. "What year did you jump from?"

Vesta gulped her martini, swallowing hard. If she was to be the catalyst for changing world events, to be Shiva the destroyer of worlds for the twenty-first century, then she was going to stand up and take whatever came next.

"1999," she said looking around the secret circle. "I came from 1999, two days ago." She held her breath again scanning the caliche parking lot and the highway beyond. Nothing was changing, the ground wasn't shaking, no abyss opened before them.

"Makes sense," Liam said nodding. "That's when you went all looney-tooney on us."

Vesta lifted her chin. "I felt like I handled it all pretty well."

Liam scoffed. "Hardly. You didn't have a clue about that little girl's birthday party you dragged me into."

"You didn't know who Serena was. You didn't know about the tablet. And the big one, you wore the same dress two nights in a row," Amara said.

Vesta winced. That was a big tell.

Sandor snorted. "You told me you had been volunteering all day to build a children's playground."

"Ha!" Liam almost shouted. "We know that would never happen."

"Okay, so I got a few things wrong."

Jared sat down in his chair. "The kicker for me was when we arrived you asked me to unlock the car." One of those devastating smiles only Jared Schultz can create slid across his face. "You told me when I bought it last year that it wasn't a car. It was a Range Rover. Big difference you said. Telling us all never to call it a car."

Vesta slowly nodded. "That sounds like a huge slip-up."

"It was the nail in your coffin," Liam said.

Sandor set his glass on the arm of his chair. "So, tell us about the chronicle. Gus, you said? And why he told you not to tell us about your jump."

"Well, I guess it's okay if I'm not going to cause the world to end." Vesta sipped her cocktail before detailing the entire story: Luna transporting her to Meri's tomb to show her the prophecy where Agrippa would change the future and cause the trionfi to stop reincarnating as the trionfi, Gus arriving and taking her through the portal to Austin in 2024, the card game he lost to Agrippa, meeting Agrippa at the party, reading tarot for him, her InSight at Justine's and almost being run over minutes earlier.

"Now we know why Gus lied," Jared said.

"Why?" Vesta asked.

"Because he will be in serious trouble for divulging how to time jump," Amara said.

"Serious trouble to who?" Liam said getting out of his chair.

"The Elders and any other entities who have the mental bandwidth and who are committed to a peaceful, productive universe," Jared said.

"Does that mean we're just the mindless drones here on Earth doing their biding?" Liam shrugged as he walked away from the trionfi. "In that case, I'm headed for more libation and a chat with that cowboy inside."

"That's not what he means," Sandor called after him.

"Then, what does it mean?" Vesta asked.

"It means, if we don't fix it, help you fulfill the prophecy of stopping Agrippa, then the world will become the vision you saw," Amara said. "And we will cease to exist as the unit we are now. Maybe without our gifts from the Elders. The trionfi has helped this world survive for two thousand years. We can't let him succeed."

Vesta blew out a long breath. Help had arrived. "I have no idea what Agrippa, or Henry Page as he calls himself now, has in mind."

"It's something related to Odin," Jared said. "That has to be why he invested more than ten million dollars in the company two weeks ago."

"Ten million dollars? Where did he get that kind of money?" Vesta asked.

"Clearly, he's been here longer than you have, and he's found a resource," Sandor said. "I'll do some hunting to see if I can track where it came from."

"I first heard of him at that point," Jared said. "My CFO alerted me to the investment. It's not unusual, nor an unusual amount. A lot of money is pouring into AI right now. It's the new gold rush."

"The question is," Amara began. "What is he going to do that will change the timeline?"

"I have no idea," Vesta said. "How do we find out?"

"By hiring the best private investigator in Texas!" Liam shouted as he walked toward the group again. In step with him was a man who appeared to be in his forties. His thick, black-frame glasses and shaggy brown hair reminded Vesta of a young Stephen King, one of her favorite authors. Dressed in a time-worn Ramones T-shirt, he and Liam could have been part of a post-punk fraternity, except his jeans were blue and loose-fitting rather than Liam's skin-tight black preference.

"Meet Lars!" Liam's arms spread out dramatically like he was introducing someone on stage. "He's going to figure out who tried to flatten Vesta."

"Hi, how are ya? Lars Wagner." A deep, resonating voice flowed from him as he walked around the circle, shaking hands with everyone. "Is it okay to shake hands again? No fear of Covid? Let me know if you don't want to," he said.

Lars grabbed her hand in a tight grip. "I hear you were almost roadkill out here in the parking lot. Did you get a look at the vehicle and the driver?"

Vesta nodded. "Yeah, both."

"Great. I'll turn on the recording app on my phone and get your statement."

"My statement?"

"Lars," Jared interrupted. "I think Vesta might be more comfortable talking if she got to know you a little, how you work. Have you been a private investigator for a while?"

"It's actually more of a passion than a profession for me. By trade, I'm an architect." He swept down into a cross-legged position on the grass inside the circle. "But I notice everything. Being detail-oriented is a job requirement in designing houses. And I'm really good at it."

"Noticing everything?" Amara asked.

"And building houses. My clients spend a lot of money and expect everything to be perfect, so I'm their man. This area has become off-the-charts popular for the big money in Austin."

He smiled while looking around the circle. "I'm probably preaching to the choir though in this group."

"Actually, our ranch has been inherited for generations," Amara said. "But I understand your point. I've seen a lot of changes out here in the past ten years."

"It's crazy! And not just people from Austin but from all over the world. I'm finishing up a house out here right now for a guy who's from Russia. Interesting dude with stacks of money but you wouldn't know it to look at him. Long scraggly beard walking around in a beat-to-hell cowboy hat, you wouldn't think he could own a trailer."

"Wait a minute! Does he drive a red pickup truck?" Vesta asked, her pulse quickening.

Lars nodded vigorously. "Yeah, do you know Rascal?"

"Rascal?" Sandor's eyebrow popped up.

Vesta looked at each trionfi member. She knew they were all coming to the same realization at once. Rasputin, represented as the Devil on the ancient tarot was in Fredericksburg. The last time she saw him, he lay dead on the stone floor of an ancient Templar cavern deep underground beneath a chateau in

France. Killed by Gui Wei, the grandson of the King of Wands. Raz had shot Li Wei, killing him. A senseless murder that still haunted Vesta. That was twenty-six years ago. And now, here he was, reborn. Was he the source of Agrippa's money? Vesta was willing to bet on it.

"Yeah, he's a wiry little dude with a pot belly but boy, can he get the women." Lars shook his head.

A major ick factor swept over Vesta at the thought.

"That's okay, I've got the perfect woman in my life."

Lars nodded toward the door of the speakeasy where Vesta saw Serena walking out.

"You're dating Serena?" Vesta asked.

"No," Amara said. "That's her twin, Faith."

Vesta caught the subtle edge in Amara's voice, a faint crack in her usual calm. Something was off—something just beneath the surface.

"How long have you two been dating Lars?" Jared asked.

A faint twinge between her brows sharpened with Jared's question, a signal that deepened her awareness. Something wasn't right.

"Only a week, but she's my girl." He hopped up and hurried toward her. "Hey, kitten, come meet new friends." He wrapped his arm around her waist.

"Oh, I know them already," she said as they walked to the circle.

"We're old friends," Jared said.

"That's great!" Lars replied gently pulling her down onto the grass beside him.

"Jared is the reason why I'm here," Faith said.

"That's right," Jared rushed in to say. "Amara and I lined up her server's job."

Lars drew her in close. "I can't thank you enough. Best day of my life when I stopped by for a drink and she was here."

Vesta took note of Amara's relaxed body language shifting. More alert? And the way she and Jared exchanged glances was different from normal.

Lars looked up at the trionfi. "Anyway, back to Rascal. You know him?"

Sandor began a slow nod. "Yeah, we sure do." He cocked his head studying Lars. "Can we trust you, man? I mean solid trust?"

"I vetted him myself," Liam proudly announced.

"Right," Sandor replied. "But we can pay you well for complete discretion."

"For sure, you have my complete loyalty. And discretion." He kissed Faith's hand. "For bringing this exquisite being into my life, I will give you whatever you want."

"You said you're still working on Rascal's house?"

"I sure am for another week probably. It's almost finished."

"Then we must act quickly," Sandor said. "We need to know if a certain guy shows up there. Describe what he looks like Vesta."

"European accent. Aristocratic looking, well-trimmed mustache. Dark hair and hawkish eyes."

"Oh, that dude!" Lars exclaimed. "Yeah, hawkish eyes are the perfect way to describe him. Sure, he's been there. I saw him today, just before I left to come over here."

The trionfi traded nods around the circle. "Can you tell us what kind of car he drives?"

"Oh man, he has a driver chauffer him all the way out here from Austin. They tool around in a black Mercedes sedan. One of those sleek ones with four doors. Real sweet."

Sandor lowered his chin as he spoke. "Are you headed back there today by any chance?"

Lars shrugged. "I could be. Always something I need to check on."

"Great," Sandor said. "Now, we aren't asking you to do anything illegal but if you should happen to hear anything of a..."

"Suspicious nature?" Lars said. "I gotcha."

"For any pertinent information you give us we will be happy to compensate you," Amara said.

Lars waved her statement away. "I love doing this stuff. And I'm really good at it. You'll see." He wrapped his arms around Faith again. "I'm gonna go do some private eye stuff, kitten. I'll see you tonight after you get off, okay?"

Faith nodded and stood up. "Okay, now I need to check on my customers inside."

Lars grabbed another quick hug before turning her loose. "Fly my angel!"

Liam, who had been gazing in the direction of the highway, shifted his attention toward Lars. He blew out a plume of vape smoke and seemed to be on the verge of saying something.

"We appreciate any help you can offer us," Amara interjected before he could speak.

"You got it. I'll check back in with you later," Lars called over his shoulder heading toward the parking lot.

"I hope he's a better snoop than wordsmith," Liam said when Lars and Faith were out of earshot.

"Give him a break, he's clearly in love," Amara said.

Vesta caught the glance Jared made toward Amara and her response of pressing her lips together while raising her eyebrows. Something was undoubtedly going on that they weren't willing to verbalize with the group.

"He's a member of one of the oldest and wealthiest ranching families out here. Maybe they aren't concerned with a big vocabulary," Amara said, shifting the conversation's focus.

"How do you know that?" Liam asked.

"I remember when his great-great-grandfather bought their

land here in the 1840s. They came from Bavaria looking for opportunity and to recreate a piece of their homeland. Jared and I helped them secure a loan from a bank in Austin."

Vesta's reaction registered surprise even though she tried immediately to hide it. But the recollections from past lives, ones she obliterated with her memory spell, always caught her off-guard. Sandor and Liam responded with emotionless nods. They had all their memories, and this was just another blip in their two thousand years of being together.

"So, Raz is alive and living out here?" Vesta asked circling back to her mission.

"That was news to us, too, him living out here," Sandor replied. "Last I heard, he was still making trouble with his Russian buddy in Ukraine."

"Something brought him this way," Jared said.

"And it was before Agrippa arrived," Amara added.

"Any ideas?" Sandor asked.

Jared shook his head. "I'm concerned that he's after Odin technology too."

"I'm sure a lot of countries would like to get their hands on what you're cooking up," Sandor said.

"His interest in the area means the word is probably out about our satellite lab on the ranch."

"I don't think anyone could get past your security system," Vesta said. "I've never seen anything like it."

"You're used to security from twenty-five years ago," Sandor said.

Jared took a sip of his cocktail. "It can be breached, but it won't be easy."

"What's in the lab?" Vesta asked.

"A lot of works in progress."

"Now I'm nervous about someone breaking in," Vesta replied.

"Don't be." Jared pulled his phone out of his shirt pocket. "I would get an alert if anything unusual happened. Right now, I want to know more about this time rip chronicle. We need to question him about Agrippa."

"I don't know how to contact him. He shows up when he wants."

"It's his job to observe, to witness, not interact with humans, even though clearly, he does. And I'm certain he's paying attention to us right now because he knows if you don't fix this problem he's caused, he will suffer a consequence he desperately wants to avoid," Jared said. "Summon him to appear before us now."

"He lied to me," Vesta said.

"To cover his ass," Liam added.

"I don't know how these things work. In fact, this may not have happened on this planet before. I've never heard of it, so the chronicle understands how serious this is. Get him here," Jared said.

"Okay." Vesta closed her eyes. A warm pulse stirred on her forehead expanding rapidly from its spot between her brows. It radiated beyond her head enveloping her neck, chest, and torso filling her body with a vibrating lightness. She sighed at the intoxicating sensation and stretched her InSight wide hunting for Gus. No images, no sounds, or flashes of awareness came to her. No trace of the chronicle appeared from her clairvoyance nor any other of her heightened senses. She called out to him with her mind demanding he appear, but no answer. After several minutes, she turned loose of the thrumming frequency and opened her eyes, shaking her head.

"He either didn't hear me, or he's ignoring me."

"It's the latter," Jared said. "We'll all summon him together." His voice, calm yet authoritative, didn't leave any room for discussion or dissent.

Liam slipped his vape pen into his pocket. Amara slid forward to the edge of her Adirondack chair to sit in a more erect position, and Sandor set his cocktail on the arm of his chair. Vesta held her pose perched on the edge of her chair and closed her eyes again.

"We the trionfi, designated children of the Elders, summon the chronicle who calls himself Gus."

She could feel the warm pulsation again but now it moved as a dynamic heartbeat around the entire group. With her InSight, she saw the throbbing wave of energy ebbing toward the center of the circle, then rushing up, down, and in all directions, expanding further with each beat. Every contraction pulled the fierce energy toward the center again so that something akin to what she could only describe as a black hole began forming.

Vesta gasped at the magnitude of what they were creating, but no Gus appeared. She frowned, stiffening her back to ground herself even more.

"We the trionfi, designated children of the Elders, demand that the chronicle who calls himself Gus, the one who ripped the fabric of time by sharing the secret of time jumping..."

The ground shook as though it was cracking beneath her.

"Stop talking already! I'm here."

Vesta opened her eyes to see Gus standing inches away.

"And turn off that whirlpool thing you have going before you cause a calamity," he shouted.

All the trionfi opened their eyes, the energy pulse vanished and with it the swirling vortex in the center. Everything around them was motionless except for Gus whose heavy breathing sounded like a steam engine pulling into a train station.

"You're speaking to my family about causing a calamity?"

Jared raised his hand just enough in a gesture indicating that Vesta should squelch her indignant tone.

"I'm known as Jared Schultz..." he began.

"I know who you are," Gus interrupted. "Of course, I know who you are. And all of you." He pointed his dismissive finger around the circle.

Jared squinted, which he rarely did, in Vesta's decades of knowing him. It always meant his patience was thread-bare and rectification was about to be served up cold.

"You are responsible for sharing information with potentially catastrophic results to a human about time travel. What are you doing to resolve this problem?"

"It is she," he pointed to Vesta. "Who will solve the problem." He shrugged while shaking his head. "It's written on the walls of a tomb five thousand years before this time by your Elders. Who am I to argue with that?"

Jared's squint intensified. "Because you're the one who caused the problem."

"What do you expect me to do?"

"Answer all of our questions and do whatever we ask of you to make certain neither Cornelius Agrippa nor any of his associates succeed with his plan."

"I'm a Chronicle, in charge of a Class II planet. I can't devote prolonged resources toward something that's out of my control. Humans are especially busy right now and my full attention is mandatory."

Jared stepped toward Gus. "I do know how to contact the Elders, and I will, telling them everything about your involvement in this situation."

"You know how to speak to them? You've actually spoken to them?" Gus's wide-eyed stare revealed the bluff he was trying to pull on Jared. Little wonder he lost at poker with such transparent emotions.

"I do and I will unless you talk truthfully to us right now."

"He's a grand manipulator, that Agrippa. But I think your

High Priestess here, especially with your help, can send him back to his own time without causing any damage."

"What is he planning to do?" Jared asked.

Gus shook his head. "I have no idea."

"You have some idea because why else would he have chosen to come here at this time?"

A scoffing sound, one Vesta had heard before from Gus, issued forth. "Oh, I don't know," he muttered. "Perhaps I mentioned some of the marvelous inventions of this time, self-driving cars and phones that not only allow you to speak to someone hundreds of miles away but also see them."

"And maybe a tablet with a battery that will never die holding the ability to instantly calibrate a concise history of a future date giving the user effectively a forward-looking time machine? One that allows them to alter the timeline by their actions if used improperly? One that could be taken back to the 1500s to catastrophically change the history of the world?"

Gus looked down at his feet. "Well, I... I don't know."

"You did, didn't you?" Jared took another step toward him.

"It's a game-changing instrument, game-changer, don't you agree?" Gus fumbled through his words emitting more puffing sounds along the way. "To change the course of history as you go and see how the results play out decades, hundreds of years later from the little device you hold in your hands. A minor action here could majorly adjust the course, and the history on the device changes, history rewritten. The absurd power it possesses."

"Yes, it does. And you told Cornelius Agrippa about it, didn't you?"

Jared stood eye-to-eye with Gus, equal in height but vastly different in every other way. The Emperor wearing a blue work shirt and jeans with no-nonsense but expensive Lucchese cowboy boots, compared to the Chronicle's untold layers of thread-bare multi-colored robes over an ancient Grateful Dead T-shirt and dirty red plaid kilt. Even worse, his shaggy mustache and beard carried a distinct odor of roasted chicken. Vesta wrinkled her nose at the sight and smell.

"Tell the truth, Gus. If you want us to stop Agrippa, you must tell us everything."

The Chronicle met Jared's gaze. "Yes, I told him about your device. But you must understand he got me positively pickled and kept letting me win at cards! He's a grand manipulator, I told you."

"Buddy," Sandor said standing up. "You're up to your eyeballs in trouble. You'd better help us in every way you can."

"I've told you everything I know."

"When did he arrive?" Sandor asked.

"A month before your priestess."

"Why did you bring her here later than him?"

"Time jumping isn't always precise. I did the best I could."

Sandor studied his face. "I don't buy it."

"Neither do I," Liam said rising to his feet. "My guess is Agrippa threatened you somehow. He was a decent alchemist but a brilliant one for assessing a situation to make it benefit him."

The Fool pulled his vape pen from his pocket waving it at the Chronicle. "You had to wait until he wouldn't notice Vesta's arrival. That's why he was surprised when he found out she had time jumped too."

"It's all out in the open now," Gus said.

"How did he hook up with Rasputin," Amara asked.

"Oh, that." Gus pressed his lips together hesitating for a long moment. "I may have mentioned how the Devil of your little gang was trying to steal your Gateway gadget. He obviously found a way to contact him and join forces."

The expressions on the faces of the trionfi grew to contain a mixture of anger, fear, and disbelief. Every word out of the Chronicle's mouth seemed to make the situation worse.

"We need to get back to the ranch," Jared said. "And you," he pointed at Gus. "You show up the second any one of us summons you from now on. Is that clear?"

"But I've told you everything."

"I doubt that."

Chapter Ten

Rasputin Dragomirov floored the gas pedal of his 1955 Chevrolet pickup skidding onto Highway 290 to head east. His plan had only a fifty-fifty chance of working and he knew it. Even though he didn't hit her, he succeeded in letting the pompous High Priestess know she was his target now.

He pawed at the tangled ruff of his beard as he drove. The only problem now was almost certainly the other meddling trionfi knew she had time jumped. Agrippa warned him that their window of killing her was short if they wanted to keep his true identity hidden. By this point, what they were after would be known to Jared, the insufferable Emperor. No matter. They would get it anyway. And maybe Jared wouldn't know exactly what they sought. Odin was developing several artificial intelligence devices and had perhaps even achieved artificial general intelligence capable of knowledge reasoning and recursive self-improvement.

Rasputin licked his lips. What a prize that would be. He could set any price he wanted and get it, not to mention the delightful destruction he would cause by putting it in the hands of their greatest enemies.

"Ha!" He laughed out loud, pulling his tattered cowboy hat down further on his head. The hot wind blew hard through the open windows of his truck, but he loved it. He was John Wayne just like in the movies he used to watch in his life before this one. Movies from America were rare in his homeland at that time when he was a boy, frowned upon by the government. But like all contraband they got through. It wasn't a horse he was steering but another jewel from the filthy capitalists, a restored Chevy pickup, shiny Communist red. Those days were past though. Communism in his homeland had been replaced with something else. He wasn't precisely sure what to call it, but the leader was certainly carving a name for himself in history with his present war-making. Rasputin was proud to call him a friend, as much as he could ever really be a friend to anyone. Again, he laughed, downshifting the truck to turn right off the highway onto his private road. He grabbed the remote control to open the steel gates.

Agrippa stopped pacing and stood at the edge of the driveway as the truck approached on the long stretch of caliche. Behind him lay the almost-completed house, a sprawling traditional Texas ranch that stood proudly on the dusty expanse of caliche. Its familiar low, wide silhouette reflected the rugged practicality of the American West, but the three onion domes crowning the second-story roof gave the home an exotic, almost surreal quality. These domes, carved from pale marble and polished to a gleaming finish, sparkled in the sunlight like scoops of vanilla ice cream, their delicate curves contrasting sharply with the house's otherwise angular design. The unpainted wooden walls, weathered and rough-hewn, lent the structure a rustic authenticity, grounding its grandeur in the raw simplicity of the land.

The domes were a tribute to Rasputin's homeland, a piece of old Russia transported to the heart of Texas. Their presence made the house impossible to ignore, a statement as seemingly out of place as the man who commissioned it. It was as if the house itself told a story: part frontier grit, part Old World elegance, a place where the vast, open skies of the West met the intricate architecture of Eastern orthodoxy. The steeply pitched rooflines, typical of Texas ranches, now seemed to cradle the domes like a crown, blending two vastly different worlds into one harmonious, if unconventional, vision.

Lars had indeed achieved an admirable feat, balancing the two aesthetics in a way that felt both natural and deliberate. Wide verandas wrapped around the lower level of the house, their sturdy posts adorned with subtle carvings that hinted at Russian folklore. The windows, tall and narrow, were framed with decorative wooden trim that mirrored patterns Rasputin remembered from village churches in his youth. Every detail had been carefully considered, from the deep overhangs that shaded the porches to the curved wrought-iron railings that echoed the domes' flowing lines.

And Rasputin loved it. This house was more than a place to live; it was a symbol of his triumphs, his ability to merge the worlds he had conquered across his many lifetimes. He saw himself in every contradiction it presented: wild yet refined, rooted in cunning yet always grasping for control over the eternal.

The Texas ranch spoke to his love of the untamed West, while the onion domes whispered of his beloved cultural roots, a subtle reminder of his legacy. To him, the house was alive, a reflection of his ambition and his unyielding ability to thrive, no matter where or when he found himself. It wasn't just a home—it was a declaration of power, one that would leave an indelible mark on anyone who saw it.

The Devil kept his foot hard on the gas pedal until the last possible second before reaching the end of the driveway. Hitting the brakes, he sent a thick spray of caliche dust into the air. Such a simple yet thoroughly delightful thing to do. He never tired of it. Agrippa, on the other hand, now resembled one of the living statues that haunt tourist spots for tips. He was coated, coifed head to Italian leather toes in fine white chalk where he stood.

"Pffft," Agrippa said spitting out dust. "Did you do it? Is she dead?"

Rasputin got out of his truck slamming the door, another satisfying action.

"Nyet," he replied with his Russian accent on full display. "We must therefore move up our plans."

"Have your men finished the tunnel?"

"They have. It would be best for the trionfi to be gone from their ranch, but we must attack before they have time to move the tablet."

"And you know it is definitely there?"

"Of course. I would not propose such a mission if I did not," Rasputin said walking past him toward the front door of his house.

Agrippa turned to follow but the Devil thrust his arm out, stopping him. "Dust yourself off before you enter my home."

Achieving his goal would take patience. Agrippa knew that. But putting up with the childish antics of this savage from the steppes wore his patience threadbare.

Inside the wide entry, a grand staircase with heavy, polished wooden railings dominated the center of the room, a symbol of permanence and power. Each step groaned slightly underfoot, a sound Rasputin found oddly comforting as if the house itself acknowledged his presence. The staircase curved gracefully upward, splitting at the top into two wings that led to the upper rooms. To the side, a long hallway stretched to the rear of the house, its dark wood floors gleaming under the filtered light streaming in from tall windows. The walls were adorned with wainscoting and subtle carvings of oak leaves, an homage to the forests of his homeland but softened by the rustic charm of the West.

Large rooms flanked either side of the entry, their double-width doorways framed with ornate trim that hinted at luxury but didn't overwhelm the house's rugged character. The room on the left held a sprawling library with shelves built from rich mahogany, lined with leather-bound volumes of Russian history, philosophy, and Western classics. A massive stone fireplace with an intricately carved mantle commanded the space, its hearth still dusty from disuse but ready to roar to life when winter arrived. To the right, a parlor radiated warmth with its low, leather furniture and a Navajo-patterned rug that stretched nearly wall to wall. Rasputin had insisted on American touches, finding the juxtaposition of his Russian roots with the cowboy aesthetic satisfying.

Above the front door hung the mounted head of a massive buffalo, its glassy eyes catching the light in a way that made it seem alive. Beneath it stood a hall tree crafted from the twisted horns of longhorn cattle, its rustic yet artistic design both practical and striking. Cowboy hats of every shape and size hung neatly from the hooks, a collection that had grown from both his purchases and gifts from locals eager to earn his favor. Below the hall tree, a bench covered in soft, tanned deer hide completed the ensemble, its surface worn smooth from use.

Rasputin admired every detail of the house with a pride that bordered on reverence. To him, this wasn't just a dwelling—it was the personification of him. The American West, with all its vastness and rugged individualism, mirrored the untamed spirit he carried within him. Yet, the house also spoke to his more refined tastes, a blend of barbarian and aristocrat. He scratched his scruffy beard and smiled.

The mounted buffalo head represented dominance over nature, while the handcrafted hall tree was a tribute to the culture he had chosen to embrace. The heavy woodwork, the rich textures, and even the faint scent of leather and pine that lingered in the air made the house feel like a fusion of his many lives, each carefully orchestrated to claim power, wealth, and legacy.

The house wasn't merely a sanctuary; it was a trophy, a monument to his ability to conquer and adapt. It stood as a physical testament to his mastery of this time and place, a reminder that even here, in the vast expanse of the American West, he could bend the world to his will. This life was already proving itself to be one of his favorites, and he couldn't wait to see what came next.

He pulled his cell phone out from his plaid Western shirt pocket. He was only twenty-three years old, but he had access to more money than he would ever need, thanks to the powerful allies he had made. The only thing he needed more of now was power, and he would have that soon enough when he had Odin's technology in his hands.

Rasputin was speaking Russian rapidly into the phone when Agrippa entered the house.

"Da!" He said before ending the call.

"Everything is set then for this evening?" Agrippa asked.

"It is set."

Agrippa nodded. "And I will have the tablet in my hands tonight?"

"The tablet will be acquired tonight."

Agrippa's stance tightened. "Yes, and you will hand the tablet to me once it's acquired."

"That was our deal, wasn't it?" Rasputin took off his hat and added it to the collection on the wall.

"It is our agreement," Agrippa pressed. "You may have the Gateway and all the other inventions, but I must have the Horizon tablet."

"So, you will return to your time to control the destiny of me for every lifetime going forward? I will be at your mercy," Rasputin waved his hand. "Along with the rest of the world by making a little change here, a big change there, and seeing the results on your little screen so you can rule over Europe, and perhaps Russia too."

Agrippa shook his head. "No, I told you. I will travel to Moscow when I return to my time. That's where you were living, yes? I will go there, and we will make changes that will benefit us both. I told you that, and we agreed on it."

"Yes, but agreements change."

"I promise you I will do it."

"We could both travel to that time perhaps and use the device together."

"That would mean you would abruptly arrive in a land foreign to you. Whatever business you were involved with in Russia would instantly cease."

Rasputin cocked his head. "It was an enjoyable time. Prince Vasili was happy for me to do as I pleased. I brought him much tax money from the villages and anything else I found interesting." A sinister grin played upon his lips at the memories.

"Stay in your country. I will come to you, and you can tell me what you want. Together we will make decisions and act on them checking the changes on the tablet every step of the way to make it exact to your desires."

Rasputin shrugged. "Okay."

"Excellent!" Agrippa smiled. "Are we staying here tonight while the plan is being executed?"

"Nyet. We will return to my home in the city. They will deliver the products there."

From the corner of his eye, Rasputin caught movement on his driveway. A car was kicking up dust as it approached the house. Quickly, the Devil walked into the room closest to him off the entry. He pulled a set of keys from his jeans pocket and opened a large wooden armoire. Reaching his hand inside, he picked up a nine-millimeter Beretta pistol, his favorite gun. He locked the cabinet, then strode to the front door.

As the black Ford pickup truck pulled next to his truck, Rasputin realized it belonged to Lars. He tucked the pistol in the waistband of his jeans before walking out on the porch.

"Howdy!" Lars called out. "I wanted to check on the backup generator that was installed yesterday. I forgot to check on it earlier, make sure they wired it up to code."

Rasputin studied the man who approached him. Initially, he had dismissed the reports of this man being a first-class architect. In Russia, such men would be properly dressed in a suit or at least pants and a shirt befitting an important role. But he had taken the chance on Lars based on the admirable reports, the portfolio he had shown him, and the driving tour of some of the local homes he had designed. He was happy he did.

Lars always walked with a slightly hunched posture as though a deep thought perpetually consumed him. It reminded Rasputin of the old men in Russia who walked that way. But Lars was much younger than them and very American, smiling and friendly for no reason. Behavior Rasputin was suspicious of at first but came to believe was just his foolish, benign American behavior.

"Is it okay to go through the house?" Lars asked as he stepped on the porch.

Rasputin shrugged. "Yes, it's fine."

They walked inside where Agrippa still stood.

"Oh, hey! I'm Lars Wagner." He stuck out his hand. "I've seen you around but never formally introduced myself."

Agrippa didn't like shaking hands or touching people in general, but he understood it was common in this age, so he gave Lars's hand one quick shake before turning it loose. "I'm Henry Page."

"I like your accent. Is it German? My family came from Germany a long time ago."

"Yes, I'm German."

Lars seemed to hunch over even more as though he were leaning in for Henry to say something else, but Henry was finished talking.

"Well," Lars said. "I'm gonna go check on that generator." He started toward the back of the house but stopped beyond the staircase, calling out. "Are you fellas headed out for dinner tonight by any chance? There's a nice new restaurant in town."

"No, we're not. We will be leaving the house soon for the night," Rasputin said.

"Okay, gotcha," he said.

Rasputin was silent, putting his finger to his lips for Agrippa to be silent as well. Moments later they heard the back door open then close. Rasputin looked at Agrippa, making a point to stare directly into his eyes.

"I plan my lives carefully. They have all worked out well for me in most ways. As I have said, I enjoyed my time when Prince Vasili ruled Russia. Catherine, the Great, as history has called her was enjoyable in other ways for me. The most fun has been with Tsar Nikolai and his empress Alexandra. Pious woman who trusted me with her children and her soul." Rasputin clucked his tongue against his cheek. "Never do that." He wagged his finger at Agrippa. "I do not want any of that history disrupted by an idiot turned loose with a time device."

Agrippa held up his hands. "I swear to you I won't disturb

your life. Any of your lives. It is only my one life I wish to change. To enrich." He began pacing the length of the entry area. "I am a brilliant alchemist. Educated in many disciplines. I would be an outstanding leader of what you now call Germany, or of England, or France. Especially more competent than either that bloated Henry or fragile Francis. And to apply what I have seen and done during this time? It would be glorious. The changes would be extraordinary for Europe." Agrippa stopped. "But I would make certain nothing changed for you or Russia. I would be in a position of power to work with you. To make your life even better during that time."

"We will see," Rasputin said.

"You wouldn't have known about the Horizon tablet without me," Agrippa said. "You might have overlooked it while in Odin."

"We would have taken it."

"Why? You might not have known what it was even if you picked it up. It looks just like all the other computer tablets that I've seen everywhere in your age except that it has Odin written in red on the cover. Why would you pick that one up?"

"You've seen it?"

"Not yet," Agrippa said. "But I believe what that old wizard said."

"The one who brought you here?"

"That's correct."

"And where is this wizard now?"

"I don't know."

"How do you know you can return to your time?"

"Because he will come when I call or suffer the considerable consequences."

"I see." Rasputin scratched the matted thatch of red hair on his head. "And so..."

The sound of the back door opening stopped Rasputin mid-sentence. Heavy footsteps echoed through the hallway announcing the return of Lars. He wiped his forehead with his shirt sleeve when saw them.

"Whew! It's still hotter than a five-dollar pistol out there." He smiled as he stopped in front of the men. "I'm glad I checked. The lid on the inlet box wasn't closing like it should. So, I fiddled with the spring and fixed it. You don't want any water getting in there. She's good to go now."

Rasputin nodded. "Good to know."

Lars looked from Rasputin to Agrippa then back to Rasputin. No one spoke. "Is that it guys? Anything else I can do for you?" Lars asked.

"No, that will be all," Rasputin said opening the front door.

"Well, okay then," Lars said flashing a big smile. "Let me know if there is. And again, nice meeting you sir." He nodded at Agrippa whose hawkish eyes studied the architect's face. Lars paused for a few seconds waiting for a response, but Agrippa stayed silent. "Yeah, okay. Good," Lars finally said as the silence became awkward. "See y'all later." He waved and walked out the front door.

Agrippa scowled as the men watched Lars get in his truck.

"Idiotic Americans," Rasputin muttered with disdain.

Lars hopped into his truck and drove back to the highway. Once he was a mile down the road headed to the speakeasy, he pulled over. He grabbed the small voice recorder from his pocket and hit the play button.

Chapter Eleven

The trionfi were walking across the yard of the speakeasy to leave when Lars wheeled his truck into the parking lot. He could barely contain himself enough to park before jumping out.

"I'm glad y'all are still here," Lars said catching his breath as he ran up to them.

"Did you find out something?" Jared asked.

"Whowee, boy, did I!" He pulled the voice recorder from his pocket.

They stood together at the gate. The trionfi on one side, Lars on the other. His words flew fast and jumbled. "They're aliens... or from another time... or another dimension. I'm not sure, but I know it's something big dealing with time travel. And they're arguing about something of yours. A Horizon tablet? They're gonna try to steal it."

"Lars," Jared interrupted, his calm demeanor halting the word frenzy. "Would you play what you recorded?"

Vesta admired Jared because his pulse had to be racing like hers with this news. Not only was Agrippa trying to get his hands on Odin technology, but now Lars knew about his time jump. Not that any sane person would believe him, but having information like that out in the open was dangerous.

Lars pressed the button on his recording device, and the conversation between Rasputin and Agrippa began. The Devil's thick-tongued accent and Agrippa's thin, tinny voice crackled through the speaker. Vesta listened, getting angrier by the moment as they haggled over what they were planning to steal and how they planned to use it. As she listened, she became confused about exactly what the Horizon tablet was. They referred to it as having the ability to change the course of history. That would align with what Meri carved onto the wall of his tomb. But how could a tablet do that?

Jared stared out into the distance as he listened, his tanned face and porcelain blue eyes registering no emotion. Amara, on the other hand, had that spark in her blue eyes Vesta had seen before. She was ready to confront them and end their plans by any means necessary. Sandor stood with his arms crossed and his lips drawn into a tight bow, a sign he was motivated to jump into action, too. And then there was Liam puffing anxiously on his vape as if it might be the last time he could. All the trionfi were worried.

The conversation ended and Lars stopped the recorder.

"How about that?" he said with a wild stare in his eyes.

Jared patted him on the shoulder. "Good job Lars. Thank you. We need to head back to the ranch right now. But I have something for you–a token of our appreciation. I'll make sure you get it soon."

Lars dismissed Jared's comment with a wave. "Not necessary. I love doing this stuff. But shouldn't we call the FBI or somebody like that? This sounds serious."

"Those men are talking nonsense. They've probably had quite a bit to drink and got carried away. Don't worry about it in any case. We've known Rasputin, Rascal, as you call him, for a long time. We know how to deal with him and his friend." Jared shook Lars's hand. "Thank you again. You've helped us a lot."

"But I have access to the house. I can find out more."

"Rasputin said they're leaving the house for the night. There's no need to risk yourself by returning there."

A look of utter dejection enveloped Lars's face but he nodded.

"Hey, buddy," Sandor said. "You're a trusted confidant of us now." He walked through the gate, slung his arm over Lars's shoulder, and began walking him to his truck. "When something else comes up, don't worry. We will call on you. And be on the lookout for whatever Jared's sending your way. I'm sure it will be something rad from his high-tech toy collection."

Sandor made sure Lars got into his truck and drove away before heading back to the group.

"Rad?" Vesta said shaking her head. "Is that a twenty-first-century word now?"

"Not really," Liam said. "Old people use it."

"Hey! You're older than I am in this life," Sandor shot back.

"Yes, but I'm much cooler."

The trionfi piled into the Range Rover to head back to the ranch. Outside, the sun settled uneasily behind a rocky outcrop on a ridge as they approached the hill. Its spiked rays of dull orange and red shot into the sky. Enid always said sunsets like that meant trouble was coming. Maybe it was the memory of her mother's words or the fact her third eye began to itch, but without thinking, she blurted out "Hurry!" from the backseat.

Jared turned off the highway onto the winding one-lane road. In the rearview mirror, she could see Jared's face. He looked anxious as he sped up. The itch flared into a searing burn between Vesta's brows, sharp and insistent. She shut her eyes, reaching deep into her InSight, desperate for clarity. But the void answered her—an oppressive, suffocating blankness that swallowed her vision whole. The realization crept over her like a shadow: Agrippa's thoughts were beyond her reach. Rasputin had shielded them, or worse, he had taught Agrippa to wield the same power, leaving her blind to their actions.

The vehicle swayed with the curves on the blacktop road as they zoomed down the private drive. The motion felt hypnotic. Vesta could sense movement–movement within her and without her. Flashing into her mind's eye, she saw the ranch. It was almost dark, but she was running close to the ground. Her breathing became rapid, trying to assess what was happening. She was running toward the house, now beyond the house to the lab. A shrill beeping sound began. Vesta realized it was inside the vehicle, not within her InSight. She kept her eyes closed, but she could hear Jared.

"Breach in the lab," he said. His voice tense now.

"I have eyes on the exterior," Vesta said. "I don't see any breach."

"How do you have eyes on it?" Sandor asked.

"I'm not sure."

"The dogs," Jared said.

Vesta frowned. How could she be seeing through the eyes of a robot dog? She looked closer at the scene playing out in her mind. It was clear she was low to the ground. There were three dogs at her eye level. Where was the fourth? A knowing crept inside her. She was the fourth. These dogs were sentient. Jared and Odin had achieved AGI, augmented general intelligence. They were conscious beings.

The vehicle pulled to an abrupt stop. They must be at the gate. A brief pause then the forward motion began again. The sound of beating wings grew from faint to loud. Vesta opened her eyes. Outside she could see a black helicopter against the dark blue sky. It was hovering above the lab.

"Stop the car!" Amara shouted.

She jumped out while the car was screeching to a halt. Vesta thought her sister was going to lose her footing, but she stayed upright, finding her balance. Amara flung her arms above her head, her lips moving, but Vesta couldn't hear the words. Wind whipped up from the south, roaring as a mighty gust from nowhere.

Vesta slid out of the vehicle and joined the other trionfi who had gathered near Amara. They watched a long rope drop from the helicopter, a large cage attached at the end. Figures dressed in black appeared on the roof of the lab. The rope lengthened, dropping the cage lower. The figures began loading something into it.

Amara roared with a sound humans couldn't possibly make. Something like a clap of thunder issued from her throat, making the ground shake. The intensity startled Vesta as the wind began circling the helicopter. It was so intense she could almost see the air currents swirling. The helicopter began to tilt side to side, the cage swaying wildly. The two figures on the roof grabbed onto the cage as it swung past them. When they did, the helicopter began rising higher in the indigo sky. It swerved to the left, almost on its side, but pulled back into position, rising higher. Amara began pushing her arms in an upward motion, whooshing and howling sounds coming from inside her. The helicopter veered to the right, making a whining noise. The figures were hanging onto the cage but were being tossed around like pieces of ribbon. Vesta thought it was going to crash as the helicopter dipped close to the ground but regained its bearings and sped away from the ranch. Amara gave one final thrust with her arms before dropping them to her side.

"Quick thinking to call on the wind. Great job!" Jared stepped beside Amara wrapping his arms around her.

"Not good enough," she said, exhausted bitterness welling up in her voice.

"Come on, let's see what they got," Jared said hopping back into the vehicle.

Amara signaled for him to go without her and began walking toward the lab. Vesta caught up with her.

"You were the only one who even thought of some way to stop them. Don't be angry at yourself."

"If I'd had even another thirty seconds, I could have completed the funnel."

"You were creating a tornado?"

Amara nodded looking down at the ground.

"How did they get on the property without being detected sooner?"

"I don't know," Amara said. "But so much of what Jared and his team have created can be used in very harmful ways."

"Like what?"

"I'll let Jared explain. But you've already heard a little bit about Horizon."

"That it's some kind of time-altering device?"

Amara nodded.

"Why did he create weapons?"

The Empress looked up at Vesta. "They weren't created to be weapons but like anything good and powerful they can be used to harm. Jared and the team are brilliant and curious. They are going to push the limits, the boundaries of what's possible."

"Same old story."

"It's in our nature," Amara said.

"To destroy ourselves," Vesta added.

The sisters made their way to the lab. At the steel door, Amara stood in front of a retinal scan while placing her right hand on another scanner. Vesta heard a loud click, and Amara pulled the door open. They stepped into a windowless interior space that looked small compared to the exterior size of the building. Everything inside was white, the walls, the tables, the chairs, and the floor except for the dark hole near the north wall. The question had been answered about how the intruders got in.

"It's not too bad," Jared said when he saw them. "Horizon is safe. They didn't have time to blow the door for the antechamber." He pointed to a white steel door. "They got Gateway though."

"No, they didn't." Vesta heard Sandor's voice call out above her. Looking up on the east wall she saw him on a white steel ladder that stretched to a trap door in the roof. Nestled in the crook of his right arm was the device she had worn two nights earlier.

"They dropped it in their hasty retreat thanks to Amara's little summer breeze," he said.

"Okay, so that means they only got Face 2 Face," Jared said.

"That treacherous little machine."

Vesta whirled around to face the west wall where Liam sat in the only comfortable-looking chair in the place.

"What's Face 2 Face?"

"Lord, we're having to explain everything to ancient Vesta," Liam taunted. "It's this hideous little gizmo you can point at anything, or anyone, and get a detailed history."

"He doesn't like it because it shows photos of his face before he got all the plastic surgery," Sandor said handing the Gateway helmet to Jared.

Liam hissed.

"They didn't get anything associated with Embellish?" Amara asked.

"No, all of it was in the antechamber. The only reason they got Gateway and Face 2 Face was because I foolishly left them out here when I was working on them earlier today," Jared said dusting off the helmet.

"It doesn't sound like what they did steal was that big of a deal," Vesta said. "You can search the internet for photos and information about anything now."

"Yeah," Jared began. "But this is different. There's a lot of bogus info out there. What Odin created sorts through all the misinformation, biases, and deepfakes to share the plain truth."

"And it updates as fast as Horizon?" Amara asked.

"It does," Jared said. "Okay, we know Rasputin and Agrippa won't stop trying to steal the tablet. And they want Gateway, too, but they are out in the open. We can be certain their next target will be our headquarters because they know we will move all technology to that location."

"That place is impenetrable," Sandor said.

"From the standpoint of breaking in, it is. But..." Jared looked down into the hole in the floor. "Anything can be breached."

"I thought you had motion detectors underground too."

"We do but they went deeper and have obviously been planning this for a long time. Now we know for certain Rasputin was after our work well before Agrippa traveled here."

"So, who gets Horizon?" Sandor asked.

Jared shrugged.

"The one who can outsmart and out lie the other," Vesta replied.

Jared walked to the handprint scanner by the antechamber door. Amara stepped over to a keypad and retinal display six feet away from the door. Simultaneously they activated the scanners and Amara typed in a code. Jared pulled the door open revealing another stark white room lined with shelves. Vesta stepped closer to peer inside. Most of the shelves were empty but two were littered with keyboards, monitors, small hand-held devices, and a tablet with the Odin logo emblazoned in red. Jared placed the Gateway helmet next to a keyboard and monitor.

"They scratched it up when they dropped it," he said trying to wipe away a black mark.

"Can I take a look at Horizon?" Vesta asked.

Jared glanced at her. He didn't seem to be in the mood for any demonstrations but nodded. "Sure."

He picked up the tablet from the shelf, flipped the cover open, and held it up to his face for another retinal scan. A pale shade of blue blossomed on the screen with the word Horizon fading in one letter at a time in bright yellow. Jared touched the screen to bring up the browser bar.

"What do you want to look at?"

"I don't know. Anything. I just want to see how it works. How it can show the future and how that changes when someone alters it."

"Hmm. Let's see. I suppose the easiest way to do that is for you to change something in your life. Let's start by searching your name."

The Emperor typed Vesta Beauvais into the browser then hit the return key. The screen filled with links. Vesta had never browsed her name before and was startled by the number of times it appeared on the screen.

"Let's choose Wikipedia. That's usually benign while somewhat accurate," he said clicking the first link.

The screen populated with text and two photographs. The first of her at age thirty-five when she became CEO of Sybarite. She was smiling in her new Calvin Klein navy wool suit. Vesta smiled back at it. Such a happy time. The second was five years later when she spoke at her alma mater, Columbia University. In the photo, she was standing on the stage of the university auditorium with its polished black columns behind her. Again, she was smiling. The occasion was a forum about women breaking the glass ceiling of the corporate world. Vesta felt a twinge in her throat. That event was only one year before she would resign from her dream job.

"So, what do you want to change?"

Jared's voice jolted her back to the present.

"Um, let me finish reading it."

The article contained all her biographical information about her date of birth, June 27, 1959, and place of birth, Crested Butte, Colorado. It listed both Enid and Cyrus as her parents, calling Enid a naturopath and Cyrus an international salesman with an unknown company. Vesta snickered at the way Strength and the Chariot of the tarot were described in such humble terms. She kept reading about where she went to school, her jobs at Sybarite, and then her resignation in 1998. Vesta swallowed hard but forced herself to keep reading. After that, the article said she became a world-famous tarot reader with celebrity clients spanning the globe. She stopped reading to stare at Jared.

"I read tarot for celebrities?"

"Un-huh, you do."

"No, I don't. I dealt with them enough at Sybarite." She pointed at the sentence on the screen. "That's what I want to change. I'm not reading tarot anymore for anyone."

"You sure? That's a big change. It will affect more than just you."

"I'm sure. I can't believe twenty-five years ago I went from CEO of a major fashion and luxury brand to being a fortune teller. What was I thinking?"

The Emperor looked at her with patient eyes. "If you read some of the other articles, I'm sure you'll find interviews you did over the years explaining how it happened."

"Can you give me the two-sentence synopsis?"

"A Sybarite client reached out to you after you left. Without prompting you picked up on an accident she was about to be involved in. You read her cards for more details and told her what to avoid. The accident happened but she wasn't involved. She spread the word to all her famous friends."

Vesta replied with a slow nod. "I see," she said after a pause. "It sounds like I've done my good deeds and can give it a rest now. So, I'm giving notice that I've retired telling fortunes."

"You'll need to put it in writing."

He opened a blank Word document and slid the tablet to Vesta. She typed a statement declaring she would no longer read tarot. No reason given.

"Okay," Jared said. "I'm sending this to my contact at the New York Times." He typed rapidly on the keyboard for a few seconds then wrapped it up by tapping the return button. "Done." Jared handed the tablet back to Vesta. "Hit refresh and take a look."

Vesta followed his instructions and saw the change in the article. 'On August 20, 2024, Beauvais retired from reading tarot professionally.' She kept reading. For the remaining seventeen years of her life, Beauvais withdrew from social engagements entirely, becoming a recluse living in a high-rise apartment in Austin, Texas. She died on October 8, 2041. Her ashes were scattered on her request at Chartres Cathedral in Chartres, France."

"Oh my God! I become a recluse?"

"Yes, if that's what it says."

"Why?"

"I don't know."

"But I can change it?"

Jared nodded.

"What do I need to do?"

"See," Jared said taking the tablet from her hands. "When we know the future and try to alter it, unexpected things happen. There are changes in the future of others now, I'm sure because you've chosen not to read your cards any longer."

"Great guilt trip you're shoving on me there."

"It's life, Vesta. It's what happens. You can't control everything. But you can see how dangerous this can be in the wrong hands."

"Why did you invent it then?"

"Because he could," Liam said stepping into the room.

Jared shrugged. "Yeah, I guess that's the most honest answer."

"Well, I'm not going to become a recluse," Vesta scoffed.

"If you return to 1999, the other Vesta will be back in this time. She chose to make a career out of tarot reading. Your action just now may trigger something in her that causes her to retreat out of society," Jared said.

"What? You're not going to read your cards anymore?" Liam almost shouted before he leaned close to Vesta. "Do you know how many addicts you've helped by telling them to get off the stuff or die?"

Vesta frowned.

"You don't know because you're in old Vesta headspace, but you've helped a lot. Not to mention your advice on smart career moves. Of course, you haven't helped my career all that much. But I am undaunted."

"Let's move this conversation into the main room," Jared said looking at his phone. "My security team is here to transfer this equipment to our main vault."

Vesta eyed Horizon in Jared's hand as they joined Amara and Sandor. An obsessive desire to search through it planted itself in her mind. Based on what she found out from it when she returned to 1999, she could make some phenomenal decisions, maybe getting her job back at Sybarite, maybe at a different fashion house. The possibilities were endless for her to achieve even more than she already had.

Amara walked to the door leading outside of the lab. "The rest of you, let's go in the house to get ready for dinner."

Vesta caught Sandor looking at her with an odd expression on his face. "What?"

He shook his head. "Nothing."

They followed Amara through the back door into the kitchen. She turned on the oven and began pulling baking dishes out of the refrigerator.

"It won't take long," she said. "I prepared several things from the garden before you arrived."

"I'm headed for a nice Gilpin's. Is it still in there with the cold cuts?" Liam asked.

"It's the coldest place to keep it without risking it in the freezer."

Liam took the bottle of gin out and walked over to the bar area next to the kitchen. "How many martini glasses am I getting?"

"I'll drink wine," Amara replied.

"Scotch for me," Sandor said.

"I'll wait for wine too." Vesta slid onto one of the kitchen stools letting the lingering thought of the tablet stay in her mind.

"I'm going to get out of these boots and put on a clean shirt," Sandor said heading upstairs.

"Liam, I almost forgot," Amara said. "I have martini glasses chilled in the refrigerator. Did you see them?"

"Oh, that sounds much better than an old room-temperature glass."

He strolled back to the refrigerator. "Where are they?"

"They may be hiding behind my bay leaf facial jar. Just push it to the back."

"What's a bay leaf facial jar?"

"It's an amazing recipe I came up with using bay leaves as the base. You know they naturally restore collagen to your skin."

"That's okay," Liam said pulling a chilled martini glass out. "I'll stay with the facials Reginald gives me. No offense."

"None taken. Vesta, do you want to try it? I can put a mask on you after dinner or tomorrow."

Vesta ran her hands over her face with a sigh poking at her saggy jawline while tenderly touching her crepey neck.

"Will it fill in all these gutters and cracks?"

"If you use it often it will affect some of the fine lines."

"I'm telling you," Liam said bringing the Castelvetrano olives out. "You need to go with me to my surgeon. She'll get rid of those lines."

"No thanks," Vesta said.

"I'm going in for a consultation for my cheek implants next week. You should come with me to talk to her."

"Liam, you don't need any more surgery. Definitely not cheek implants."

"Yes, I do. It's what's missing from restoring my youth. I have to look fresh for my new television show."

"What new show?" Amara asked.

"I'm going to be on the new season of Love Island."

Vesta squinted. "Where is Love Island?"

"It's not where, ancient Vesta, it's what."

"It's a reality show, right?" Amara asked. "Where people couple up to win money?"

"It's more than that. You stay in a fabulous romantic villa, meet new people, and have fun for a month or two. It has millions of viewers. It will be great to launch the next phase of my career."

"Why do you want to subject yourself to that?" Vesta asked. "Wait. Scratch that. You're a drama queen, so this will be something you will excel at. And you'll probably win."

"They don't know what they're in for." Liam raised his Gilpin's martini. "Here's to me showing them how to have some fun."

"I suppose I could look up your bio in Horizon," Vesta said. "We would already know if you won."

Amara turned around from the sink to face her sister. "That would be a gross misuse of the tablet."

"Lighten up. It would just be for fun."

"Now do you see why Rasputin and Agrippa want it so badly?"

"I wouldn't misuse it. Only check it for a laugh."

"It's not a party game." A blush rose in Amara's cheeks. Vesta knew it meant she was angry.

"Whoa, don't bring storm clouds in here," Liam said trying to lighten the mood but failing to do so.

Vesta understood why Amara was upset. The Horizon tablet wasn't a game. She also understood how Agrippa manipulating the events during his time for his own gain could destroy life as they knew it. And how it could cancel their reincarnation as members of the trionfi. They would be RanChans. Vesta didn't like the name Sandor had coined for humans who reincarnated into random lives, but at that moment, that was the name that popped into her mind. Jared was right. Now Agrippa was out in the open with his intentions. Having the aid of Rasputin added another staggering layer of difficulty in defeating them. Vesta caught Amara's gaze.

"I'm sorry I suggested that. I really am. I get it. Horizon can be turned into a destructive weapon. That's what Agrippa would do if he took possession of it."

"We'll see if our Devil would let him have it," Liam said, polishing off his martini.

"That unholy alliance is an uneasy one for sure," Amara said turning back to the sink to finish washing the salad greens.

"Now that we know they're both after it," Sandor said, walking back into the kitchen. "Let's make sure they turn against each other."

"What's your plan?" Vesta asked.

Before he could answer, the back door swung open. Jared walked in. "All devices are headed to our headquarters in an armored truck with two escorts. Tomorrow a crew will repair the lab floor after installing deeper ground vibration sensors. I blame myself for the break-in and loss."

Amara picked up a large bowl of salad greens, tomatoes, cucumbers, and carrots from her garden and carried it to the rustic table on the edge of the kitchen.

"Let's turn loose of all that for an hour to have dinner. Everything is from the garden except the wine."

"And the gin," Liam called out from the bar.

"Fair enough," Jared said.

"Is this solid oak?" Vesta asked, admiring the table.

Amara smiled. "It is. You don't remember, but you were with me when I bought this in the 1920s from a carpenter whose family still lives out here."

Vesta returned her smile. No, she didn't recall the purchase. Her memory spell had obliterated huge chunks of her lives, and now time travel had stolen more.

One by one, the trionfi sat down at the table in sturdy wooden chairs made of the same blonde oak. Vesta loved it when they were all together. Her family. There they sat, in their sixties, with wrinkles and gray hair. Except for Liam. He was the Fool who would always buck the system, who would always push the envelope.

Amara passed around the salad, a squash casserole, a tureen of lentil soup, and freshly made whole wheat rolls. Jared chose a bottle of 2019 TX RG from Calais Winery in Hye, just outside of Fredericksburg. Conversation ceased for a minute as everyone dove into the meal.

"What has been your favorite thing about this time Vesta since you're three days into it now?" Jared asked pouring wine for everyone. "So much has changed since 1999."

"It has to be the mobile phones." She shook her head. "I have the internet where I can hunt for anything, shop for anything. And it has a camera on it." Vesta nodded at Jared. "I had the idea of somehow putting a camera on a phone a long time ago, by the way."

"I recall you mentioning that to me." Jared smiled.

"Wait, did my idea inspire you?"

Jared smiled. "Odin wasn't the first to put a camera on our portables, but I think we've done a better job with optics than anyone else."

"This is one of my favorite lives so far. I love how youth can be sustained in this age. And I'm not only talking about my cosmetic enhancements," Liam said. "In most of our past lives, I would be considered irrelevant now. Instead, I feel vibrant and revived by all these young people I associate with. Even all of you are young-minded. I'm happy all of us are still relevant."

"It's scary to think this could be our last life knowing each other as members of trionfi," Vesta said.

"We won't let that happen," Jared replied, looking up from his plate.

"It has been lovely that we have spent so much time together in this life. There were many lives where we rarely saw each other, remember?" Amara said. "Travel was difficult, plus we had crises we were dealing with in our own parts of the world."

"Or we couldn't leave because we were forced into damned servitude," Liam said.

"I know, buddy," Sandor said. "But out of that little

medieval mayhem, you created the whole troubadour craze." He nudged Liam's shoulder, sitting next to him. "That launched a career you're still in today."

The Fool shrugged. "It's true. And I was living in castles with nothing to do all day but come up with witty lyrics to amuse my master. I'm glad that nasty Javier is gone from this life though. He deserved that ending."

Vesta knew Liam was referring to Javier Garcia, the King of Pentacles, who fell to his death from the tower of Saint Jacques in Paris in 1997. She, Liam, and Sandor were all there to witness his ugly demise after trying to shove Vesta over the ledge. That event was still fresh in her mind, but according to where she was now, that was twenty-seven years ago. Linear time seemed so irrelevant to her.

"There was also the one before this one where I had to perform for those filthy Nazis." Liam shuddered.

"They were filth, but you were spectacular in your cabarets. That was a time when we were all working together for a common cause," Amara said.

"Those crazies were after total world domination," Sandor said. "Glad that didn't work."

"You know that's what Agrippa's after, right?" Vesta said.

"So, what's the plan?" Sandor asked.

"The short form is we capture him and throw him back to his time," Jared said.

"How do we do that?"

"Grabbing him won't be too hard. We need to get the chronicle to send him back without any way to return to this time or any other time."

"Can't Amara concoct one of her plant recipes and dispatch him?" Liam asked.

"No!" The other trionfi members shouted.

"His death would have huge consequences in the timeline."

"What? One less slimy alchemist."

"Even slight alterations cause big consequences," Amara said. "We can't know what they are until the alteration unfolds. But no, we cannot kill him."

Liam shrugged.

"We have to send him back with a one-way ticket," Sandor said.

"Where is he living?" Vesta asked.

"Wherever Rasputin is living," Jared said. "He wants to keep his eyes on Agrippa."

"I'll find out where the little weasel is living. We know he has at least two places. The ranch house Lars has built and somewhere else. Probably Austin," Sandor said.

"After we send Agrippa back, then what do we do about Rasputin wanting the tablet and other Odin things?"

"Either blackmail or a bribe. Something he wants even more than the technology," Sandor said.

"What would that be?" Amara asked.

Sandor shook his head. "I don't know yet."

"How are we going grab Agrippa?" Vesta asked.

Jared picked up his glass of wine and looked around the table. "By giving him what he came after."

Chapter Twelve

By mid-afternoon the following day, the plan was set. Odin would host a pop-up event to unveil the cutting-edge technology it had in the works, including the Horizon tablet. Jared explained to Vesta how pop-up events had become popular over the last decade and how Odin rarely held one. But when it did, everyone in the tech industry would drop everything to attend. News of the gathering would be impossible for Agrippa to resist.

According to the plan, Vesta would approach him under the auspices of threatening him but would secretly drop one of Amara's potions into whatever he was drinking. Jared and Liam would then get him into the waiting arms of the chronicle who would send him back to Bavaria at the exact time and place he left in the 1500s. Next on their list was to contact Gus to tell him the plan.

Standing in the study off the left wing of the house, the trionfi called out to the chronicle.

Vesta closed her eyes, focusing on his image in her mind. She spoke as if she were giving simple instructions to someone. "Gus, we want you to appear in this room. Come join us now."

The trionfi waited for a long moment. The room was so quiet that the faintest whisper would have sounded like a scream. But there were no whispers, no sound at all.

"Now!" Jared's voice boomed off the walls loud enough to make them crack.

A loud exhale whooshed through the room, causing Vesta's hair to brush against her face.

"Yes, yes, I'm here."

The voice preceded the image by a half-second before the chronicle materialized in the middle of the room, He was dressed as usual in his faded Grateful Dead T-shirt with layers of lightweight cotton kimono robes overlaying it. In his hand, he held a large, charred rib. The odor of smoked meat hung in his tumbleweed hair and long, scraggly beard. Vesta wrinkled her nose.

"We have devised a plan to solve your Agrippa problem," Jared said.

"I would say it's more than just my problem. But," he said pointing the rib at Jared. "What do you have in mind?"

"We're going to hand deliver him to you, and you are going to immediately send him back to exactly the time and place he came from."

"And you're going to seal up, permanently close his access to any time jumping ever again," Sandor added.

Gus huffed. "It's difficult to transport someone against their will."

"Luna took me to an ancient Egyptian tomb fifty feet underground during another time without my approval."

Again, the chronicle huffed. "You didn't know you were about to time jump, did you?"

"That's not our problem, buddy, that's yours," Sandor said.

Gus paced around the room, gnawing on the rib. "These things must be handled delicately," he said, shaking his head.

"You see, if the abductee struggles, he could land in another time altogether."

"We can't let that happen," Jared said.

"Certainly, but what if he does?"

Amara took a step toward him. "Agrippa will have drunk a potion made by me. He won't be unconscious, but he will be impaired."

"That definitely helps matters," Gus said.

"Then we're all agreed," Jared said.

"Er, ah, well." The chronicle cocked his head to one side. "There is the matter of him not accessing the portal again. Closing it as you put it."

"What's the problem?" Sandor asked.

"Well, it's not as simple as all that. You see, there's no way to actually shut them."

"Figure it out," Sandor said.

"I do wish it were that simple," Gus said shaking his head again. "But it's not."

The trionfi locked eyes with each other briefly. Their tightened jaws, raised brows, and quiet frustration needed no explanation.

Amara's face brightened. "I know what to do. Along with the sedative, I'll mix up a memory potion, so he won't remember how to access the portal."

"Brilliant!" Gus bellowed.

"But there is a crucial aspect to it," she said, turning to Vesta. "When he drinks the potion, you must say to him, 'You will forget how to time jump now and forever.'"

Vesta nodded.

"It will only take a few moments for the potion to begin to take effect, and he will know instantly by your words that you have drugged him." She looked at Sandor. "He will need to be immediately restrained."

"Got it. No problem," Sandor said.

"Well, then. Everything is in hand," the chronicle said. "I'll be ready."

"We're counting on you," Amara said.

"And don't show up with any food," Liam added. "Whatever you're eating is positively disgusting."

"I'll be at the ready. Don't worry," Gus said before he took another bite of the rib.

A gust of wind shot through the study and the chronicle disappeared.

"Call me crazy," Sandor said picking up some paper blown off a table. "But I am worried."

"Me too," Vesta said. "This might be our only chance to get him. If we fail, he's going to be even more difficult to catch."

Jared pulled his mobile phone out of his pocket.

"Okay, the email about the pop-up has arrived in everyone's mailboxes. It went out to all Odin investors, staff, and media. Tomorrow night at eight o'clock in the Roosevelt Room downtown. The venue will definitely work. There's a first floor where all the tech will be and a mezzanine level at the back. That's where Sandor and Liam will take Agrippa once Amara's potion hits him. Gus better be waiting up there."

"You're going to demonstrate Horizon to all those people?" Vesta asked.

"Yeah, we have several versions of it. I'll bring a different one from the one I showed you yesterday. We'll also talk about the LESTAT proprietary battery that will never die as an option where they can pop out the regular battery and put LESTAT in. We'll point out the screen and speaker quality advances and the mode they can select where they can get AI unbiased information on their searches."

"Nothing about how you can see the future?"

"Correct. That's too sensitive to share."

"You know the nerd circles online are already talking about it, right?" Sandor asked.

"I know. If someone asks about it, I'll neither confirm nor deny it."

"Won't Agrippa suspect this is a trap?" Vesta asked, feeling a sense of unease.

"Probably, but he won't be able to resist coming."

"That wretched alchemist thinks he's smarter than all of us," Liam sneered. "He'll have a plan to counter our trap."

"I'm counting on it."

Jared spoke with calm confidence, instilling Vesta with hope. All her years lusting after him had clouded her awareness of his steadiness, wisdom, and unbiased leadership. She didn't regret the physical yet shallow relationship in their twenties and thirties, but she appreciated this connection more.

"I need some time to put the potion together," Amara said. "It will be tricky combining the sedative with the memory sweep. I don't want to cancel his other memories or disturb the trajectory of his life as it historically played out. He was, after all, a feminist, believing women were equal to men. He also challenged his peers to keep questioning their conclusions, which led to modern-day scientific skepticism. So, he did make some worthy contributions during his life."

"And don't forget he inspired Marlowe's Faust," Sandor said. "This raises the question: was it his experience of time jumping here, retold to others, that inspired the idea? Was making a deal with the Devil of the tarot behind the story?"

"So, you're saying his time jump did happen in the history of his life that we see already written? That this wasn't an event stepping out of the historical timeline?" Vesta asked.

Sandor shrugged. "I don't know."

"Time fidgets on the periphery of human awareness, haunting with its presence. Inescapable, fleeting, spent and wasted time. Contorted into conforming into a linear structure by anxious minds desperate to comfort themselves but never able to master it. Blinding themselves to its true nature. Past, present, and future arranged into a rudimentary comprehension to ease their anxiety," Liam said.

Vesta, Amara, Sandor, and Jared all turned to stare at the Fool, who had been silent since entering the room. Sandor's mouth hung ajar slightly as if he were going to say something but couldn't decide what.

Liam's eyes widened as he clasped his vape pen between his teeth. "So, can I just stick to my frivolous behavior and not worry about any of this?"

Amara smiled. "Time is certainly a conundrum that can twist your thoughts into knots if you try to make it conform in a strictly linear way. Yes, Liam, enjoy yourself in this moment because this is the only moment." She patted him on his back. "I'm going out to the garden. Does anyone want to join me?"

"We are headed back to Austin," Vesta said, looking at Sandor.

"Can I ride with you?" Liam asked. "I need to round up some of my fringe musician and filmmaker friends to come to the tech rave tomorrow."

As Vesta slid into the passenger seat of the Tesla, a sharp pain shot through her right leg.

"Ow," she muttered.

"I wish you would get that fixed," Sandor said starting the car.

"What?"

"Your hip."

"It's fine."

"No, it's not. Test results revealed you have age-related osteoarthritis in that hip. New Vesta probably doesn't know that though."

She frowned. The pain subsided, but that likely explained why her little fingers and middle fingers felt stiff and didn't flex all the way any longer. Age-related too no doubt. She had tried to forget about her current age and focus on stopping Agrippa, but it was difficult. By Sandor's proclamation to get it fixed, did that mean surgery? That would be a decision the other Vesta would make after she returned to her healthy, younger self in 1999 when she was in her early forties.

"You breezed through your cataract surgery a few years ago," Sandor continued. "You're back to twenty-twenty vision. They'll do the same with your hip. And remember the great job they did on my heart? Yeah, I guess you don't, but primo job. It's not like lifetimes before when you just had to live with it."

"That little ticker of yours always seems to get you," Liam said, sprawled in the backseat.

"Yeah, but I think I'm going to set a personal record in this life. Shooting for eighty, baby!"

"Hm, me too, but I'm aiming for ninety and beyond. Why not? Look at William Shatner. He looks great. I found out who did his eyes, and I'm making an appointment," Liam said.

Vesta shook her head, pulling down the sun visor to reveal a mirror. Adrenaline coursed through her as she looked at herself. Fine traces of lines in 1999 were now fully etched, plus new ones added. The loose skin on her neck was the biggest problem, along with its endless wrinkles stacking one on top of the other. But her skin tone looked healthy, and her blue eyes were as clear as the Texas sky. She pressed her lips together and sighed. She could go the route Liam had taken. The internet was littered with images of celebrities she had as Sybarite clients who had taken Liam's route. Some had restrained work done, just enough to tidy up the biggest wrinkles and sagging skin, others had gone full transformation into losing any resemblance to their original faces. She glanced again at her reflection. Even though it was still a bit jarring, she was glad for the choices she'd made.

Liam was still talking. "I don't know what Jared is expecting out of me," he was saying. "I do have a bad back. I mean how much muscle is he thinking we can exert on that nasty alchemist?"

"He's going to be drugged, buddy. We just need to make sure we put him in the chronicle's hands. That's all."

"Why isn't Jared doing that? He's much stronger than I am!"

"Because, like you said, Agrippa will know we're setting a trap. He'll be thinking it's Jared who would be grabbing him. But Jared will be busy showcasing Horizon or one of the other devices. He's smart. He knows we don't want to kill him and alter his timeline. My guess is he will think our trap comes as he's leaving the bar or walking down the sidewalk or something like that. I don't think he's guessed what our plan is."

Liam clucked his tongue. "I wouldn't be so sure. I've seen him in action."

"Just do your job. We'll take care of the rest."

The oppressive August heat pressed down on Austin like a giant thumb trying to squash a bug. The buildings and intricate web of concrete roads absorbed the soaring temperature holding it fast. Vesta and Sandor dropped off Liam at the Continental Club on South Congress. The iconic live music honky-tonk had become one of his beloved places since moving to the city. He could always find someone interesting to talk to there, and the staff adored having a British music legend hang out. He even kept one of his guitars, Delilah, a 1960s Stratocaster, parked in the manager's office for any time he wanted to sit in with the band. The guitar was named after the song made famous by another British superstar, Tom Jones. Nothing made the club-goers lose their minds more than when he would wail the cover tune in his rock and roll style.

While drinking cheap gin and swapping stories at the bar might not seem like a good way to prepare for what lay ahead the next day, Vesta understood that was how Liam handled everything in his life. She adored that about him. It was a carefree attitude she could never embrace, no matter how hard she tried.

Instead, she and Sandor drove the short distance to their apartment, where Sandor changed into his swimsuit for a solid hour of swimming laps in the rooftop pool. That was his method of burning nervous energy while putting details into place. As for her, she carefully surveyed outfits in her closet, not only to familiarize herself with her wardrobe in 2024 but to decide on the perfect ensemble to wear to the pop-up. It needed at least one pocket, cocktail attire without being too dressy. Within minutes, her hands landed on a silky floral Mary Katrantzou dress with pockets. Its long bell sleeves would make slipping something into Agrippa's drink easy, and the deep pockets would hide the vial Amara would give her. She decided to pair the dress with ice-blue Manola Blahnik slingbacks and carry the fuchsia Fendi baguette sitting on a top shelf. A tingle of excitement ran through her. She knew this was deadly serious business, but no one said she couldn't look fabulous saving the world.

The remainder of the evening passed quietly. Vesta and Sandor walked across the street to Bob's Steak and Chop House. They sat at the bar eating salmon and sharing a bottle of burgundy wine, the Magician explaining the concept of cryptocurrency to her.

The next day sped by with calls, emails, and texts from tarot clients in a panic because she had suddenly retired from reading cards. Because of the chaos involving Rasputin's thugs breaking into Jared's lab, Vesta had forgotten about her abrupt decision to quit. Word spread quickly. As she read through the list of names, Vesta's reactions ranged from amused to stunned by her clientele. She was accustomed to working with famous people at Sybarite. The fashion and luxury goods house attracted wealthy, notable names, but the list of people who desired her tarot insight into their futures was as impressive, if not more so. Did they all come to see her inside the Hotel Emma Spirits tank? The answer she discovered was no. She met with them via her computer laptop through something called Zoom. So much had been born since the beginning of the new millennium. She had to admit she felt a decent amount of guilt canceling all the readings, but the idea of being a tarot reader for money nevertheless smacked of tawdriness.

A ripe apricot sun slid into the western horizon. Vesta watched the vibrant colors slowly fade into washed tones from the apartment's wall of windows. Sandor was at the pool again, burning off pent-up anticipation. She was already dressed for the Odin event, carefully double-checking that small objects she placed in her dress pockets wouldn't show a bulge. She paced in front of the windows, debating what to say to Agrippa so he wouldn't become suspicious, distracting him so she could drop Amara's potion into his drink.

"Did you see Horizon over there? I know you're interested in it." She frowned. "I have to stop rehearsing," she mumbled to herself. "I'm going to overdo it if I don't stop."

Long tense exhale. What could she do instead? She looked down the hallway, nodding her head. Walking quickly, she stepped inside the bedroom, approached the antique Japanese cabinet, opened it, and took out her Thoth tarot deck. Pulling cards for herself didn't happen often. Her InSight guided her in most instances, but she had trouble seeing how everything would go over the next several hours. When dealing with altered humans, like the trionfi, or half-humans like Lucy Jane, it was impossible to foresee the outcome. And Rasputin had blocked Agrippa's mind from being read, or he had taught the alchemist how to do it, so that wasn't a viable option. The power of the cards could overcome any block in gaining guidance. Why that was so, she wasn't sure. She just knew it was true.

Vesta walked back into the living room. She sat down on the sofa and began shuffling the cards. The question she repeated in her mind was, *what will be the result of the trionfi's efforts tonight to stop Agrippa?* Over the short few years after coming to know she was the High Priestess of the tarot and coming to know how to read the tarot, she understood that what the cards said wasn't irrevocable. It was the trajectory based on current factors with a ninety percent chance it would happen. Free will was the wild card for humans, though. The saving grace or curse, depending on the circumstances.

She sensed the deck was shuffled. With her left hand, she pulled the top card. The nine of Wands, known as Strength, she laid on the table. Relief spread through her. The sun on one end of the long staff, the moon on the other. Traditional symbols of male and female energy. A good indication the trionfi would be working effectively together. Vesta drew in her breath and pulled the second card. The Wheel of Fortune turned over in her hand. Vesta frowned, knowing the card could represent smooth sailing through the plan or it could signal a sudden turn of events. Being in the challenge position of the spread concerned her that it could be the latter.

The third card was the course of action called for. Maybe it would mitigate the duplicity of the Fortune card to reveal its clear meaning. Vesta pulled the card from the deck. The Fool. Vesta stared at it. Of course, Liam was the Fool of the tarot, but the card could also represent the energy of taking a risk, trusting intuition, and being willing to set out on a path even though the destination wasn't certain. This was the course of action called for. The trionfi were going to trust their intuition and take a risk with their plan. By doing that, the challenge energy of the Fortune card could work in their favor, or their plans could go terribly wrong. Vesta realized she was still holding her breath. She let it out and rubbed the spot between her eyebrows, which tingled as though pins were being stuck into it

The front door opened as Sandor hurried into the room.

"I'll be ready in ten minutes or less. I took a shower in the pool house."

He spoke over his shoulder, walking down the hallway in his ridiculously plush pool robe. But in exactly eight minutes, the Magician stood before her, looking undeniably handsome in his dark gray Ralph Lauren suit and white button-down shirt. The silver threads sprinkled throughout his raven hair added a distinguished touch, highlighting the flecks of gray in his amber eyes to complete the total look in a fetching way.

"Are you ready to do this?"

Vesta nodded. She didn't want to tell him about the cards.

Chapter Thirteen

Heat wasn't the only challenge in Austin in August, Vesta was quick to learn. Humidity played an enormous role in the comfort level, too. Sandor pulled up to the valet stand in front of the Roosevelt Room on 5th Street in the heart of downtown. Even in the short walk to the door, oppressive air filled with sticky moisture pummeled her. A cocktail dress with spaghetti straps would have been much more appropriate for the evening but not for her mission.

They walked through the door to the foyer where a gentleman wearing a black suit and white shirt with a smart charcoal tie greeted them at a reception podium. He knew them by name. Vesta smiled as if she knew him too. He parted the golden veil of the beaded string partition to allow their entry where a crowd was already assembled.

The shotgun-shaped space dripped with sophisticated elegance. Deeply padded black banquettes lined the wall on the right where large, framed images in black and white – a moody woman smoking a cigarette, white roses floating on a black background, and a jazz musician blowing on a trumpet – hung on a pale brick wall above them. Odin engineers lined the opposite wall behind black high-top tables pushed together, forming a long row. The newest devices from Odin were laid out on the tables in front of them. The engineers wore high-quality black cotton T-shirts with the Odin logo in white, the trademark lightning bolt dotting the I. The white gloves they wore sent the subtle message that they alone should touch the products.

A sleek, twenty-foot bar stretched beyond the tables, flanked by black-and-white portraits of Theodore Roosevelt on one end and his cousin, Franklin, on the other, both standing watch over the space. At the far end, a staircase led to the mezzanine level, completing the room's sophisticated design.

Amara walked up, embracing them both. As she completed Vesta's hug, she let her left hand slide down to Vesta's right hand, where she placed a tiny bottle. It felt warm and heavy. Vesta's heart beat faster as she carefully slipped it into her pocket.

"I'm going upstairs to check out things," Sandor said. "Will you order their best Macallan's for me?"

"Sure."

"He's not here yet," Amara spoke in a quiet voice, barely audible, moving her lips only slightly.

"You can bet someone is watching us though," Vesta replied, in the same soft tone.

Amara smiled in agreement.

Vesta walked toward the bar, spotting either Serena or Faith bartending. Her polished ebony hair cascaded around her flawless pale face, accented by vibrant red lips. She wore the same black suit attire as the host in the foyer, setting off her skin tone and dazzling obsidian eyes.

"How are you tonight, Serena?" Amara asked as they arrived.

"Very well. Ladies, what can I get for you?"

"Hello, Serena. Nice to see you again. Macallan's, whatever is the oldest, neat please, and a sparkling water," Vesta said.

"Nothing for me, thanks," Amara replied.

The Empress, dressed in a simple black boatneck cocktail dress, long blonde and gray hair plaited down her back, leaned in close to her sister.

"Try to empty it."

Vesta nodded, sensing the minuscule weight of the tiny bottle in her pocket.

Serena returned with the drinks. Vesta picked them up and turned around, surveying the faces in the room. She supposed any one of them could be working for Agrippa, but probably not the ones sitting in the banquettes laughing and drinking. Some of the people clustered by the device tables were clearly journalists, taking notes, pointing at the devices, asking the engineers questions. But two men dressed in plaid shirts and dark denim jeans seemed to be watching the room more than what was on the tables. One with a thin frame and thick push-broom mustache made eye contact with her, but only for a second. He let his eyes casually drift from her to Amara, then across the room. Vesta caught her sister's eye, following her gaze to the man. He was watching them—of that, she was sure. The other man looked as if he could have been a wrestler at some point. His hulking appearance amplified by his gleaming bald head.

"I'll see you in a while," Amara said, walking toward the stairs.

Vesta took a sip of her water, surprised by the dryness of her throat. Sandor weaved through the crowd, taking his drink when he got close.

"Good?" she asked.

"Great. And just as expected."

He nodded toward the front entry where Agrippa strolled

through the golden veil of beads, stroking his finely groomed beard, his hawkish eyes taking in everything.

More guests had arrived, packing the room, but Vesta never let her attention stray from the alchemist as he moved steadily down the long row of tables. He listened intently as each Odin engineer described the function of the device before him, asking questions, completely engaged with every bit of information. Occasionally nodding, his focus never left the table, even though she was certain he knew she was watching him. When he reached the last table where the Horizon tablet sat, she would be standing at the end of the bar. Maybe four feet separated the table from the bar. She would be in a prime position to approach him.

Vesta watched Serena's twin, Faith, approach Agrippa, asking if he would like a drink. He shook his head, his gaze still on the engineer and device in front of him. Vesta pressed her lips together, her mind racing. If he refused to drink, how could she get the potion into him?

Minutes crept by. She had drunk the glass of water and asked Serena for another to not arouse suspicion standing by the bar. Agrippa was almost to the end of the row. He had seen Odin technology devoted to healthcare, diagnosing diseases much sooner and treating them with new therapies constructed by artificial intelligence. He saw home and professional security equipment combining cyber and physical systems enhanced with the latest 3D printing. An entire table he visited was devoted to new sustainable technology for building construction using solar and wind power. Mini televisions showcasing the latest high-definition images with LED and OLED sat beside next-generation virtual reality and augmented reality gear.

At last, he came to the table where the Horizon tablet rested on a clear plexiglass display stand. The Odin employee demonstrated how the device worked, answering a barrage of questions

Agrippa threw at him. Hair on the back of her neck stood up, her third eye spun like a wheel caught in a whirlwind. He was monitoring her every move even though his gaze never left the tablet.

How would she get the potion into him? Muscles in her jaw tightened. She could feel the subtle weight of the tiny bottle resting at the bottom of her pocket. This plan had to work. It was their only chance to stop him. She let her eyes leave Agrippa for a moment, feeling an energetic tug from someplace else. She caught Amara glancing at her from a banquette where she stood chatting with a man who was taking notes. Vesta's expression must have conveyed her frustration because Amara gently excused herself from the journalist to walk toward the rear of the room. She gave a subtle blink of her eyes, telling Vesta she understood. Did her sister have a plan to help?

Agrippa maintained his laser focus on the table where Horizon sat. The pupils of his eyes grew larger as he looked at it. This was his target. She could feel the energy in his body increase, but in that moment, she could feel something else. The temperature in the room seemed to be rising. Her long sleeves felt stifling, even the light silk fabric of the dress began to feel like heavy wool. She needed more water and took a step further down the bar to get Serena's attention. Immediately, she noticed that taking one step away from the table changed the temperature in the room by ten, maybe fifteen, degrees. She cut her attention to Amara, who stood near the stairs. She had her mobile phone up to her ear as though on a call, her eyes closed. Vesta knew the Empress wasn't talking to anyone, she was conjuring a column of intense heat bearing down on the table and Agrippa.

Drops of sweat rolled down the engineer's forehead. He wiped them away with the top of his glove. He continued the demonstration, holding Horizon in one hand and pointing out features to Agrippa with the other. Vesta noticed a security cord attached to the bottom of the tablet. The only way Agrippa could steal the tablet would be to whip out some serious wire-cutting scissors. And while she wouldn't rule that option out, she guessed he had another plan.

Agrippa leaned forward to get a closer look at the screen. Vesta saw a drop of sweat run across his forehead and down his nose. The engineer pulled the tablet away from him before the droplet fell, plopping on the table. Agrippa looked over to Serena, who stood behind the bar. He made the motions of drinking something. She pulled two bottles of water from the cooler and handed them to him across the bar. Agrippa unscrewed the cap and took a long drink. Vesta's pulse shot into overdrive. This was it, the moment to act. But how? Agrippa was holding the water bottle in his hand. He needed to put it down.

"That's quite a tablet, isn't it? Would you like to hold it?" Jared asked as he walked up to the table.

The alchemist turned around squinting his eyes as he studied the Emperor's face. "Yes, I would," he replied in his crisp Germanic accent.

Jared looked over to the engineer. "It's okay, Steve."

The engineer, looking relieved, handed over the tablet and reached for the other water bottle. Agrippa placed his own bottle on the table and took the tablet with both hands, the security cord taut as it stretched across the surface.

"Let me show you a couple of special features," Jared said, making sure he positioned Agrippa with his back to Vesta.

"Why are you doing this?" Agrippa asked, wiping more sweat from his forehead.

"I know you went to a lot of trouble trying to get a good look at this. And," Jared said tugging on the security cord. "It's not like you can steal it. This is a carbon fiber cord. It's not going anywhere."

As Jared began showing Agrippa the features of the tablet, Vesta scanned the room for the two men who were his accomplices. Both stood near the front, watching Agrippa. From the crowd, Amara emerged and walked up to them. Whatever she was saying to them took their attention away from their boss, who was now fully engrossed in the tablet he held in his hands.

Vesta pulled the little bottle from her pocket, popped the tiny cork off the top, put the bottle in her left hand, and took two steps to the table. She stood directly behind Agrippa, so close she could feel the heat coming off his body. Sweat began to bead up on her forehead and palms, causing a panic inside her that she would drop the bottle. Pretending she was looking over Agrippa's shoulder to not give away her actions to the Odin engineer, she felt for the alchemist's water bottle with her right hand. Her long sleeves paid off at last. She was able to pick up the bottle without notice, concealing it underneath her sleeve. Steadying her nerves but afraid to breathe, she turned away from the engineer and poured the contents of the bottle into the water bottle. Agrippa stayed fully focused on the tablet while Jared continued to talk. Vesta placed Agrippa's bottle back on the table in the same spot. She smiled at the engineer who was watching the demonstration while drinking his water, paying no attention to her.

Jared slid the tablet from Agrippa's grasp and handed it back to the engineer when Vesta moved back to the bar.

"But something is missing," Agrippa said. "Where is the aspect of immediate updates on the timeline? Can you show me that?"

"I'm not certain I understand what you're referring to," Jared said, keeping his cool even though he, too, was coated in a glaze of sweat.

"You know, mighty Emperor. You give me a taste of this treasure but not the full portion?"

Jared dabbed his forehead with a handkerchief he pulled from his pocket. His subliminal suggestion worked because Agrippa grabbed his bottle of water, draining the remainder of its contents. Like a switch turning off, the heat abated rapidly around them. Agrippa wiped his forehead with the sleeve of his jacket.

"This heat... How do you tolerate it?" His words already slurring.

Vesta stepped beside Agrippa, her mouth close to his ear.

"You will forget how to time jump now and forever."

As she raced to the stairs, Sandor strode past her, headed for Agrippa. Liam followed close behind. Each one stepped alongside him at the table.

"What do you want?" Agrippa's speech almost incoherent.

"We're going for a little stroll, buddy," Sandor said.

"Take your hands off me..."

But Agrippa couldn't put up any fight. Sandor seized his left side, wrapping his arm around his back. He told Liam to do the same on his right. Together they walked Agrippa toward the stairs. Jared moved quickly ahead of them.

"Apologies," he said to a cluster of people taking notice. "A little too much to drink."

They wove their way through the crowd to the stairs where the three began hoisting him up.

"Nasty alchemist," Liam taunted. "Getting a little payback here, aren't we?"

"Is the chronicle here?" Jared asked.

"Yep, been here for ten minutes," Sandor said, pushing the No Entry stanchion out of the way at the bottom of the stairs.

They carried Agrippa to the mezzanine level, where Gus sat on a low-slung sofa sipping a high ball of whiskey.

"Oh, so soon?" he mumbled, struggling to stand up.

"Get that vortex open," Sandor shouted.

Amara, who was standing beside the sofa, grabbed one of the chronicle's arms to help him. A loud bang brought everyone to a standstill. The door behind them had been kicked open. Out from it walked Rasputin with a revolver in each hand, looking like a modern-day Yosemite Sam. His misshapen cowboy hat, long red beard, and western shirt with longhorns on the plackets were comical, but his expression was pure deranged maniac.

"Agrippa's coming with me," his words spat out as he pointed one of the guns at Amara. "Or your Empress is dead."

"Put down your guns, Devil," Sandor said. "You have no use for him."

The viper smile slid across his face. "Oh, but I do. I have twelve bullets, more than enough for each of you. Who wants to be first? But wait, I have another little surprise for you. Look over the railing."

Jared, already at the mezzanine railing, glanced at the crowd below. His eyes landed on the two men Vesta had spotted earlier as accomplices of Agrippa's. Wedged in between them was Faith, whose dark eyes telegraphed true fear.

"No!" The Emperor swung his attention back to the Devil. "Turn her loose!" He looked at Amara. "They've got Faith."

Amara lunged at Rasputin. He stepped back cocking both guns. "One more step, Empress, will be your final one for this life." His raspy Russian accent made the words sound more like an invitation than a threat.

"Amara, stop!" Jared shouted. "What do you want Rasputin?"

"I want the alchemist. You two," he pointed at Sandor and Liam, still holding up Agrippa who was now unconscious. "Walk him to my truck parked in the alley. My associates will take your dark-haired girl. The trade will be simple. The girl for the tablet. Otherwise, she dies." Rasputin cocked his head and smiled. "Simple, yes?"

"She's played no part in this," Jared said.

Rasputin shrugged. "That doesn't matter."

"Wait," Sandor said. "Let's discuss this. We can come up with a better idea for all of us."

Rasputin cackled. "My plan is the best plan and already in motion. The girl is gone until you deliver the tablet."

Jared glanced over the railing again to see that the two men and Faith were indeed gone from the bar.

"What guarantees do we have that you will keep your word?" Jared asked.

"None! You have known me for two thousand years. You know my record. Take from that what you will."

"Rasputin," Amara spoke up in a calm voice. "I do know you. You were once the wisest among us, knowing that material objects and power over others were transitory and worthless. You would teach this around the world, bringing enlightenment to so many, helping to create some of the greatest religions that still exist in the world."

The Devil spat on the floor. "Humans are consumed with violence and greed. It's in their DNA. I grew weary of such fruitless endeavors and understood my greater value was to show them the results of pushing their ravenous instincts to the limit." He let out a venomous cackle. "It's much more fun too. Yes?" He looked at Sandor. "You and the Fool take the alchemist down the back stairs now. No more delays, or I will take pleasure in using my Western gun on your Empress."

Sandor scanned the room. "Where's the chronicle?"

"He vanished the second Rasputin kicked open the door," Liam said, struggling to hold up Agrippa.

"Your doorway has closed. Do as I say now," Rasputin barked.

Sandor frowned looking at Liam. "Let's go."

"I will follow," the Devil said. "If any of you do something foolish, I will shoot the one closest to me and continue shooting. I'm a real cowboy now." Another wild cackle burst from his mouth as he waved the gun in his left hand in the air.

The Magician opened the door to the stairs, slowly he and the Fool hoisted Agrippa down to the red pickup truck where they dumped him into the passenger seat.

"Where do we meet you for the trade?" Sandor asked.

"All in good time," Rasputin said, hopping into the driver's seat. He started the engine, put the truck in gear, and floored the gas pedal. His screeching laughter could be heard to the end of the alley, where he turned the corner and disappeared.

When Sandor and Liam returned to the mezzanine, Vesta was the first to speak. "Did either of you think to check the rooms up here?"

The Magician scowled. "Of course we did."

"Who checked the one Raz came out of?"

Liam looked down at the floor. "I suppose it was me."

"Then how did you not see him hiding in there?"

"I don't know," he said, his voice shrill, flipping his mop of black hair out of his eyes. "I'm going to have a cocktail." He went downstairs.

Vesta knew he was embarrassed, even angry with himself, which rarely happened. Sandor stepped inside the room.

"There's a desk in here. It looks like an office," he called out. "My guess is Rasputin hid behind it when Liam looked in."

"He wouldn't take Faith to his house," Jared said. "She could be anywhere now. We'll have to wait for him to contact us. We have no other choice at this point."

The Emperor gave Amara another look Vesta couldn't quite decipher before he walked downstairs.

"He's right. We must wait," Amara said before following him.

Sandor ran his fingers through his hair, the mischief normally glinting in his eyes had faded. Vesta knew he was worried

"Can you tune into Faith with your InSight?"

She was already sitting down on the sofa to find out. She closed her eyes, blocking not only her sight but the noise of the crowd below, as well as the smell of stale alcohol that was always present in bars. She focused on opening her third eye.

"Aah," she murmured. The instant relief of tuning out the physical world, entering the tranquil, expansive universe of nothing but everything always had the same effect on her.

"Faith, Faith, where are you?" she whispered.

Rapid-fire images exploded in her mind. Buildings, store-fronts, parked and moving cars created a dizzying collage in her awareness. As she continued to watch, the crowd scene downstairs layered in on top of the street images of faces of Odin engineers, invited guests in the banquettes laughing, and glimpses of the artwork hanging on the wall above them. She saw Jared leaning in to talk to Amara, and Liam drinking a martini while holding court with a group of people near the bar. Everything felt chaotic; the images of speeding through the city mingled with the bar scene. Vesta grabbed her head.

"Are you getting anything?" Sandor asked.

"I am but it's very confusing."

As she spoke, all the images vanished into complete darkness. Vesta looked up at Sandor, describing what she saw. He nodded, looking over the railing to the scene below.

"What is it?" she asked.

"Just a hunch. I'll tell you later. We need to go to Fredericksburg."

"Why?"

"Rasputin will want to make the trade outside of the city. He thinks it's the Wild West out there. His base is there. Let's get the others."

Sandor raced downstairs. Vesta sat still, recalling the images she'd seen with her InSight. Why was there such a flurry of disconnected scenes and then nothing? She closed her eyes again, calling up her powerful gift. Only a veil of black came forward when she tried to find Faith. Blowing out a long exhale, she walked downstairs. Sandor had collected the other trionfi who were ready to leave the Roosevelt Room. A plan was in place, he said, when she caught up to them. She hoped it would be more successful. The Wheel of Fortune card was more than a challenge; it had foretold utter failure.

Chapter Fourteen

It was past midnight before Vesta and Sandor arrived at Amara's ranch. Even after she finally lay down in bed, it was impossible to sleep. Her monkey mind kept jumping from thought to thought, no matter how hard she tried to make it stop or slow down. Faith must be terrified. By all appearances and based on Vesta's intuition, Faith was the epitome of a naïve young woman. Vesta assumed she had been raised in Fredericksburg along with her sister, Serena, and that their remote upbringing gave them little exposure to large urban environments or a wide variety of experiences outside of their rural location. It was rare to meet someone with such remarkable innocence. A protective nature for them had sprung to life within her.

Thoughts about what Rasputin and Agrippa had planned also kept her awake. She knew they would have a scheme for the Odin pop-up, and it turned out to be one that worked to decimate the trionfi plan. She never underestimated either one of them, but now she was fearful of what they might do, especially with Faith in their clutches.

And then the trionfi plan caused her worry. Jared

mentioned that Agrippa noticed the Horizon tablet at the pop-up wasn't the upgraded model when he demonstrated it to him. For someone from the sixteenth century, he grasped new concepts exceptionally fast. If he was handed that version again, he would know. What would happen to Faith at that point? Vesta knew. Rasputin had no regard for Faith. Cruelty had over-taken him ages ago as his primary motivation. Vesta shuddered. The trionfi couldn't let Faith be murdered.

She got out of bed. Sandor was already asleep, his face turned away from her, but she could hear his deep, rhythmic breathing. Some portion of comfort came from knowing such a dynamic man as him felt safe in the moment, safe to rest and dream. Maybe his dreams would mingle with Faith's or Agrippa's. She doubted either would happen. Since she couldn't gain InSight from Agrippa and now Faith, she would bet that Sandor accessing their dreams would be impossible too.

Vesta walked out the balcony door of their room. The intense heat had abated some, a breeze caught her short, bleached blonde hair, tossing it gently. Above her, the clear sky silhouetted a thousand diamond stars. A satellite catching the sun's rays from the other side of the Earth silently sailed in the inky sea. She felt the muscles in her back relax a bit. This was a magical place for her, feeling among the stars. Memories of Enid teaching her about the constellations from their home on the side of the mountain near Crested Butte reached out to her. Enid would bring the quilt she made that covered her bed from their cabin to spread on the grass. Together, they would lie on it, side by side. Vesta would listen for hours to her mother talk about why the constellations had their names. They would count the shooting stars, having a contest to see who could spot one first. Vesta allowed a smile to slide across her face. She was glad to have those memories.

An owl hooted close by, with another responding from a

greater distance. Her favorite bird since childhood, Enid taught her that when an owl flies, it makes no sound because of the unique serrations and velvety texture of their feathers. Several kinds of owls lived in the dense forest around their cabin. The great horned owl, the screech owl, and her favorite, the barn owl with its heart-shaped face, they would spot on their nocturnal walks. She couldn't decide which kind she was hearing at that moment, but its haunting calls were comforting.

Vesta closed her eyes, asking her InSight to tune into Faith. The spot between her eyebrows warmed into a gentle glow, but she could see only blackness. Nothing came to her, no sights, no sounds, nothing. She walked back to the bed and laid down to count backward in French from one hundred to zero, eventually falling asleep.

The intoxicating aroma of coffee brought Vesta to full consciousness in the morning. Pale sunshine played on the hardwood floor by the windows like a child with a treasured toy. Sandor was out of the bed, out of the room altogether. She hurried through a shower and got dressed. The night before, she had carefully chosen to bring a pair of black jeans, a black T-shirt, and hiking boots, which seemed the most all-purpose attire for whatever lay ahead.

All the trionfi except for Liam were assembled in the kitchen when she arrived. They were focused on a text message on Jared's mobile phone. He held it up as she walked into the room.

"Okay, Enchanted Rock at noon."

'Big place," Sandor said. "Where?"

Jared shook his head, "Doesn't say."

Vesta knew from her research since arriving in Fredericksburg that it was a Texas state park encompassing hundreds of acres near town. A dome of solid pink granite soared over four hundred feet above the surrounding landscape, which is why it's called Enchanted Rock. The ancient local tribes of Comanche and Tonkawa revered it as a sacred site while also believing spirits haunted it.

"Now visitors must make a reservation. You can't just walk into the park," Amara added.

"Something tells me Rasputin has already taken care of that." Jared set the phone down on the counter. "We need to leave here in three hours."

"Let's eat and go over our plan once more," Amara said.

It was straightforward. Jared would hand Rasputin or Agrippa a dummy Horizon looking identical to the one he wanted.

"What he spotted when he commented on the tablet last night," Jared explained, "was that the icon for the Visionary app was missing." He pointed to a tiny gold letter V logo on the upper right portion of the browser by the download button. "That's what he's after."

"How did he know about the Visionary app?" Vesta asked.

"Online chats about tech probably. It's been in development for years."

"Are your employees, your engineers trustworthy?"

"Yeah, NDAs and all that, but things leak out. Always have. Speculating about it isn't the same as having it in your hands."

Jared didn't seem too concerned about what information had gotten out. It had been the same in fashion. Sybarite would try to launch their new collections with a big unveiling, but every season, someone had already shared one or more of the designs with the media or online.

"Won't he want to demo it right there?" Vesta asked.

"Sure, and I've planted several dummy future scenarios in this clone app."

She nodded. "So, you hand it to him, and he gives us Faith?"

"That's the plan. Then he jumps back to his time."

"And when he realizes it's a dummy, then what?"

"It will take him a good while to figure that out."

"And then?" Vesta asked.

"Gus finds the way to close the portal so he can't jump here again."

Jared's plan sounded solid. Again, the trionfi was in the position where this had to work. Faith's life was at stake, and the fate of the world as they knew it. The thought sounded incredibly dramatic to her, but it was true.

Liam walked in to join them, and everyone fell silent to take in the sight. He stood dressed head-to-toe in traditional native American clothing from the 1800s. His buckskin leather shirt, leggings, and breechcloth were trimmed in finely cut fringe dotted with sterling silver crimps. He wore a hairpipe breast-plate of water buffalo bone and horn and carried in his hand a cluster of eagle feathers, snowy white except for the brown tips. On his feet were moccasins, the same soft beige leather as his outfit.

"I can't wait to hear this story," Sandor said.

"We're going to sacred land today," Liam fanned himself with the feathers. "Quanah Parker gave me all of this." He lifted his chin while doing a slow twirl.

"The Comanche chief from the 1800s?" Vesta asked.

"That's the one," he replied picking up one of Amara's freshly baked whole wheat biscuits from the counter.

"Now, how would you know someone like that?" Sandor asked.

"I helped him out once."

"How?"

Liam nibbled on the biscuit for a moment before answering. "Let's just say he needed to accomplish something of an esoteric nature, and I was able to lend a hand. I was made an honorary member of the tribe. Since we will be on their land, I want to honor them in return."

Sandor shook his head. "You never cease to amaze me."

"As it should be."

"It's a good look on you," Jared smiled. "I have some things to attend to before we leave. I'll see everyone here at eleven-thirty sharp." He walked toward the library on the far side of the house.

Liam saluted him as he left the room. "Yes, Big Chief."

"There are a few last-minute items I would like to check on too," Amara said walking out the back door.

Sandor looked at Liam, pursing his lips as though he were thinking something through before turning to Vesta. "So, what have you got up your sleeve? We know it's not going to be a walk in the park up there."

"I tried to locate Faith last night after everyone was asleep." She shrugged. "Nothing. Chaotic images making no cohesive sense right after she was abducted, then nothing. What have you got?"

Sandor shook his head. "I'll be on guard for whatever they pull. Rasputin's a wily one but Agrippa feels just plain dangerous."

"Trust me," Liam said, adjusting his breastplate. "He is. And he won't stop until he gets what he wants."

The trionfi made their way to Enchanted Rock in silence. Jared drove, Amara sat in the passenger seat next to him. Vesta positioned herself in the back seat behind Jared, Sandor behind Amara, and Liam in between them. He toyed with the silver crimps on the fringe of his buckskin shirt, picking at them aimlessly during the drive.

Passing through the town of Fredericksburg, Vesta couldn't help noticing the large number of high-end restaurants, bars, and shops filled with art, antique shops, and other fine goods. As expected, it was sprinkled with a generous dose of German-style places to eat, a sign promoting Oktoberfest, and cowboy-themed gift shops. It echoed the spirit of the European settlers who had quarried the local limestone for commercial buildings and homes. Over a hundred years later, they had solidly weathered the passage of time. As they left it behind, turning right onto another highway, the buzzing between Vesta's eyebrows began. She closed her eyes to tune in.

Pressure bore down on the top of her head. The throbbing grew intense as images flowed in her mind's eye. A vast expanse of green dotted with hills of varying sizes came into view. Dusty pale pink granite lay beneath her. She knew the view had to be from the top of Enchanted Rock, but the images churned in her mind again, turning chaotic. Juxtaposed with the view was the interior of a car and the face of the guy with the push-broom mustache laughing. She began to feel off balance as the view of hills bathed in bright sunlight returned, crashing into his face. Vesta grabbed her head, opening her eyes to make the InSight stop.

"What did you see?" Amara stared at her from the front seat of the Range Rover.

"Whew, I'm not sure. I mean, I know it was from Enchanted Rock, but the images were jumbled. Faith is definitely there already. But something strange is going on. I can't get a clear picture. There's interference as though someone else is inserting their images."

As she spoke, they rounded a bluff, bringing the faded pink hilltop she saw with her InSight into view.

"That's it, isn't it?" she asked, rubbing her forehead.

Jared nodded. "Let me lead the way up. Sandor, you bring up the rear. It goes without saying, but I'll say it anyway. The goal is to rescue Faith with no injuries to anyone. I spoke to the chronicle earlier. He'll be waiting to take Agrippa back to his time as soon as I tell him to. Let me make the call."

Vesta cast her gaze around to the other trionfi. Everyone kept their eyes straight ahead, even Liam. That, most of all, made her nervous. Where was his flippant attitude? Where was Sandor's sarcasm? Not even Amara chimed in with one of her typical overly optimistic comments. Vesta thought about the prophecy carved by the Elders on the wall of Meri's tomb thousands of years ago. Why was her image carved there instead of Jared's, who was leading the trionfi, who laid out the plan? It was all coming down to this. History from this point forward rested on what was going to happen on top of this giant rock. Vesta swallowed hard.

They pulled up to the entrance gate. The park attendant, a burly yet friendly man who reminded Vesta of Smokey the Bear in his park ranger's uniform, identified the car as being on the list for the "surprise party" that had rented the entire park for the day.

"Surprise party, indeed," quipped Liam as they drove beyond the gate.

The road took them past the ranger headquarters and tourist center another mile before they arrived at a gravel parking lot. Two black SUVs sat side by side at the far end. Jared stopped the Range Rover, and they got out. Popping open the back door, Jared pulled out a khaki-colored backpack that Vesta guessed must contain the Horizon tablet. He handed a second one to Amara.

The Emperor looked at each one of the trionfi, blue-sky eyes clear and calm. "Ready?"

Everyone nodded. He turned, and all fell in line. Amara stepped behind Jared, Liam behind her, Vesta next, then Sandor. They walked to the Summit trailhead sign, leaving the parking lot to begin the ascent to the top of Enchanted Rock.

The noonday sun blazed in the cloudless sky. Vesta wondered if Amara might call up a nice cooling rain to give them a break, but she knew better. The Empress never used her gift of controlling the weather for her own personal reasons.

Knee-high switchgrass lined the flattest part of the trail, with live oak trees standing in clusters alongside scrubby buttonbush and yucca plants. A jackrabbit darted across their path. Vesta thought about the white rabbit who sat beside her all day in Monument Valley, her last day in 1999 when she was in her early forties. She had to return to that time. She would not be robbed of twenty-five years of her life. The muscles in her jaw tightened.

"Get the job done," she whispered to herself. "So you can go back to your life."

How would she live it differently knowing what she knows now? Maybe she would find another job in the fashion industry or work with Amara's foundation, Conscious Evolution Partners. Anything but reading tarot for a living. Vesta shuddered. She may be the High Priestess, but she didn't have to live steeped in the job. From what the others told her, she had spent many lifetimes doing exactly that. Of course, she couldn't remember much of those lifetimes because of the memory spell she cast on herself, but she had made a clean break of it so far in this lifetime and wanted to keep it that way.

She looked up, turning loose of those thoughts, to see that they had left the path, beginning the climb on the pink granite. Vesta wondered how Liam's buckskin moccasins would hold up against the coarse grain of the rock. But he seemed to be doing amazingly well ahead of her, nimbly moving around the small and medium-sized boulders dotting their immediate landscape.

The hiking boots she discovered in her closet were perfect for the task. Their muffled crunching as she stepped along reminded her of walks she would take in the forest around her childhood home. Enid would call her attention to the different kinds of trees and shrubs, the names of a multitude of wild-flowers they would pass, and how to identify the birds and animals they would encounter. Vesta rarely needed to call upon that extensive education once she moved to New York, but she was always glad to have it.

No one spoke as they continued to climb. It was a long trek up to the top, with the heat unrelenting. Vesta felt a nudge to her right hand and looked down to see Sandor handing her a water bottle. She didn't like to admit it, especially to herself, but he did look after her. Gratefully, she took it, taking in a long drink. At last, they neared the top of the massive rock. A bird called out from a lone live oak nearby.

"Whip-poor-will!" The shrill call made them pause.

"Was that a Whipper Whirl?" Amara asked.

"Couldn't be," Jared said. "This climate is too hot for them."

"Oh, but it is," Liam spoke in an uncharacteristically serious tone. "And its call is an omen of death to the Comanche tribe."

Silence fell among them until Sandor cleared his throat. "Well, we're not Comanches. Let's get back to business."

Vesta felt relieved for his sarcastic comment. It took the edge off her growing sense of doom.

After five more minutes of uphill climbing, they reached the top of Enchanted Rock. It sprawled out hundreds of feet in front of them in shimmering waves of pale pink. Scrubby live oaks, cacti, and shallow vernal pools filled with hardy succulents lay scattered across it. Granite boulders, large and small, littered the landscape. Jared stopped, with the trionfi following suit. No sound except for a soft breeze rushing past them.

"Ah, you've arrived at last," a voice called out, the Russian accent all too familiar.

Rasputin stepped from behind a huge boulder thirty feet away from them. In the glare of the noonday sun, he looked even more like Yosemite Sam than he had the night before with a Colt six-shooter in each hand. His wide-brimmed black cowboy hat failed to corral the greasy red hair underneath that strangled the collar of his black shirt. His droopy red mustache and wild, stringy beard trailed down toward the oversized gold belt buckle featuring a rearing horse. Even with his black-on-black choice of jeans, shirt, and boots, his short stature of barely five feet six inches made the overall effect of his attire comical.

Rasputin motioned with his right hand. From behind the same boulder, the massive brute with the bald head from the Roosevelt Room emerged, tugging on Faith, whose hands were tied behind her back and mouth gagged. Her dark eyes staring wide open told the story of the desperate fear rampant within her.

"Oh my God," Amara whispered.

"Turn her loose," Jared called out. "I brought what you want."

"Are you certain?" Agrippa asked as he stepped from behind the boulder. "Chances are you are trying to trick me again."

If Rasputin looked like Yosemite Sam, Agrippa looked like Sam Elliott as a cowboy; the absolute opposite of Rasputin's sloven style. With his well-groomed dark brown beard and mustache cropped close to his face, his high forehead, and his elegant Patrician nose, he exuded refinement. Vesta loathed that she allowed those thoughts in her mind. He wore a white button-down shirt, blue jeans, and hiking boots. Instead of a cowboy hat, he sported a burnt orange University of Texas cap with the white Longhorns logo prominently displayed. His look was pulled together and attractive. Again, she hated herself for having the thought.

"Let me see what you brought this time," Agrippa said.

"My only concern is getting Faith to safety. If this," Jared took off his backpack and held it up. "Is what it takes, then fine. Let's make this exchange. Can I step forward?"

Agrippa eyed him for a long moment. "Yes, bring it to me."

"Hold it right there!" A voice shouted.

Vesta whirled around. Behind them stood Lars, the architect, and trionfi spy, with a rifle pointed at Cornelius Agrippa.

Chapter Fifteen

"**Y**ou've got my girl," Lars said, looking through the scope atop his Remington 700. "Let her go, or you're going to have a bullet right through that pea brain of yours."

Agrippa squinted in the bright sunlight. "Wait, aren't you the handyman?"

"Yep, I'm the handy man with a rifle. Let her go right now."

"He's the builder of my house," Rasputin said. "He's no assassin."

"Lars," Jared's voice calm. "Lower your rifle. I'm making an exchange right now to get Faith to safety."

"These guys are real spies or aliens or something. I heard them talking. There's something wrong about what they're doing, I'm sure of it, and you wouldn't listen to me. Now they're gonna hurt Faith."

Jared took a step toward Lars. "I'm listening to you now. If you want Faith to be safe, lower your rifle. Let me handle this. I have what they want."

"And what's that?" Lars asked, not moving his eyes or his aim from Agrippa.

"A tablet." Jared unzipped his backpack. "That's all."

Lars slid his attention toward Jared's backpack. "Let's have a look in there," he said. "The truth is, I don't know much about any of y'all."

"Sure." Jared took three steps to stand beside Lars.

Carefully, the Emperor pulled open the backpack, revealing its contents. The architect moved his head slightly to peer inside, then looked at Jared.

"Okay, give it to him." Lars moved his eyes back to the rifle scope.

"Do you mind lowering that so I can walk over there? I would feel a lot better if you would."

The steady tone of Jared's voice must have instilled some confidence in Lars because he lowered his rifle.

"Thank you," Jared looked at Agrippa. "I'm headed your way."

With easy-moving steps, he covered the roasting surface of the rock, stopping directly in front of him. From the backpack, he pulled out a tablet.

"Here you go. Now, turn Faith loose."

"That simple, huh, you hand me this treasure, this power. It is all too easy." Agrippa eyed the tablet in his hands. "Let me make certain you're not trying to deceive me again." He flipped the cover off the tablet, woke up the screen, clicked the Visionary logo, and began typing. A smile crept across his face.

"See?" Jared looked at the bald thug holding Faith. "We're good. Turn Faith loose."

Agrippa turned to Rasputin with a slight nod.

"The Emperor does not part with his precious objects so easily. Are you certain that is the correct one? He is experienced with his deceptive games." Sweat dripped into the Devil's beard as he spoke.

"I handed him the Horizon tablet with the Visionary app.

He just tested it for himself. Some of us value life over material things and will make choices based on that simple principle."

A broad grin broke across Agrippa's face. "A fool's choice, but no matter. Now I have the unique tablet."

"Hey!" Lars called out to Jared. "So, who gets the other tablet in your backpack?"

An almost imperceptible wince crossed Jared's face, but Agrippa caught it. His smile vanished.

"You tried to trick me again. This one is a fake!"

"Kill her!" Rasputin shouted.

Before Jared could take a step, the huge man holding Faith picked her up and threw her with all his might in the air, hurtling her over the edge of the rock. She was gone. At the same moment, the Devil pointed his guns at Lars and the trionfi, firing as fast as he could. Vesta grabbed Amara, pulling her behind a large boulder. A flurry of bullets struck Lars in the chest, abdomen, and legs, landing with dull thuds at each point. But Lars had already raised his rifle once again, and while looking through his scope, he pulled the trigger, hitting the Devil squarely between his eyes with a .270 Winchester bullet. The impact knocked the black cowboy hat off Rasputin's head, sending it into a small outcropping of cacti two feet away. A stunned look of surprise registered on the Devil's face as he fell board-stiff backward onto the pink granite rock.

"Don't kill me! Don't kill me! I'm unarmed," Rasputin's thug yelled.

Jared grabbed him with one hand as he pulled zip ties from his backpack with the other. He shoved the hulk's arms behind his back, wrapping several ties around his wrists.

"You won't get out of these. They're carbon fiber. Now lie down!" He wrapped his ankles with more ties. Jared's actions were fluid and fast but not fast enough. Agrippa snatched his backpack and now held both tablets in his hand.

"Don't move! Or that one dies too," Agrippa shouted, motioning over his shoulder.

Jared looked where the alchemist pointed to see the other thug, the one with the push-broom mustache, holding Serena tightly in his grip near the edge of the rock where her sister had vanished. Her hands were bound, and her mouth strapped with electrical tape. Her eyes revealed the same terror and confusion as her sister.

Jared started toward her.

"I said stop, or her fate will be the same as the other," Agrippa said.

The Emperor froze, the muscles in his face tight with anger, his eyes icy blue.

Agrippa smiled holding up the tablet emblazoned with the Odin logo in red he had taken from Jared's backpack.

"My instincts tell me this is the real Horizon I want."

He opened the device and began typing. He looked up at Jared.

"Yes, it has already recorded the death of young Russian businessman Rasputin Dragomirov. Tragic hunting accident. Is that so?" Agrippa laughed. "Okay. Whatever, as you like to say in this century."

He closed the tablet.

"Admirable of you to be willing to give me the real one as a last resort to save the girl's life. Many would not do such a thing. I may be from a time not as technologically advanced, but I do know human nature. Better than even you, perhaps. Admirable Herr Schultz, or should I say, Emperor." He laughed again.

"You have what you want. Please let Serena go!" Amara shouted. She had emerged from behind the boulder and was crouched over Lars, his head in her hands.

"Why do you bother with him? He's quite dead. I can see that from here," Agrippa smirked. "Him too." He nodded

211

toward Rasputin. "I would thank the handyman if he were still alive. He did me a great service. Now I'm free without having to deal with your Devil. Unsavory character, don't you agree?"

"Lars was a decent man deeply in love."

"By the way, Empress, your herbal potion sent me into a peaceful slumber for many hours, but I still know how to access the portal. Neither you nor your handyman succeeded in your efforts against me."

"You might not have to answer to Lars," Liam shouted as he walked toward Agrippa, speaking for the first time since they had arrived on the rocky top. "But what about them?"

The Fool lifted both his hands, gesturing to a rise nearby, the highest point on Enchanted Rock. There, in the blaze of brilliant daylight, four figures, at first barely visible in their transparent state, took on solid form. Agrippa and everyone else stared in stunned silence. They wore the same clothing as Liam but without all the ornamental details of the breastplate and tiny silver crimps. Their faces, chiseled with prominent, lean cheekbones, held grim expressions. Their eyes glittered like polished ebony.

"No more blood will be shed on this sacred ground." The voice seemed to come from nowhere, yet everywhere. It spoke English as though sounding out the syllables for the first time.

"Who are they?" The push-broom mustache guy yelled.

"They're the spirits who protect this place," Vesta said, walking from behind the boulder. "I summoned them. Turn Serena loose and leave."

"No! Kill the girl, I'll take you with me like I promised." Agrippa shouted to the thug. He waved his arms in a circular motion in the air, chanting an ancient form of Latin.

"He's calling the portal!" Jared shouted.

Sandor took advantage of the distraction to use his gift of momentary invisibility. He stood beside Vesta one second, the next, he evaporated, materializing behind the thug holding Serena. He reached around the guy's head with both hands, shoving his fingers into his eyes. Jared rushed toward them, slamming his fist into the man's face. He crumpled to the ground. The Emperor caught Serena in his powerful arms as she fainted.

A whooshing noise Vesta recognized caught her attention. She shot her attention toward Agrippa. Beside him, the rock and sky beyond seemed to shimmer, vibrating as though intense heat was rising from the rock's surface. But that wasn't what was happening. Agrippa had called forth a portal, determined to time jump with the tablets.

He let loose a wild cackle as he placed one foot in the shimmering circle. From Vesta's peripheral vision, she saw Liam fly through the air and crash into Agrippa, knocking him back from entering it. The Fool grabbed at the tablets, but Agrippa held on tight.

They struggled, both evenly matched in size and weight. Agrippa kicked Liam in the stomach; he bit him on the ear. Liam howled in pain, but he held on. He rolled on top of the alchemist, slamming his knee into his chest. Agrippa let out a scream but never turned loose of the prize. He flung his leg around Liam, hauling himself on top in a swift move. With his one free hand, he punched Liam in the face.

Vesta ran to them. With one well-executed roundhouse kick she'd learned years earlier in self-defense class, she landed her heel on Agrippa's back. He gasped as though it might be his last breath. Vesta thought he might turn loose of the tablets as he paused in the struggle, but he held on, regaining his focus and head-butting Liam with a horrendous force. The crack of bone was a sickening sound. Liam groaned and collapsed, turning loose of both tablets. The alchemist stood up but with a definite wobble. He scrambled toward the shimmering portal, leaped in, and vanished.

Vesta rushed to Liam. "Oh my God! Are you okay?"

She hoisted his head into her lap. Blood trickled from his mouth, his eyes fixed in a locked stare.

"No, no, no!" she shrieked.

Amara stood up and ran toward them, but in her path, the four Comanche spirits appeared. They surrounded Liam and Vesta. Their images flickering as if they were caught in candle-light. They wore the same buckskin clothing as Liam, their long black hair parted in the middle and separated into two braids resting against their chests. Their dark eyes glistened with a mesmerizing, ethereal glow.

"He is our brother," the tallest one said. "He will not die. He helped another brother save many lives in our tribe. We will not let him perish on our sacred ground."

The four extended their arms to form a tight circle around the Fool and the High Priestess. A soft vibration pulsated around them. Vesta could feel it in her bones; she could taste it in her mouth, feeling the cool, moist air touch her face, watching the pulse manifest as a glowing white orb filling the circle.

When Liam entered the kitchen dressed in tribal clothing that morning, her InSight told her that the guardians of the ancestral rock would be near if needed.

She relaxed into the intoxication of the moment. The exquisiteness of it was beyond anything she had ever felt. It reminded her of being rocked as a baby in Enid's arms, knowing she was safe, loved, and protected. Liam twitched his head, bringing her focus back to him. He coughed, then groaned.

"Ow, that hurts," he mumbled.

"Liam, you're okay!" She scooped him even closer to her.

"Easy, those parts hurt too," he said.

Vesta looked up at the Comanche braves. "Thank you for

saving his life. And thank you for coming when I called out for you."

"You are our sister, priestess. We know you will care for our brother." They spoke in unison, their voices coming from everywhere, but nowhere.

Their images rippled, becoming more transparent until, a moment later, they were gone.

Amara and Sandor swooped in. The Empress pulled a first aid kit from her backpack filled with herbs and potions she had made. Out came a compress scented with lavender and eucalyptus that she placed on Liam's forehead and eyes, followed by salve in a tiny jar for his temples smelling of rich cardamon and wild honey.

Sandor crouched beside Vesta gently hugging her.

"You okay? How did that white light feel?"

"It felt amazing, but I failed," she heaved out the words. "The prophecy will come true now. Agrippa got away with the tablets. He's going to change the world into the nightmare I saw with my InSight and that Luna described when we were in the tomb. We will no longer reincarnate with the gifts the Elders gave us. We won't know each other as our tarot family in our next lives. And life for everyone on the planet is going to be hellish."

Vesta spoke at such a frantic pace she had to pause to catch her breath The trionfi were silent, absorbing all she shared until Liam slid the compress up from his eyes so he could see his trionfi family.

"That nasty alchemist may have gotten away with the tablets, but they won't be much use to him without these."

The Fool raised his arms slightly and opened his fists to display a LESTAT battery in the palm of each one.

"Damn! How'd you do that buddy?" Sandor exclaimed patting Liam on the shoulder.

"Ow, that hurts too," he winced. "When Vesta smacked him with that roundhouse it distracted him for a few seconds. Long enough for me to grab them."

"That's brilliant!" A voice tinkling like windchimes in a light breeze called out.

The trionfi turned to see Luna sitting atop a tall monolithic rock several yards away.

"I watched the whole thing. It was truly fantastic. You did it, Vesta."

The High Priestess shook her head. "Liam did it. He pulled the batteries out."

"He couldn't have done without your masterful kick."

Luna hopped down from the boulder, a good eight-foot drop, landing effortlessly on the hard surface. Clad in the same black T-shirt and camouflage pants, anchored by a pair of black combat boots, Luna looked ready to deal with any predicament in any time.

"Did you create a vortex up there?" Jared asked.

"I sure did! I had to document this momentous occasion."

"Like you did at Strangelove's in New York?" Sandor asked.

"Yep!"

Vesta remembered the trionfi's wild morning at Strangelove's Bar. She had just resigned from Sybarite. Distraught, she wandered aimlessly in frigid weather before deciding to walk in. The bar was closed, but it didn't take much to convince Jason, the bartender who was there cleaning up, to pour her a drink. As it turned out, Jared, Amara, Sandor, and Liam all showed up within the hour. Shots of liquor and merry dancing ensued. The graffiti-laden walls of the bar fascinated Vesta. She recalled browsing the myriad names, attempts at poetry, and random drawings accumulated over the years when she came to a full stop in front of five tarot cards securely pasted to the wall.

The five trionfi, who were in the bar at that moment, were staring back at her from their images on the classic Rider-Waite-Smith tarot deck. They were arranged in a circle, and at the center, written in black Sharpie ink, were the capital letters T, E, and D. Vesta recalled how she touched the High Priestess card, her card, sparking instant dizziness within her. Sandor explained it was a vortex created by Luna, the Traveler, who was also part of the greater trionfi family. The letters T, E, and D, she was told, stood for The Everlasting Day. It was Luna's way of documenting a momentous time. Vesta didn't realize the significance at that moment, nor did she know Luna would pop through a vortex to join her inside a mysterious cave in Monument Valley. Of course, that lead to her popping them through a vortex to Meri's tomb to reveal the prophecy of the Elders.

The question drifted around in Vesta's mind for several months after that: was it by accident or coincidence that Luna glued their cards to the wall of a punk bar in New York that they would all end up in years later? It wasn't a question to her any longer. Time, as Liam, in a surprising moment of eloquence put it, had been wrangled by humans into a linear narrative of past, present, and future to simplify it. It made them less nervous about the possibilities. She more than understood that now.

The vortexes were how Luna traveled, but was that the same as how Gus time jumped or how he taught Agrippa? The thought brought her back to Enchanted Rock.

She looked around. Lars and Rasputin lay dead. Both hired thugs were bound at their hands and feet. Amara was attending to Serena, but she appeared to be okay. Liam was sitting up talking to Luna while Sandor and Jared were deep in discussion several yards away.

"We have to get Gus to block the portal so Agrippa can't time jump again," Vesta called out to them.

"You're reading my mind," Sandor teased. "But you knew you could do that anyway."

She was relieved to see him back to his old self. The fact was she couldn't read his mind or any of the trionfi because they had permanently blocked them to keep anyone from entering. It was one of the first things she learned how to do when her memory spell was broken.

"Do you want to call him?" Jared asked. "Make it a full circle wrap-up."

Vesta gave him a nod. She closed her eyes, even though she knew she didn't need to. Jared had put him on speed dial to pick up their calls as soon as they went out.

"Gus, we need you here now."

An encapsulated gust of wind six feet wide stormed to life. In the middle of it, Gus, the chronicle, appeared. His imposing figure stood in his usual garb of ratty robe layers and tie-dyed Grateful Dead T-shirt, long hair and beard flying loose in the tiny maelstrom. In his hand, he held a golden goblet encrusted with what looked like jewels the size of walnuts. He drank from it as he looked around at the scene.

Jared and Sandor walked close to him as the wind drew to a standstill.

"Cornelius Agrippa accessed the portal and returned to his time. Vesta succeeded in fulfilling the prophecy and stopping him from altering the current timeline. Our mission is almost complete. You now need to close the portal that you showed Cornelius Agrippa how to open so he can never use it or any other one ever again," Jared said. "And you need to do it now."

Huffing and puffing sounds issued from the chronicle. "Well, I'm not sure what you request can take place. I thought the fair lady Empress was concocting a memory potion to cause him to forget how to access it again."

"I did," Amara said. "But potions work differently on everyone. He created a portal minutes ago, and time jumped. Clearly, he remembers how. We can't have that. You must close that portal immediately and forever."

Gus began pacing, mumbling incoherently to himself.

"Is there a problem?" Sandor asked.

"As I said, I don't know if I can achieve what you're asking."

"It's not an ask, it's an order," Sandor replied.

"Well, it's impossible."

"No, it's not," Luna's windchime voice interrupted.

All eyes turned toward her. She shrugged. "He can do it." Her round face shone like the moon, even in the bright sunlight. The tight silver curls around her head and her crystal blue eyes added to the celestial effect. "Of course, that would mean he would be closing the portal for him too."

"What are you saying, Luna?" Amara asked.

"He wouldn't be able to hop around to any time he chooses anymore." She shrugged again. "He would have to stay here."

"Here in this time?" Sandor asked.

Luna nodded. "Yeah. He would still be a chronicle though, seeing everything going on in the world forever and ever."

Gus reared his head back. "No!" he shouted. "Meddlesome waif! She doesn't know what she's talking about."

"Yes, I do."

A breeze began to stir around the chronicle, rustling his robes and hair.

"Don't do it," Jared shook his head. "Don't leave. If you do, my next call will be to your bosses to tell them every rule you've broken here."

Gus stared at Jared for a long moment. Slowly, the circle of wind around him died. He glared at Luna.

"Close the portal permanently," Jared said. "Right now."

"But I will be stuck in this place, in this time." He wiped his forehead with his filthy sleeve. "It's monstrously hot. I can't survive here."

"Oh, sure you can," Sandor patted him on the shoulder. "He can travel, right Luna? He can go to other places in the world."

Luna nodded.

"And hey," the Magician continued. "You're already dressed for living in Austin. You'll fit right in."

"It's true," Amara said. "This is a place and during a time when no one judges you by what you choose to wear."

"Although you may consider a salon visit or four to clean up that beard and hair, trim those nails. I can make recommendations." Liam wagged his finger at Gus.

"I couldn't possibly resign myself to such a fate as staying in this time."

"That's the consequence you face now," Vesta said. "You dragged me into the future, depriving me of twenty-five years of my life to clean up a mess you made."

"You'll be stuck here too," he rushed to say. "You won't be able to return to 1999. Those years will be lost to you."

Vesta froze upon hearing his words. Slowly, she glanced at Luna. "Is he telling the truth?"

Luna pressed her lips together, nodding.

A ball of energy that felt like a rock hurled itself into the pit of Vesta's stomach. She looked off into the distance, staring at nothing. Staring at another choice being made for her that would radically alter her life. It would mean most of her forties, all her fifties, and half of her sixties she would never experience. She had no memories of them now, which meant she probably never would. Another gaping hole. So many details of her past lives were gone from the memory spell she cast on herself, and now this.

She drew her attention back to the group. Amara's eyes

were filled with tears. She understood. Even Liam slowly shook his head.

The truth was she never asked to be the High Priestess of this group known as the trionfi. The Elders gave her the gifts and the responsibility. Did she still owe them all her lives to come? Was she supposed to give up one-quarter of this life now, pouf, just like that, to never know those years?

Vesta's expression grew dark. If she didn't give up those years to stay where she was, then Agrippa might return to this time or another, wrecking the world, turning it into the nightmare she foresaw. Did she even have a choice about her own life at this point? She choked back the lump in her throat.

"Do it," she said. "Do it right now. Close the portal."

The chronicle scoffed, huffing out words. "It's not that simple. Not sure I can even do it."

"Buddy," Sandor walked up beside him. "You risk being deported to a planet with no people, no roasted turkey legs or rot-gut whiskey. You want that?"

Gus scowled, his bushy eyebrows meeting like a pair of wings on his forehead. "You leave me no choice."

"That's right," Sandor said. "And wait till you taste the Tex-Mex at this little hole in the wall I know in town. The first round of top-shelf margaritas will be on me."

A loud grunt was the chronicle's only response. He set his goblet down on the pink granite to use both hands. With flattened palms, he initiated what Vesta thought looked like a mime performance, sliding his hands in the air as though he were creating a doorway. He did this in all four directions, creating a space six feet in width, and six feet in height each time. When that was done, he placed both of his hands together, walking around the perimeter of what he had pantomimed, starting at the top of each "doorway" and sliding his hands to the bottom, covering all the space in between with many passes of his hands.

As he moved, he spoke ancient Latin words, or at least they sounded Latin to Vesta. Several minutes passed as he meticulously worked. At one point, the ground beneath them shook, causing small granite boulders nearby to sway back and forth. A worried look sprung up on the chronicle's face, but he kept working.

The heat felt oppressive under the cloudless sky, bearing down on everyone. Amara pulled water bottles out of her backpack and walked around, handing a bottle to each. Liam poured half of his water over his head and found a tiny patch of shade on the east side of a large boulder. Luna joined him as they huddled together for a minute, deep in conversation, before she hopped into her vortex and vanished.

At last, the chronicle stepped back. "It's done.".

"What was the shaking all about that we felt?" Sandor asked.

Gus frowned.

"It was Agrippa trying to come through again, wasn't it? He realized those tablets are useless without the batteries."

"Yes," Gus barked. "I'm sure it pleases you to know that."

"Not at all." Sandor pointed to the area where the chronicle had been working. "Aren't you glad, though, that you sealed it up?" He patted him on the back. "Otherwise, we would be right back where we started."

A snarling expression grew on Gus's face as he wiped a river of sweat from his forehead.

"Now, what?" He chugged the bottle of water Amara had handed him. "What am I supposed to do here? Live on this blasted rock? Eat berries growing in the wild?"

"You can live in one of our rental properties in Austin," Jared said. "Amara and I own several nice places. And you can work at Odin. I'm sure you have a lot of wisdom and experience you can share with my engineers. You'll earn a decent salary and integrate into this society. It's actually a really good one."

Gus snorted. "We'll see if it's a good one or not."

"And hey," Sandor cocked his head. "You could sell that big whiskey cup of yours over there for some real cash if you wanted to get a head start on living large. That has to be worth a pretty penny or two."

Gus scooped up his chalice. "This was a gift from Henry VIII when I out-drank him on a stag hunt. Last one sitting on the horse, you know." He sighed. "All just memories now."

"At least you have those memories," Vesta said.

Amara walked toward Vesta. She knew a hug was sure to follow as soon as she arrived. "No embrace necessary," she said stepping away from her sister. "I'm fine. We have a lot of work to do here. How are we going to deal with the bodies of Lars and Raz? And I can't believe no one has checked on Faith."

"I have," said Jared. "She'll be fine in a little while."

"What do you mean she'll be fine? That oaf threw her off the hill onto solid rock hundreds of feet below."

Chapter Sixteen

I t took until the relentless sun finally withdrew from its lofty perch above them, retreating into the western sky, before the entire group returned to the parking lot. Among the first down from Enchanted Rock was Sandor with the two hired henchmen in tow. As it turned out, they were from the nearby town of Kerrville with longstanding reputations of sinister behavior stretching as far back as their teenage years.

Sandor had already spoken to the Gillespie County sheriff from his mobile phone, detailing their actions of kidnapping Faith and Serena and of breaking and entering along with attempted burglary on Amara's ranch. Video footage from the lab's cameras confirmed they entered through the hole blasted in the floor.

The duo was warned about sharing information they may think they saw on the rocky top. It was highly doubtful, Sandor told them, that anyone would believe a story about Comanche Indian ghosts appearing before them, let alone someone disappearing into thin air to travel somewhere else in time.

"Try that out on the sheriff and see where it gets you," he said. "And you're lucky," he pointed at the hulk. "Faith landed on a bush when you threw her and will be okay. Otherwise, you'd have murder added to the other charges."

The two were deposited into the back of the black SUV they arrived in. The Magician had confiscated the keys to the vehicle from the hulking one's pocket and now held them in his own.

The county sheriff had also been informed about the deaths of Lars Wagner and Rasputin Dragomirov. It was an old West-style shoot-out over the kidnapping and rescue of the young women. No mention would be made of Agrippa, or Henry Page, as he was briefly known in the twenty-first century. A deputy had been dispatched to meet the medical examiner on the rock.

Vesta and Liam were the next to arrive in the parking lot with the chronicle straggling behind them. Vesta had assisted Liam in a ceremony to dispel the energy of violence, bloodshed, and death on Enchanted Rock. Working with the eagle feathers, the hairpipe breastplate, and loose tobacco Liam carried in a pouch, they made offerings to the spirits of the sacred rock. Gus watched with a bored look on his face from a tiny patch of shade.

Amara and Jared were the last to make their way off the hill. With them came Serena, walking beside the Empress, and Faith, wrapped in a blanket, resting in the arms of the Emperor. Her face was bound with gauze. Vesta could tell that one arm and both legs were lying in unnatural ways. Broken, no doubt. But why hadn't Jared called for an ambulance? Such injuries required immediate attention.

Vesta opened her mouth to ask the questions, but Amara caught her attention, waving her hand in a small gesture to stop. She did as Amara wanted but knew she would pursue it again later to find out the answer.

Sandor drove the SUV with the thugs in it to the sheriff's office in Fredericksburg. Vesta rode with him to tune into their thoughts for the possibility of more information. Tapping into the mind of a stranger was always an expedition into the unknown. She would see the trajectory they were on and how their life would play out given their current set of circumstances. Chances were high that it wouldn't be altered because few humans used their innate power of will to change the course of their lives, even when it would benefit them. Lethargy, stubbornness, capitulation, the way they were raised, and past experiences forever imprinted in their minds held most people back from ever deviating from a predictable path.

The bald, hulking man, Jasper, had been raised by a cruel father and weak-willed mother, who were still prominent in his life. When he was kicked off the high school football team for smoking pot, his father had beaten him, causing a permanent scar above his left eye. He always sought to impress his father with material things: a new pickup truck, a new gun, anything he thought would show him that he was finally a success. That's what led him to Rasputin. Quick money for doing everything he wanted and keeping his mouth shut. As far as what he knew about the Devil, it wasn't much. He had spent months with a mole boring out the tunnel from mainly solid rock under Amara's ranch. It was hard work, but Rasputin paid well. Vesta's last image of him in her mind was him sitting in a jail cell as a much older man.

As for Dwayne, the other hired thug, his father had disappeared when he was a baby. He and his mother moved in with her mother, but then his mom left when he was six. His grandmother did her best to raise him with a high moral standard, but he fell in with the wrong crowd in high school. That's where he met Jasper. Together, the two of them had broken into cars, stolen farm and ranch equipment from neighbors, and committed other petty larceny acts for over a decade. They got caught and punished a few times but had never committed crimes as serious as kidnapping. It was clear from Vesta's InSight that Dwayne would end up with the same fate as Jasper.

She let the connection to her InSight drop. She had seen enough. These men couldn't enlighten her or Sandor on Rasputin. Even less so on Agrippa. They had never been brought in close, only used for their brute strength and willingness to obey.

The drop-off with Sheriff Lancaster was easy. She and Sandor gave statements about what happened and promised Amara, Jared, Liam, and the young women would stop by within the next few days to do the same. The sheriff was a stout man of medium height in his fifties, with hazel eyes shining with alertness. Not much got past him, Vesta could tell. But he knew Amara and recounted the Christmas parties he and his wife had been invited to whenever Amara was at Blue Sky Ranch. Until that moment, Vesta hadn't known the ranch had a name.

He even pulled out a scrapbook holding some of the history of Fredericksburg to show them photos of a groundbreaking in 1924, one hundred years earlier, of their new offices and jail. In the faded black-and-white image, she saw who the sheriff identified as Amara's grandmother, who generously donated money toward the construction. Vesta smiled as she looked at her sister's face from a previous life. With her blonde hair braided and pinned tightly to her head, she was one of several people holding shovels for the historic moment. None of the other trionfi were present, but Vesta knew Jared was probably close by.

No solid memories of that time existed for Vesta. Only occasional random moments captured like snippets of an old newsreel. They were usually prompted by Sandor's comments about how they lived in Los Angeles, producing blockbuster feature films during that era. It would cause a memory to pop in as a life she once lived. One of his favorite lives. She wished she could remember more.

Inspired by seeing the photo, Sandor talked about those days with passion as the sheriff's deputy drove them to Blue Sky Ranch, but he spoke of them in the third person.

"So, Amara's grandmother's sister and her husband, are you tracking with me there?" Sandor waited for a nod from the deputy. "They were friends with all the big stars of the day. Chaplin taught her how to do a proper waltz. And Gloria Swanson was madly in love with him."

Vesta was grateful the deputy listened quietly as Sandor reminisced. But being in his late twenties, she guessed he might not be familiar with any of the celebrities he spoke of.

Once safely deposited inside the ranch house, Vesta found Liam sprawled on a comfortable sofa in the theatre room. He was watching one of his concerts at Madison Square Garden from the 1980s he discovered playing on a cable channel.

"I had to get back to a sense of normalcy." He flipped his black hair out of his face.

"That's normalcy?"

"Yes, look at me. I'm in my prime there. The crew were shooting behind the scenes, too. I miss the limousines the most, I think. And look at the adoring audience."

"You still have adoring audiences. They're just a little smaller these days."

"Don't spoil the vibe! Why don't you go join the others in Frankenstein's lab?"

"What are you talking about?"

Liam waved his hand. "Shhh! It's getting to one of my favorite parts."

On the giant screen in front of them, Liam, in his twenties, pranced on stage to the opening chords of one of his biggest hits, Play It As It Lays.

"In the moment here and now," he sang, "Let the moonlight kiss your face. Every step and every breath, find the beauty in this place. No need for searching far and wide, your heart knows what it craves. Play it as it lays, girl. Play it as it lays."

Vesta had to admit it was a great song. She glanced at Liam reclining on the sofa, his glazed eyes watching his younger self. A look of wistfulness painted on his face for those heady, youthful days. She knew he was having the hardest time of them all dealing with his sixties. But at least for the moment, he was vividly reliving those exquisite moments of being the beautiful young man preening and posing for thousands of adoring fans.

Vesta tiptoed from the theatre room out the back door of the house. As the sun prepared to dip below the hills, long shadows stretched from nearby trees. Patches of purple sunlight gleamed in between the deep, shady areas. Random patterns of sunlight and shade as she walked. This time of day always had a calming effect on her because it signaled a release from the day's grip. She had either checked off all the things on her list she needed to accomplish, or she hadn't. It was as simple as that.

The robot dogs roamed around the entrance to the lab. The head of one turned toward her as she approached. Its red eyes stared, scanning her before it turned away to resume its surveillance of the perimeter. She rang the buzzer on the door. Amara opened it.

Walking in, the first thing she noticed was the hole in the floor had been repaired. Dark gray concrete marked the spot where Jasper and Dwayne blasted into the lab. Once thoroughly dry, it would be covered with white tile to match the rest of the floor. Vesta saw Serena sitting in the comfortable chair near the door. Vesta smiled at her as she walked by, but the young woman didn't seem to notice. Her total focus rested on her sister, Faith, who was leaning back in an examination chair by the long white table in the center of the room. Jared hovered over her.

As Vesta walked closer, she realized Faith's eyes were in a fixed stare. Her face devoid of expression. Vesta froze in place. There was no doubt the woman needed emergency medical care. Why hadn't they called an ambulance earlier? She wasn't moving, not even breathing, from what Vesta could tell. Why wasn't someone doing something to help her?

She looked at Jared. He was inches away from her with one hand near the back of her head. In his other hand, he held several small objects that looked like capsules. He took them one by one with the free hand, placing the capsules in her hair.

It was then Vesta noticed the strange twist in Faith's neck, too far to the right to be normal and tilted up at an odd angle. A blanket covered most of her body when Jared carried her down from Enchanted Rock. Vesta had been walking to the SUV to ride with Sandor rather than in the Range Rover when she saw them. She hadn't picked up on anything dramatically different about Faith other than what she thought were broken legs and a broken arm. Now, the closer she looked at her, the more she knew something was terribly wrong. Her right leg below the knee jutted out in the wrong direction at a forty-five-degree angle. It was clearly broken, and her left foot dangled from her ankle. She was still wearing her white shirt and black pants, the uniform from the Roosevelt Room. Tears in the fabric revealed her skin, but there was no sign of blood. And the skin glistened in a translucent shade of pink in the bare patches, looking like spun cotton candy.

Amara walked up beside Vesta.

"Jared is tending to her," she whispered. "Don't worry. She will be fine."

Vesta turned to her sister. She could feel the deep furrows of her brow making serious inroads on her face as she shook her head. "What am I looking at here?"

"Faith is an AI assistant." She paused for a moment before adding. "Her sister Serena is too."

Vesta mouthed the words "AI assistant" as she looked over at Faith again. What did that mean? A robot? Like the dogs roaming around outside?

"Jared is giving her medications to heal herself."

"What medications?"

"Microcapsules of reversible polymers and hollow fibers so her neural and vascular networks will heal and restore. Some low melting point alloys to repair her skin."

Amara gestured to Serena. "Come closer if you want. You can watch your sister completely regenerate."

Serena stood up. Her long, shiny black hair lay against her alabaster skin, the jet-black pupils of her eyes glinting from the bright overhead lights as she stepped forward. She wore a sundress gathered at the waist, covered in tiny blue flowers. Her Birkenstock sandals made a padding sound on the tile floor as she walked. She looked as human as Vesta. Except, just like Serena, Vesta had to remind herself, she wasn't entirely human either.

Jared straightened himself to his full height, raising his eyebrows as he looked at Amara, silently saying with his body language, "Let's see what happens." Several long moments passed before Faith blinked her eyes once. In a smooth, slow motion, her head moved from the weird tilt into a natural position. After another blink of the eyes, her leg shifted into its rightful place, and so did her foot. The bright pink patches on her legs, chest, and waist began to disappear, replaced by the smooth white skin on the rest of her body. More blinking. Vesta felt her third eye begin to spin. She watched a conscious awareness grow in Faith's dark pupils. What was she seeing? Life, that's what it was. She could feel it, too; Faith was coming back to life.

She could sense the relief emanating from Jared and Amara. Her intuition told her the healing session was a first for them. Serena, who had been completely still watching the transformation take place, moved quickly to her sister to give her a long hug. They were identical to each other, mirror images embracing. Serena squeezed into the roomy chair with Faith. Their beautifully shaped oval faces now with broad smiles, perfectly straight teeth, and full lips. Vesta could understand why Lars fell crazy in love with Faith.

"Did you have to make them exactly alike?" Vesta whispered to Amara.

Her sister cocked her head toward the door signaling for them to leave. Before she did though, she stepped in to embrace the sisters. She spoke in a low voice, too low for Vesta to hear what she said. The young women smiled in return.

"Let's go to the garden." Amara led the way out of the lab. "They're identical because we weren't certain we had everything in place. The others before them didn't quite work. So, we created two at once."

"The ones that didn't work looked like them too?"

Amara nodded.

"Isn't that creepy? Do you have the rejects standing around in some broom closet somewhere?"

"Vesta, it's not like that at all. We disassembled the others entirely, moving the networks that were successful into them."

"Why two at once?"

"Through our trials, we learned a great deal about not only how to make them physically healthy but mentally and emotionally as well. In the later stages, we developed two slightly different pathways to regulate their emotional well-being. So, we decided to try both."

"Which one is better?"

"I don't know at the moment. Faith was in a relationship with Lars. This was unexpected and something we didn't know about until two days ago."

"Did Lars know she wasn't human?"

Amara shook her head. "Jared and I realized that had the potential to be a problem. We assumed we would have time to slowly introduce both her and Serena to those concepts and the societal norms associated with them. But as you can see, we didn't."

"Poor Lars."

A sigh floated from her sister's lips. "An utter tragedy."

"Where's Gus?" Vesta asked as they walked across a wide swath of land bathed in shade.

"I assigned him a bedroom and insisted he take a shower."

"Great idea."

"Fresh clothes too."

"What a difference that will make. It's going to take a while for him to adjust to being just in this time. Do you think he'll have any trouble? I mean, he's not human either."

Amara strode across her land with the confidence someone would expect from the Empress of the tarot. She reminded Vesta of Enid when she would walk through the forest near their Colorado home. The dirt and trees, the plants and animals, seemed to invigorate them both.

"I did an initial chemical analysis on the chronicle the minute we got home. Just a blood sample, but from it I saw that however he managed to do it, he manifested real skin, blood, tissue, the works. He's much closer to humans than Faith and Serena, even down to having DNA and RNA showing up."

"Will he age like we do?"

Amara shook her head. "I don't know, but it will be interesting to find out."

They arrived at the door of the massive greenhouse. Amara typed in her code on the keypad and pulled open the door.

"Gus will help us understand how to make our assistants even more human."

"Is that a good thing when it's all said and done?"

Amara flipped a switch on the panel by the door causing soft light to flood the room filled with her special plants. She smiled at her sister, leaning in close.

"Think about how many non-human and not-completely-human people you know now."

Vesta considered Amara's words. None of her trionfi family were one hundred percent human. They were in the beginning when the Elders chose them to receive their gifts, but that was two thousand years ago. Their abilities came with a spark of something extra altering their DNA. They weren't as altered as Lucy Jane, though, who was only half-human on her mother's side. Then there were the NoMorts, who were immortals because they drank the Dead Tomb elixir. They weren't completely human anymore either, and there were dozens of them roaming around the planet. Vesta's thoughts turned to her former Sybarite assistant Jessica, who Jared brought back from the dead, and Grace Garcia, who was also returned to life by the maker of Dead Tomb. Was their DNA different now, too?

"You're right," Vesta nodded. "There are a lot of not-completely-humans. But are these assistants and the newer versions to come going to be smarter than us?"

"The majority, yes."

"Could that be dangerous for the humans, and even us?'

The Empress gazed around the greenhouse. "Maybe. But the quest to create won't stop because of that. Safeguards are in place for all our assistants, and hopefully, the same is true for all the other assistants being created by all the other labs and scientists." She shrugged. "But there's no way to know for sure. And only time will tell."

"I hope we didn't go through all that we did today with people dying just to have the world end up in a war with them."

Amara smiled. "Let's not worry about that right now. I want to choose a plant to send to Lars' family." She walked down the long aisle in front of her with plants sprouting in a multitude of shapes with leaves shining in green, purple, orange, and red. She turned right at the end of the table, walked two rows over and halfway up, talking to each plant as she passed it. Smiling, she picked up a curious-looking green plant with tiny star-shaped white flowers.

"You're the one, aren't you?" She cooed in a soothing voice.

Vesta thought it must be her imagination or her exhaustion, but she could have sworn the plant's leaves and flowers sparkled even brighter hearing her words.

Amara walked back to the entrance door. "I'll put this *Memoriosa Dulcisplantia* in a lovely pot I made and send it to them with a note."

"What is it?"

"It's a sweet memory plant. It will gently encourage their memories of Lars to be happy and loving. And I'll host a ceremony to honor him on the next full moon. You're welcome of course."

"Okay. I don't have anything else to do since I will still be here instead of back in 1999 and in my forties." Vesta knew her tone was bitter, but she didn't care.

Amara leaned in, hugging her, moving too fast for Vesta to dodge it.

"You saved the world. Remember that."

"Yeah, yeah, whatever."

Chapter Seventeen

S andor and Gus sat on the wide deck off the dining room. Drinking twenty-five-year-old Macallan scotch, they shared a laugh as Vesta and Amara made their way into the house.

"Come join us," the Magician called out.

"How about we take dinner up the hill to the outdoor dining room? I think we could all use some food," Amara replied.

"Capital idea!" Gus raised his glass to her.

"Quick showers first though, right?" Vesta asked.

Amara nodded. "Capital idea."

Inside the kitchen, they found Jared and Liam preparing gin martinis. The silver shaker rattling with ice cubes sounded delicious. Amara shared the dinner plan, and Jared told her Serena wanted to take Faith to her house for the evening. Sandor had programmed his car to take them there with the agreement to all gather back together at the ranch tomorrow.

As Vesta and Amara headed through the house and up the staircase, Amara explained that the young women, new to this world, needed time to process what happened on Enchanted Rock. They were now part of the trionfi family, to be welcomed any time to any gathering, yet they were also sisters joined by an extraordinary bond. Their awareness and emotional intelligence had leaped a vast chasm during a short span of intense trauma. They needed to sort through it all in their own personal way.

After their showers, Jared helped Amara put the finishing touches on the pasta salad she had made that morning and tossed together a green salad from the garden. Vesta set the table, proud of the fact she had avoided cooking all her life, not knowing a colander from a calendar. But she could set a splendid table. All her years at Sybarite, overseeing the luxury home goods department, acquainted her with the finest in china, crystal, and silverware. The settings arranged for photo-shoots were stunning to behold, inspiring some creative muse inside her.

When all was ready, the trionfi and Gus made their way up a gravel path to the top of a hill a thousand yards away from the house and lab. A weathered but sturdy wooden table twelve feet long sat underneath a huge candlelit chandelier. The massive branch of an oak tree stretched over the middle of the table in a perfect position to hold the chandelier but not obstruct the nighttime sky dazzling above them. There was something about golden candlelight that felt inviting, warm, and protective. And the bright silver pinpoints of light in the inky sky above created the perfect contrast and balance. Intimate and infinite.

They sat down in heavy wooden chairs fitted with plump seat cushions outfitted in a rich shade of lavender. Jared poured a Viognier Reserve from Pedernales Cellars to begin the meal as Amara passed around the huge bowls of pasta and salad. Fresh bread and butter made at a local farm completed the simple menu.

Vesta glanced around the table as everyone eagerly ate and chatted. Her family. And now Gus, the chronicle who ripped time, sat with them. A shower had done wonders for him. No particles of food remained in his long beard and mustache. Vesta suspected Sandor had taken his comb and clippers to the chronicle's facial hair. It looked far tidier. Even the hair on his head was combed, parted neatly down the middle. To top it off, he wore a Polo shirt and khaki pants, no doubt from Jared's closet. The transformation was remarkable.

Liam sat next to him, looking every bit the rock star in his black shirt halfway unbuttoned to the middle of his chest, black jeans, and his ever-present medallion of The Fool dangling from a leather cord around his neck. He absentmindedly kept sweeping the mass of black hair out of his eyes as he spoke, which persistently and immediately fell back into his face.

On the other side of him sat Amara, radiant blonde and gray hair spilling below her shoulders, animated blue suede eyes wide and full of joy. Her simple coral-colored peasant blouse accented with a stunning turquoise squash blossom necklace resonated with the authenticity of the American West, old and new.

Jared sat to her right, wearing a classic T-shirt in navy with blue jeans. Few men in their sixties could pull off the look with such devastatingly handsome results. Even though he was no longer in the prime of his life, the muscle tone in his arms was still impressive. The expertly controlled chaos of his spiky gray hair would forever be a trademark for him. That, and of course, his hypnotic blue eyes, which always seemed to look into the soul of whoever he spoke to.

Sandor was next to him, to Vesta's left. He wore his ubiquitous white button-shirt with the sleeves rolled up just below his elbows. Groomed to perfection, his dark hair threaded with silver and amber eyes alive with curiosity, he exemplified the Magician's energy. Capable, surprising, and full of generosity, humor, and love, Vesta wondered why she hadn't embraced his affection more. Maybe she would now.

Gratitude enveloped her being with the people she loved and who loved her. She looked down at her hands. Fine lines across the skin intersected pipelines of blue bulging veins underneath, and they were topped with speckled sunspots. Why hadn't she used more sunscreen on her hands all those years ago? Too late to worry about that now. At least she had protected her face.

Aside from the lines and the drooping skin at her jowls, she wasn't displeased with how she'd aged. Her crepey neck was another issue, though, which she would address later. But she was wearing a gorgeous Veronica Beard black and white striped sundress cinched at the waist that fit her perfectly. And even though her fingers felt stiff, especially in the mornings, she was basically pain-free for a woman of sixty-five.

Dinner progressed, more food, more wine, and more laughter until, at last, everyone sat relaxed in their chairs, looking out over the expansive view of the nighttime sky.

"I can tolerate this," Gus said, half joking, half serious as he reached for the bottle of Macallan's sitting on the table. "Most planets with life are far worse than this. I suppose there's always the threat humans will extinguish themselves and everything else by blowing themselves up or destroying the planet with their harsh treatment of it, but that hasn't happened yet. Maybe it won't."

"I'll introduce you to my foundation, Conscious Evolution Partners." Amara nodded. "We're working very hard to make sure nothing like that ever happens and to help everyone recognize how developing a program of sustainability will benefit every living thing."

"Admirable, my dear Empress." Gus bowed his head to her. "I would expect nothing less of you. I look forward to learning more about it."

Vesta stood up from the table. "I'm going for a walk on this gorgeous night. I won't go far. Just up the hill." She picked up her wine glass, leaving the golden glow of the table behind. The shimmering stars above surrounded her as she climbed to the highest rocky outcropping. The ground below lay featureless in its solid, dark blanket. As she watched, the moon slid above the eastern horizon, waning in the shape of a slice of watermelon.

"It never gets old, does it?"

The voice, as light as the tingling of ice falling into a glass, startled her. Vesta turned to see Luna sitting beside her.

"Why did you come back so soon? Missed us?"

"I forgot to tell you something." The image of the moon reflected in her eyes.

"That's who you are in the trionfi, right? The Moon." Vesta nodded toward it. "But they call you the Traveler. It must be because of the Moon's constant travels across the sky that you have that nickname."

A crescent smile moved across Luna's face. "That's right. But unlike you, I didn't start out as human. The Elders made me like you. It was kind of the reverse of what they did with you. They were fascinated by all the emotions humans displayed, emotions they didn't possess. But they understood love, fear, and all the feelings in between were a really important part of who you were."

Luna looked up. "They also knew about the influence the moon had over humans to make them feel sad, moody, crazy, romantic and lots of other things. So, they made me to bring that awareness into even more focus."

"Was it because I was so mixed up about what to do next, was that why you came to me in Monument Valley that day?"

"Let's just say you were ready to embark on this adventure."

"Adventure? Agrippa almost got away with the Horizon tablet, battery, and all. People died. Lars shouldn't have died. What a horrible loss. Even Rasputin, as despicable as he was, loved playing out his cowboy fantasy here. I could tell he was happy. No one should have died. Death is a doorway, but not everyone is prepared to pass through it when they do."

"Spoken like the true High Priestess of the tarot."

Vesta shook her head. "I'm back in the same spot I was when you found me on the mountainside with the white rabbit. I have no idea what to do next." Vesta wrinkled her nose. "That was you, too, the white rabbit, right?"

Luna nodded. "Just a little hologram to gently lead you to what you needed to see. And to save the world from Agrippa. Of course, I knew you would."

"Was it a certainty?"

"Oh, no." Luna's crystal eyes grew wide. "Not at all. Everything would have been totally different. Truly wretched if he had been successful."

Vesta sighed. "Okay. It was all worth it then."

A smile slid back into place on Luna's face. "I need to tell you something."

"That's right, something you forgot earlier. What is it?"

Luna gazed at her with an unearthly sparkle as though she were made solely of translucent moondust. "I can take you back to 1999."

Vesta stared at her in stunned silence. "How?" she finally asked.

"Through one of my vortexes."

"I thought Gus closed my only way back. That's what he said. And you agreed with him when he said I would be stuck here."

"He closed the portal that he made and traveled through. His portal wasn't the same as my vortexes."

"What's the difference?"

Luna shrugged. "I don't know." She stood up and stretched. "Maybe they're different because the Elders made them for me to travel through, and maybe Gus created his own a different way, or it's a way chronicles around the universe travel." She shrugged again. "I really don't know."

"And you're sure you can take me back?"

"Yeah! I took you from that mountain cave at the end of the twentieth century to the tomb underground during this time. I can take you back."

"To the same exact time and place?"

Luna nodded, then paused. "But I can only do that once for you."

"What does that mean?"

"You can't change your mind and ask me to bring you back here or to any other time. See, it's easy for me to travel between all these times because that's what I do, but it's not so easy on humans or part-humans. Things can get screwed up, a little or a lot."

"Could that happen to me if you take me back?"

"Maybe." Luna cocked her head. "It's hard to say. I don't want to say no, and then you be mad at me if something bad does happen."

"But you took me to the tomb without asking and without warning me about the danger."

"Yeah, but that was different because you needed to stop Agrippa."

"I still had no choice. How is Agrippa, by the way? Have you checked on him since he returned to his time?"

"Oh, sure. He tries to impress other alchemists with the tablets. They're strange looking at first to the others, but they don't do anything, so any interest in them fades pretty fast. They chalk it up to him creating something new in his lab that's unique to look at, but that's all. He talks about living with the Devil to anyone who will listen to him. They think he's lost his mind."

"Was he incredibly angry when he realized the batteries were gone?"

"Super pissed. And you saw how he tried to come back through to your time. That made him even madder when he couldn't."

"Good."

Luna began pacing back and forth on the tiny outcropping. Vesta knew she was getting restless.

"So do you want me to take you back to the cave in 1999?"

A day earlier, she would have said yes in an instant, but now she hesitated. Life was comfortable here, and for the first time in a long time, she was happy. Going back to 1999, she would still have to figure out what she was going to do with her life. Would she stay on the path she took, becoming a tarot reader for celebrities? If she changed it, would people die from drug overdoses and accidents she would have helped them avoid? How could she not follow that path knowing the consequences? Here, she was free from having to do that anymore. She and Sandor had a comfortable life in Austin. All her family were close by.

Her thoughts came to a full stop before she allowed herself to face the next thought. Enid, Cyrus, and Raymond. They had to be young adults now. Where were they? She had been so consumed with stopping Agrippa she hadn't thought to ask about them.

The idea of seeing her mother almost brought tears to her eyes. And what about her father, Cyrus, and her uncle, Raymond? She watched both being shot to death. She squeezed her eyes shut at the thought. They must be alive. What if she ran down the hill now to ask Amara where they were, if she could see them?

Vesta glanced at Luna. She was rocking back and forth from her heels to the tips of her toes. Impatient, trying to be patient.

Here was her chance to live her lost twenty-five years, to slowly move through her forties, her fifties, and coast into her sixties, and remember those days when she arrived at this point again. Luna was offering her the opportunity to pick up where she left off that day in Monument Valley. She had yearned for it from the moment she set foot in this time. Why was she hesitating now?

"Can I think about it for a little while and let you know?" Vesta winced at her question, knowing the answer.

"I need to go." The anguish in Luna's voice was palpable. "I don't feel good if I stay in one place too long."

Vesta looked up at the moon in the sky. It had traveled higher in the heavens since Luna's arrival. She understood it was time for Luna, the Traveler, to move on, too.

"Will you come back later if I call you after I've had time to think about it?"

Luna pressed her lips together. "I don't really operate that way. I don't hear anyone calling me. I'm kinda all over the place."

"Vesta!" Amara's voice called to her from the table. "We're going into the theater to watch one of the movies you and Sandor made last life. Come join us. Jared's making espresso martinis."

"Espresso martinis? What are those? They sound wonderful," Vesta murmured to herself.

She glanced at Luna, who didn't need to say a word because her face said it all with her raised eyebrows and focused expression.

"What's it gonna be?"

"If I go back, will I remember all of what happened here?"

Luna shook her head. "I don't know."

"Will I do everything that will lead me back to this point in time?"

"I don't know that either. You try to stop Agrippa, that's for sure, but will it play out the same?" Luna shook her head again. "I don't know. There are too many variables."

The time had come to make her decision. Vesta could feel Luna's imminent departure coming swiftly. At least this time, she did have a choice. The irony was she wasn't sure she preferred it to the other way when choices were made for her. How could she possibly choose?

She looked up to the sparkling night sky to give her the answer. The first star her eyes landed on was Sirius, the brightest in the twinkling canopy, also known as the Dog Star. Liam always said that was his favorite because it was the only dog he could properly take care of in his life. Liam, dear Liam, wrestling those batteries out of the tablets. He saved the world as much as she did.

Her task was complete in 2024. Maybe she should get back to her own life.

Then, the song she heard Liam singing earlier in the night on the video began echoing in her head.

"In the moment here and now. Let the moonlight kiss your face. Every step and every breath, find the beauty in this place. No need for searching far and wide, your heart knows what it craves. Play it as it lays, girl. Play it as it lays."

Vesta smiled.

THE END

Free bonus chapters and prequels to The Tarot Legacies can be found by subscribing to victoriabelue.com

The Fairforest Witches series arrives in 2025! Four estranged sisters reunite at their father's funeral, only to uncover a perilous family legacy: a powerful **Book of Shadows** hidden in a cursed tomb, now targeted by a rival witch family bent on destruction. As they race to New Orleans to retrieve the book, battling dark magic, buried secrets, and their own fractured relationships, they must decide if their newfound bond is worth the ultimate sacrifice.

Join victoriabelue.com to be the first to know when Book of Shadows is launched into the world.